Scraps

Also by David Luck
Ghosts of Leadville
Men Are

Scraps

Fictional Fragments

By
David Luck

iUniverse, Inc.
New York   Bloomington

Scraps
Fictional Fragments

iUniverse books may be ordered through booksellers or by contacting:

iUniverse
1663 Liberty Drive
Bloomington, IN 47403
www.iuniverse.com
1-800-Authors (1-800-288-4677)

Because of the dynamic nature of the Internet, any Web addresses or links contained in this book may have changed since publication and may no longer be valid. The views expressed in this work are solely those of the author and do not necessarily reflect the views of the publisher, and the publisher hereby disclaims any responsibility for them.

ISBN: 978-1-4401-2921-6 (pbk)
ISBN: 978-1-4401-2941-4 (cloth)
ISBN: 978-1-4401-2940-7 (ebk)

Printed in the United States of America

iUniverse rev. date: 3/19/2009

To all the people who gave me the scraps that tumble, churn, and excite my life—.

Writers are vacuum cleaners who suck up other people's lives and weave them into stories like a sparrow builds a nest from scraps.
–Garrison Keillor

Table of Contents

Angelica and Carlos

Angelica blows on her ragged mittens, warming her hands. Her breath forms a cloud and steams the windshield of her car. *Where is he?* It isn't like Carlos to be late, and the fact that their son, Roberto, is with him adds to her anxiety. Her stomach is beginning to ache, and she is getting colder by the minute.

She hates to waste the gasoline, but she has to use the heater to warm up a little. He should be along any minute, she tells herself: he is never late. Angelica turns the key in the ignition, and the car grumbles to life. After a few minutes, she turns the heater fan to full, and the warmish air blasts into the cold interior of the car. She lets the car run, heater warming, for just a few more minutes, and then turns it off. Silence replaces the fan whine coming from the heater.

She rubs her mittened hands along the tops of her thighs trying to generate some additional heat. She looks out the windshield toward the lake, but has to rub away the frost before she can see. The reeds along the shore glisten with icy crystals, the lake surface's frozen sheen reflects the multitude of colors from the variety of stores across the street from the lake.

"Why did he have to meet here anyway?" she asks herself.

Angelica was only fourteen years old when she met Carlos. It was spring, April in fact, when she and her very best friend, Maria, left school early for a walk around the lake. They were about half-way around, over by the swing set that sits to the south of the lake, when they heard a low whistle, then "Ay, que bonitas!"

Neither of the girls turned their heads, but then another low whistle came and an invitation to stop and have a cold beer. Angelica made the mistake of looking back, over her shoulder, and there was a young man standing next to a tree, his left hand pressed against it, his straw hat tipped back from his handsome face.

Maria giggled, and the two started running slowly from the scene. Soon out of breath, mostly from the giggles, the girls looked back again just as the man waved to them with a big flourish of his right hand. They decided to walk around the lake again.

Angelica again turns the key in the ignition and lets the car run longer this time until the heater is blasting hot air. She slips her mittens off and puts her hands in the wash of hot air as another fifteen minutes pass, with still no sign of Carlos and Roberto.

Another week went by before Maria and Angelica were able to sneak away from school early enough to make the walk around the lake. They saw the man before he saw or heard them, which was amazing considering all the giggling behind hands-to-the-face they were doing. He was in the same spot on the shore of the lake, and he was fishing. His straw hat was pulled to the right of his head in a jaunty angle. He was busy propping his pole in a split stick and anchoring it with a rock.

The girls walked slowly by, and just as they passed, Angelica couldn't help herself, she wiggled her behind just a little as she walked.

"Señoritas, cómo están? Come see my fish." The man was gesturing toward a dented black plastic bucket.

Maria was already giggling, and as the two held their heads high, tried to keep their bottoms still as they continued walking around the lake. Angelica was the first to let out a big gasp of air that she was holding, suddenly finding it very difficult to breath.

Angelica reaches for the key and switches off the car, feeling a bit warmer although now the windows are all but completely frosted over. She notices the pattern on the side window, and it reminds her of a tree, the leaves waving back and forth, brushing the sky a clear blue.

A week or so later, just two days after school let out for the summer, Angelica began a walk around the lake. She had thought she would stop to see if Maria wanted to come, but instead, her feet took her directly to the path that wound around the lake.

The geese that wintered there had gone north for the summer ahead. There were a few ducks trying the waters, and as she walked, she startled one soon-to-be mother duck from her nest among the tall grasses growing along the shore. Three white eggs glistened in the warm sun. She was soon near the spot where she and Maria had encountered the man, and she could hardly believe her eyes: he was fishing in the same spot as if he were still there from weeks ago.

He looked up from his fishing, and smiled broadly at Angelica.

"Ah, Señorita, you have returned to see my fish."

Angelica stopped and looked at the man. She saw his broad, friendly, smiling face, his straw hat tipped jauntily to the side. He was wearing jeans, and his strong thighs were pushing at the fabric. His bright plaid shirt was unbuttoned and the tails were flapping lightly in the morning breeze. His chest was muscular and bronzed from the sun.

He was still smiling as he gestured for her to come look in his dented fishing bucket.

"Venga aquí – Mire."

The man picked up the bucket and walked half the distance to where she was standing and set it down. A small amount of water sloshed over the edge and slithered to the ground. The breeze combed through her hair.

"Dónde?" she asked.

"Están aquí. Here in the bucket."

She took two steps toward the bucket, then three, and then stood on her tiptoes trying to see, but she was still too far away. He picked up the bucket and brought it to her, setting it down at her feet, splashing her shoes with water. Inside the bucket, swimming feverishly around and around, were two small fish, their eyes on Angelica, pleading to her for a quick release.

She stood watching with the man, entranced, smelling his lotion, feeling a vibration deep inside that she had never felt before.

"I am Carlos, and you are Señorita ——?"

She looked up and into his watchful brown eyes, eyes large and soft enough to fold around her. She quickly turned, the feeling **inside** her so strong she was beginning to doubt that her legs would hold her up any longer, and slowly returned to the path and began walking away.

"Señorita ——?"

"Angelica," she said over her shoulder in a very small voice, as her feet gained momentum against the path that led around the lake.

The car is getting cold again. Angelica looks at her watch, but has to turn the interior light on first to see the hands. Thirty minutes she has been waiting, and it is now nearing 7:30.

"I'll give him fifteen more minutes, and then I'm going to go to the police station and report him." Her breath fogs out from her mouth like smoke from a chimney as she speaks, and she rubs her mittens together and bangs her knees, trying desperately to warm up.

The summer she met Carlos seems like yesterday, yet is obscured by mist and frost as time passes. How many years have passed now?

Maria's eyes were getting bigger and bigger. Her hand was pressed against her mouth, and her giggles were becoming almost hysterical as Angelica continued her story about seeing the fish.

"How big were they?" Maria asked again, although she had just asked the same question about the fish minutes before.

Angelica raised her small brown hand and swam it through the air. They both giggled. Although Maria was her very best friend, she had not told her how her legs had felt like hot rubber or how her breath welled up in her chest until she thought she was going to explode.

"Are you going back?"

"Maybe."

"When?"

"Or, maybe not?"

"Can I come with you?"

They both giggled again and hugged each other, agreeing that this was their secret, although Angelica was already thinking about how to return without her friend. As the summer days lengthened and then began to shorten, she spent more and more time at the lake. After getting up early to do her chores, she pretended to go to the library, or told her mama that she was going over to Maria's house.

And sometimes she did go to Maria's house, and they would go to the basement or out into the back of the side yard and whisper about Carlos and his fish. And once in a while, Maria would go with Angelica on her journey around the lake. But on these trips together, Angelica would only speak Carlos's name in greeting and would never, despite his protests and invitations, stop and visit.

Angelica checks her watch for the fourth or fifth time and there is still two minutes to go before her self-imposed deadline. She stamps her feet against the floorboard, sighs, shakes her head angrily and turns the key in the ignition.

They talked about everything: how fish were able to breathe in the water, and how baby ducks learned to swim. They talked about his birthplace in Chihuahua, and Carlos told about his family running the border when he was only five. They talked about green cards, his job at the hospital across town, and how he liked the evening shift because then he had time for his fishing, and now, of course, time to talk with her.

She told him a little of her family, her father's work that took him on the road and away from home much of the time, and she once talked about her brother, who had died at birth. And although he once asked her about Maria, Angelica did not tell him anything about her except that they were best friends.

They had never touched in any way, except perhaps, when she was helping him land a fish or set the bait, although she wanted him to and often dreamed of him holding her in a passionate embrace. She had long since lost the feeling of not being able to catch her breath when they were together, but at times, she would still have this odd buzzing sensation within, and her legs would still feel like hot rubber.

His fifteen minutes are up. In fact, by her watch, sixteen and a half minutes have passed since she made her declaration and it was time to go to the police, but exactly what she will she tell them, she does not know.

It was the day of her fifteenth birthday that they finally touched. Her family had surprised her with a big birthday party, a picnic at the lake. Her father was in town, unheard of in the middle of the week, and he had gathered some of his friends in a

Mariachi band to play for her. They serenaded her with *Mexican Rose*, *The Mexican Hat Dance*, and, her favorite, *La Cucaracha*.

She tried to relax and enjoy the party, but she could not help but continuously glance toward the south end of the lake where Carlos was always fishing. Once or twice she caught a glimpse of a light-colored shirt, and perhaps a hat, but she was unsure whether it was he. Mid-afternoon, as the men and boys were flying kites, she thought about sneaking away and going to the end of the lake to see Carlos. But then realizing that he would be gone for work, she was finally able to catch her breath and relax by blowing all fifteen candles out with one big burst of air.

The sun began to lean hard to the west, and the party was ending. Rather than ride home with her family, she begged them to let her walk around the lake and then home. It would, she explained, after such a large and noisy party, allow her to experience her birthday in the quiet within herself. Angelica hugged and kissed the well-wishers good-bye, even the old Mariachi men smelling of beer and stale cigars. Then she began her walk, lost in the memory of her party.

As she neared the south end of the lake, a man was sitting on one-legged stool fishing. The broad lean of his back was familiar, as was the jaunty angle of his hat pulled low over his eyes.

"Angelica—Mi ángel! Venga aquí y déjeme verla," he called as she neared. "Tell me, what are you doing here so late in the afternoon?"

Angelica continued walking toward Carlos, and just as she reached him, her legs became rubbery as the buzzing inside intensified, and she began to fall. Carlos quickly dropped his fishing pole and wrapped his big strong arms around her to steady her. In the process, his hat fell to the ground and his shock of black hair tumbled like a waterfall at midnight over his forehead. She leaned her head against his chest, and through his cologne she smelled his sweat and the buzzing fell from her heart to her stomach and beyond.

Long shadows were working their way across the end of the

lake, and several ducks swam by, quacking a chorus of sound. Carlos nuzzled her hair, whispering soft pleadings, which to Angelica's ear pressed against his chest, sounded almost like the priest during the Lenten service. She raised her face to look at him, and his huge brown eyes had narrowed in a way she had never seen. And at that moment he picked her up and carried her to the tall grass under the large tree along the edge of the lake and laid her tenderly down among the softest of the grasses. In a moment Carlos had shed his shirt and was down beside her with his hand under her skirt, causing the buzzing to turn to a thump in her ears.

Carlos was soon on top of her, his heavy frame pressed strongly against her small self, and as she watched the tall branches of the tree, the leaves waving back and forth, gently brush away the clouds from the sky, the electricity spread in one great rush from the very center of her body to the very tips of her fingers and toes.

Angelica turns the key in the ignition while her left foot taps the floorboard in exasperation. Perhaps her father has been right after all, and Carlos is not to be trusted, although in the three years she has known him, he has always been true to his word. It is very unlike him to be late.

"Maybe," she thinks, "I should go home and see if he has been trying to call me. At least at home I could be studying instead of wasting my time like this."

She puts the car in gear, lets in the clutch and starts to pull out of the parking lot, rubbing the frost from the windshield as she moves forward. She quickly brakes, and backs into the same space she has just vacated.

"Five minutes. I'll give him five more minutes and then I'm going to the police station," she says aloud, renewing her angry determination. She leaves the car running, enjoying what little warmth is beginning to flow from the heater.

Carlos wanted to marry her, little she with the big belly. Her father would not permit it saying Carlos was too old, and besides, he could not be trusted.

"What kind of man is this? Living in this country for twenty years and still working on a green card? What kind of a man, I ask? And he wants to marry my daughter? After getting her pregnant!"

Her parents pulled her from school, against her pleading, her "everyone else that's pregnant keeps going to school," and finally "I'll run away with Carlos if I can't stay in school."

None of it helped. Other than an occasional visit from Maria (against her mother's wishes), she might as well have been an outcast on some remote island in the middle of the Pacific. She began sneaking away from the house and walking around the lake, but it only made her feel worse. Carlos was no longer fishing there.

Roberto had just turned two years of age when the two of them were sauntering around the lake one fine day in late May. As they reached the south end of the lake, heading for the playground swings, there sat a man on a one-legged stool, fishing. The broad lean of his back was familiar, as was the jaunty angle of his hat pulled low over his eyes.

"Angelica—Mi ángel! Venga aquí y déjeme verla," he called as she neared. "Tell me, what are you doing here so late in the afternoon, and who is that handsome niño so close to your side."

Angelica stopped. The two, Carlos and Roberto, stood looking as if at a mirror, except one was big, and one was small. Carlos removed his hat and the cascade of black hair falling down his forehead mirrored the face of Roberto. Roberto reached for his mother's hand, but after a moment, he released it and started walking toward Carlos.

Carlos dropped down on one knee, laying his fishing pole on the ground. Roberto stopped about a foot from Carlos until

Carlos opened his arms in greeting, and the boy stepped into his embrace.

The old forgotten buzzing began within Angelica, and panicking, she cried sternly, "Roberto, come here!"

Roberto turned within his father's arms, and then as Carlos released him, he walked slowly towards his mother, his brown eyes every bit as large as Carlos's. As Carlos stood, a smile spread across his face, and Angelica was not unaware of his thighs pushing against the fabric of his jeans.

A police car is driving down the street, and begins slowing as the driver apparently sees her car, alone, in the parking lot of the lake. Angelica quickly thinks of flashing her lights to gain more attention and after stopping him, will report Carlos and Roberto as missing. But she does not. She can not. Tears well in her eyes, and one tear makes a hasty exit down her right cheek. She raises her hand and brushes it away with her mitten.

The three have, as Maria tells her, a strange existence. With hard work and help with Roberto from her aunt, Angelica has earned her GED, and is now studying at the Community College to be an x-ray technician. She has a job at the hospital just south of the lake, and with help from Carlos, she was able to move from her father's home a year ago into a small basement apartment. Even though she wants to, she has not told Carlos the address of the apartment.

In just the last six months, she has been allowing Carlos to take Roberto for one weekend a month, and until tonight it has worked well, giving her a weekend to herself, and Roberto time with his father.

Angelica is watching each car as it comes down the street, watching for an old beat-up, red-colored Ford, for a slowing, a turn signal, any sign. A red car passes. A car signals, but turns on the street before the park. A horn sounds from someplace in the distance. She begins to shake not knowing whether from the cold or from the fear building inside her.

Another car, a dark blue, passes. Another comes, white, and goes on by. The car is warm now, but her shaking is no less. She has a cold feeling lodged in the pit of her stomach. Another car, and yet another, red, a signal, turning into the lot. The car pulls along side her car, and she fights to get the frost-laden window rolled down.

Carlos's window is already down, and she is met with those huge brown eyes and his broad smile. Behind Carlos, through her tears and the frost, she can see Roberto strapped in his car seat in the rear of the car.

"Lo siento mucho, mi ángel, pero hace mucho frío esta noche. It is too cold, the car would not start, and I had no way to call and tell you what happened. I am sorry if you were to worry."

Angelica opens her car door just as Carlos does the same. She starts walking toward Carlos, and just as she reaches him, her legs became hot and rubbery as the cold feeling inside turns to buzzing, and she begins to fall. Carlos quickly drops Roberto's small suitcase and wraps his big strong arms around her to steady her. In the process, his hat falls to the ground and his shock of black hair tumbles like a waterfall at midnight over his forehead. She leans her head against his chest, and through his cologne she smells his sweat and the buzzing falls from her heart to her stomach and beyond.

Colita

Seating himself on a bench by the lake, the old man takes a photograph from his breast pocket and searches the image for clues, for something missed the other hundreds of times he has looked at the picture.

The picture, ragged at the edges, the colors dimmed with years, shows a huge flock of geese. In front of the geese, and mostly to the right, are sea gulls, a seemingly strange bird to be in Colorado, so far from the ocean. In the back, some of the geese are just taking flight, the others craning their necks as if to see where they were going.

He leans forward, this old man, his elbows on his knees, the photograph still pressed in his hands as he rubs his cracked and callused fingers over the surface of the picture, as he has done time and time again, coaxing a clue or uncovering a hidden thing he has not seen before. With his sad eyes, he stares at the photograph maybe four or five minutes, and then, hanging his head slightly, he puts the picture gently back in the pocket in the bib of his overalls.

Sitting back on the bench and squinting his eyes, he looks out over the surface of the frozen lake. The sun is hanging low in the south, and dark clouds are gathering. It isn't more than twenty feet from where he sits that it happened, and hearing the honking, he turns his gaze toward the advancing geese looking for a handout. He chokes back a lump gathering in his throat.

"Get out of here, you sons-a-bitches," he mumbles to the geese as he waves his hands in a feeble gesture. "You'll get no bread crumbs from me. Now git! Váyanse!"

The geese stop momentarily, necks pumping, looking for the first crumb. A small group of sea gulls land just behind the geese, startling a few in the back as they crowded, pecking through the herd, making their way to the front.

It could have been 1990, almost ten years ago to the day. Colita, his granddaughter, and he were walking around the lake. It was a crisp December day, with little warmth from the sun. The breeze was slightly chilly and blowing from the north. Christmas was just a few days away.

"What is Santa going to bring you, Colita?" he asked her in Spanish. She was only six, and she was holding his hand and smiling up at him.

"Una muñeca," she answered. "You know Pappa, a dolly."

He loved their walks together, and he loved the way she called him Pappa even though he was truly her Grandpappa. But after all, she didn't know her father. That bastardo!

He remembered the year his beautiful daughter, who had been working for an airlines in Texas, came home pregnant. Because she knew he would have walked all the way to Texas just to kill with his bare hands the scoundrel who had made her with child, she never spoke of him. Only once had the old man tried to get her to tell him, but instead she cried, and he had held his daughter awkwardly in his bear-like arms until the huge tears stopped. He had never asked her about it again.

Now, Colita had dropped his hand and skipped ahead. The geese, hundreds of them, were grazing the grass above the lake just ahead. Colita was carrying a sack of stale breadcrumbs and had been looking forward to giving the geese some Christmas dinner.

He caught up with Colita as she stopped and began calling the geese, throwing a few crumbs ahead of her on the path. The geese, gawking and squawking, stopped grazing and moved toward the pair. A flock of sea gulls landed to the right of the geese and moved toward them expecting the same Christmas handout.

The sun, which had been out a moment ago to slightly warm the air, had disappeared behind a dense black cloud. A few fine snowflakes drifted lazily down. Looking up, he thought, "Looks like a white Christmas after all."

He reached into his jacket pocket and brought out an old camera, removed it from its soiled case, brought it to his eye and stepping back, readied himself for the picture of his beautiful Colita feeding the geese Christmas dinner.

"Forward a little," he called to Colita.

He waited until Colita was completely surrounded by the geese and the gulls, and as his finger pushed the small red button, there was a sudden flapping of wings. Before he could get his eye away from the camera, the gulls and the geese were in flight and the last of the gaggle were running for takeoff.

Momentarily blinded by the dust of takeoff and the sun, angled far to the south and blazing through the intensified snow as it peeked out from behind the black cloud, he called out, blinking once, then twice, looking again.

"*Colita*," he shouted. "*Colita—*."

Going Postal

Maggie had been on the street for nearly three years, and she liked it. She liked the freedom and the fact that she didn't have to talk to anyone unless she wanted to, and, most often, she didn't want to. Occasionally, when she was sitting on a bench looking out over the lake, someone would speak to her, and once, a man on inline skates had stopped to offer her chocolates. It was Mother's Day. And what was he thinking anyway; he was old enough to be her father.

When an event like that happened, she would just continue to stare out over the lake and not speak, even when the man all but shoved the chocolates in her face. Oh, he probably meant well, but she just didn't need the conversation.

She was glad spring had finally come, the warm sun on her tanned, leathery face felt good, and if the warmth continued, she would be able to rid herself of the heavy wool coat that had sustained her through the winter. Once, in January, it had gotten too cold even with the coat, and she had had to seek a cot in a downtown shelter for a few nights. She hadn't stayed long; people were just too friendly—and nosey.

Along about noon, she got out her sewing. Maggie was

embroidering flowers on a denim skirt and vest she had purchased at a thrift store. Once done, she would sell it to a little shop she had discovered that would take her work, putting a few dollars in her pocket for a coffee and another denim garment of some sort. Although she had embroidered many different items over the years, she liked the heavy thick feel of denim under her fingers as she worked.

Geese, waddling along the lake's shore, were honking a ruckus: probably a mating call. A pair of Mallards were swimming by, barely rippling the water. The grass along the lake's edge was greening fast, and if it got any warmer, she would have to move to the shade, or take off her coat.

In the afternoon she would walk to the other side of the lake where she could see the mountains that were now behind her. She liked to look at the peaks and think about all the people that may have climbed them although she had only seen the mountains up close once, long ago. This time of year they were still snow covered, and they looked cold. She couldn't imagine climbing them in the wintertime, or even in the spring when the sun was warming.

Her fingers passed swiftly over the fabric, and the large heavy sewing needle flashed in the sun, sending light semaphores out across the lake. For Maggie, it was a fine day.

Merna was busy sorting the mail for her route. Because of an accident on I-25, she had gotten to the station a little later than usual making her feel terribly cranky and irritable, mostly with herself. She hated to start her route any later than nine thirty, and today it would be closer to ten. In her twenty-four years of delivering mail, she prided herself in her work, especially the accuracy of delivering the correct pieces to each mailbox along her route.

Her practiced fingers raced through the piles of mail, sorting and stashing the letters, cards and junk pieces into pigeon holes numbered for each person on her route. When finished, she banded and stacked the tidy groupings into square baskets in order of delivery, with the fliers piled in a separate basket.

Her thoughts drifted to yesterday when her boss, out of the clear blue, had asked her if she was contemplating retirement. That little sawed-off son-of-a-bitch. What business was it of his anyway whether she thought about retirement or not? Through her teeth, she had told him, "Hell, no, and retirement isn't even a word in my vocabulary."

She liked her work, and planned to work forever if her legs held out. Maybe sometime after she had thirty years in she would think about it, but certainly not until then. Besides, the retirement benefits would be so much better if she waited. That little prick. To hell with him anyway.

Finishing her sorting, Merna placed the baskets into her mail wagon, made sure they were in order, and then stopped by the bathroom. As she washed her hands, she glanced in the mirror above the sink.

"Damn good do," she said about the short, mannish style to her graying hair.

Drying her hands with paper towels, she saved one back and used it to pull open the door. Merna didn't like touching the door handle with her hands.

"No telling what damn fool forgot to wash her hands," she murmured under her breath as she left the bathroom, stopping by Accountables for any registered or certified pieces of mail.

Finding none for her route, she was out the door and behind the wheel of the van driving off toward the start of her route. Although, except for January, winter had been relatively dry and mild, she was glad spring was here. She liked the color of the spring sun early in the morning, and today, a little later than usual for her route, it was hot. Merna wished she had put on her shorts instead of the slacks she was wearing.

"What the hell," she said to her reflection in the rearview mirror as she backed from the parking space and drove from the lot behind the post office.

Jasper felt chilled. Cold to the bone in fact. It didn't matter what time of the year it was or what the temperature registered, he felt chilled. Maybe it *was* the war. That's what one doctor had suggested years ago when he had first felt cold. Now that he thought about it, he had never warmed up since his tour of duty in France. God it was cold in the winter of '42, slogging through the snow chasing Krauts. He had told himself that if he lived through the fight for Houffalize and the cold, he would settle in Bermuda— even if he had to wait tables for a living.

Instead, he had settled in Denver, and had not waited tables, but first worked in advertising, then owned an agency, and over the years, had done very well. He had never married, although he had always had a lady friend: to travel and to be seen with in restaurants and clubs. His sexual preference was really for men, but he had always been much too afraid to act on this impulse.

Jasper never felt himself lucky or charmed in any manner, so he didn't gamble or take bets of any kind. He attended Centennial Racetrack on summer evenings to be seen and mingle with clients and potential clients, but he never bet on the horses. He liked a sure thing, something he could touch and put in a file for safekeeping, or for that matter, hang on the wall where he could study and admire what he had purchased.

So it was a complete surprise, and a lucky one at that, when sometime in the '50s he had purchased a huge wheat farm far east of downtown Denver. On the day of the signing, he patiently walked behind the previous owner, an eighty-year-old tired and wrinkled man, as he explained the workings of the farm, and especially how to start the stubborn and ornery Farmall tractor.

No, Jasper had never farmed the place, and certainly didn't want to live there. He leased the land to neighboring farmers who, dependent entirely on rainfall to water their crops of dry land wheat, would enrich him one year but impoverish him for several more before hitting another good crop. Most took good care of the land, except during the especially dry and windy years when no one could keep the soil from blowing no matter how hard they tried. The buildings were harder to lease, and finally

Jasper quit trying. The years finally took their toll when the last building fell to ruin sometime in 1979.

He had purchased another small piece of real estate when he opened his advertising agency. It was an old brick office building on Blake Street. The building had not been used for at least ten years, and you had to step over homeless bodies sleeping in the doorways to get in the front door, but it was cheap, and the cleaning and fixing up had not been very expensive, especially in the '50s. When finished, it was a splendid home for his agency, and there were rooms above that could be leased if he ever chose to fix them up. He did fix up a small complex of rooms, and that is where Jasper lived and hung his acquired art on the walls. And from where, as he used to kid his staff at the advertising agency, he could walk to work.

Like a speed walker nearing the end of a race, summer always had a way of stepping by. In small steps maybe for some days, but here it was approaching September, and the steps were getting longer and faster. There was a slight chill in the air early this morning, and Maggie pulled the collar of her jacket up a little more snugly around her neck. The sun was comfortably warming her legs as she stretched them out from her usual morning spot on the bench near the west side of the lake. Maggie tipped her head back a little so she could see under the long bill of her yellow sunbonnet and squinted into the sun to stare at a branch of leaves waving over the lake. There was already a hint that they would soon be changing color.

She reached to her left, uncovered her grocery cart of belongings, and took out a denim vest. Her embroidery hoop snapped off as she pulled the fabric toward her, and the top hoop rolled like a silvery, loose tire across the sidewalk, across the small grass strip, and into the lake. The slight turbulence the hoop made in the water interested some partially feathered young geese and honking loudly they began swimming in Maggie's direction.

Just as she stood, she heard the scurrilous scrap of inline

skates coming around the curve in the sidewalk. It was the old man, and although he never spoke or stopped again since he had offered the chocolates, he skated around the lake two or three times a week. Chocolate Man, she called him in her mind, and what was he trying to prove at his age? He should be sitting in a nursing home at a card table playing bridge.

Once, maybe in June, Maggie had seen Chocolate Man giving some fishing poles to some kids fishing along the shore of the lake. They were using fishing line wrapped around a bottle, or as one boy was doing, a can. They were getting some pretty good casts, but, of course, reeling was a little slow.

Chocolate Man was carrying three or four poles, and when he saw the boys fishing, he stopped skating and watched them for a little while. Then he offered them each a pole. He showed them how the reel worked, and how to cast with the pole, and sure enough, the boys had it down in a jiffy.

Later that afternoon, as Maggie pushed her cart past the place at the lake where the boys had been fishing, she saw their discarded cans and bottles still wrapped with fishing line. (Generally, her habit was to let trash lie. If people wouldn't pick up their own crap, it wasn't her job to do it.) But rather than see a duck or a goose get tangled in a line, Maggie picked up the debris and threw it into a nearby green trashcan.

Merna not only liked delivering mail, she especially liked her route. It lay in a diverse part of Denver, around St. Anthony's Hospital. Some of the area was a little rough, migrants and drug dealers, but she had pretty much shaped up the people on her route, and they knew she wouldn't take any crap from any of them. By and large, the people on her route stayed out of her way, except for rare occasions on Saturdays when someone eager for their mail would meet her at the gate or by their box.

She also had few dogs to contend with. When she had first taken over the route, many dogs were loose, or at least loose in a yard she would have to traverse to get to the mailbox. Merna would turn in a viscous dog report, Form # 876, and quit delivering the mail until the dog disappeared from the yard. Sometimes she wouldn't deliver their mail for a month, then put a card in their box to come to the post office to get all the back-mail. Damned if she was going to carry it out to them when it was their own stupid fault for having a dog in the first place.

The thing she liked most, and today she began humming as she thought about it while she drove to her starting point, was to take her lunch break at Sloan's lake. She liked the trees and the view of the mountains, which was incredible if she sat on the east side of the lake. And, she wouldn't have to talk to anyone while she ate. It really pissed her off to eat with people, talking with their mouths full, laughing and spewing food bits all over. People could be so stupid.

Her morning had gone well, and the mail load was not too heavy today. At eleven forty-five, she pulled her van into the south parking lot at Sloan's, took her little cooler, and walked over the outlet bridge to sit at the first green, metal bench she came to.

Across the lake, in the distance, was Mount Evans, mostly bare from snow except for a few patches, Squaw Mountain with Papoose and Chief rolling up behind, and to the south of Evans, Rosalie Peak. At one time or another, Merna had climbed them all and many more of the peaks in Colorado. She liked to think of mountain climbing as a way to keep in shape for her mail route.

She loved to get some part-time postal employee such as a relief carrier cornered and tell them about her climbing. They would most invariably try to correct her and suggest that her mail route was what kept her in shape for her mountain climbing. Merna would always shake her head slowly from side to side, look them straight in the eye and tell them no, it was the other way around. It was her mountain climbing that kept her in shape for her mail route. She loved to watch them squirm, as it made no sense to them, and then she would get real close, right in their face and say, "I'm sure of it." By now, the trapped person was ready to flee in any direction, and it always made Merna feel good when she let the exchange end.

Today, the lake was lying very still and reflecting the bright green of the willows angling from the ground to her left. As she began eating her scrambled egg sandwich, she noticed a hint of yellow coming to the leaves in the reflection. It would not be long before the fall colors would be showing themselves like a multicolored quilt. When the weather got too cold, she would take her lunch in St. Anthony's cafeteria, or sit in the van parked near the lake.

She was on her second bite of sandwich when an old man on inline skates swept past her, gliding with big swoops of his skates. Merna was impressed with his speed. "Pretty good for an old fart," she thought. He was out of sight for a few minutes, behind the giant stand of willows along the south shore, but soon she could see him speeding along the sidewalk that wove through an area of newly planted grass.

Her gaze returned to the mountain range, and she thought ahead to the coming weekend when she would be hiking in the more southern parts of Colorado: the San Juan Mountains. Merna had wanted to climb in the San Juans for years, but for some reason other ranges and peaks had come first. She would be traveling through Lake City, camping along Henson Creek before climbing Uncompahgre Peak and maybe Wetterhorn, both fourteeners. On her way home, she hoped to stop in Ouray and soak in the hot springs. Next to climbing, soaking in hot springs was the second love of her life, and she had taken Monday off from her postal route just so she could spend some leisure time in the soothing, steaming pool.

Skateman was on his third lap around the lake as Merna finished her lunch. Instead of slowing, he seemed to be gathering speed as if a hungry pack of wolves were nipping at his heels. Some geese, young ones leading the flock, scooted out of his way, plopping into the water as she stood and began walking slowly back to the van, enjoying the sun on her back as she climbed in and started the engine.

She caught herself smiling, as she thought about Skateman hitting a sidewalk crack and flying through the air, ending up crumpled in the grass. She would be the first one there to help, or as she thought later, step on the neck of the old fool and be done with it.

"It would serve the old bastard right," she said, then added, "Dumb son-of-a-bitch."

Jasper was on his third lap around Sloan's Lake, and was finally beginning to feel warm when he passed a man on the sidewalk that reminded him of a real estate man he had known years ago: heavy set, jolly jowls, no neck to speak of. Of course that man would now be as old as he was, and the man on the sidewalk was just a young fellow.

He recalled when the man, the real estate agent, appeared one morning at the advertising agency wanting to speak with him in private. It was 1978, and Jasper had a feeling it was something important. After the usual morning pleasantries, the real estate man cleared his fat, wobbly throat and got down to business. He began by saying he understood Jasper owned an old run-down farm out east. The way the man had emphasized run-down made the hair stand up on the back of Jasper's almost-bald head.

Why yes, Jasper had admitted, he did own an old run-down farm of sorts, emphasizing the run-down part just as the man had. Too bad the buildings were in such bad shape, or the property might be worth a little something. The agent's slick-shaved upper lip had begun to perspire even though the air that morning was cool.

Well, the agent had said, he had a farmer-client that was interested in the land, you know, wanted to expand his farm now that wheat prices were going up and the weather had been cooperating with a little rain. Would Jasper think about selling it or was it an old family piece of land that made it emotionally valuable? His client, the agent had added, couldn't afford much, but thought that old run-down place was just what he was looking for.

Again, the accent on "run-down."

"Give me something to think about it," Jasper had told the man, watching the beads of sweat on his lip merge together and run down to his mouth. It was fascinating watching, considering Jasper was colder than usual that morning, and had no concept of needing to sweat. Yep, he'd said. He'd think about it, and the man could leave his card and he'd get back with him.

Something was up. His old run-down farm suddenly seemed to be valuable to someone, and Jasper wasn't in any hurry. He figured the longer he waited, the more valuable it would become, so he'd just sit back and wait until he heard something. He had a feeling it wouldn't be long in coming. Meanwhile, he had work to do. His agency had just gotten a new account, and he planned on doing a real fine job for the law firm of Milton, Jobs, and Snod.

Jasper never thought of himself as political, not in the least way, but it was hard to be in the advertising business and not hear the scuttlebutt around town. It wasn't long until he had his ear on the goings on out east of Denver. There was talk of a new airport. It was hard to imagine, for an advertising man with accounts at Denver's Stapleton Airport, the need for a new one. Stapleton was considering enlarging, it was convenient, it worked well, and business was thriving. Who in the world would want to drive way out east to an airport?

It wasn't long until the line of real estate agents that wanted to buy that old run-down farm had stretch to the corner of the block. All had some old farmer-client that wanted it, and still Jasper waited for one of them to come clean and tell him the real reason for their interest. It was pretty much centered where the new airport would be placed, and if they could buy it cheap, they could make some big money reselling it to the Airport Authority.

Well, Jasper had been in no hurry, and finally in 1989, he sold the old run-down farm directly to the Authority for enough money to make his blood feel warmer for two or three days. Enough that he hadn't even needed a blanket to cover him while he slept those first few nights after the papers were signed.

It had been a beautiful fall, the brilliance of the sun slanting long over the lake, the breath-taking October-blue sky. Maggie looked out across the lake towards the mountains, a hazy, darker blue skyline of jagged peaks and valleys. She took a long breath, and then did something she rarely allowed herself to do. She thought back to when she was a child and her parents and sister had driven with her across the desert first and then through the mountains from California to Denver.

She thought how she had cried when she had to go potty and her father had angrily jerked the car to the side of the road, stopping long enough to let her out to pee, and how her feet had stung on the hot, desert sand as she squatted, making her pee to the side as she lifted first one foot and then the other, urine running down her chubby legs, sizzling as it disappeared in the sand.

And then remarkably came the cool green mountains with the tall trees, and the cool breezes and the freezing cold creeks. And the rocks. She had never seen such huge rocks towering on each side of the road, and she became fearful that they might tumble onto their car as she watched out the window. But none fell, and then there was Denver.

A cawing crow in the trees to the south of the lake and the answering echo from its chick in a farther tree brought her thoughts back to today. Maggie let out one long sigh. It had been too many years, her parents dead at least twenty, found in an alley, a drug deal gone bad. She had no idea where her sister was or if she was even alive.

The crow chick's calling was becoming more frantic. Maggie looked in the direction of the trees just as Chocolate Man whizzed by in front of her. From under the long-billed sunbonnet, she watched him corner the tight approach onto the bridge, and then he was gone. Soon there would be snow, and Chocolate Man would no longer be able to skate at will, and Maggie would be digging out her heavy coat and the three pairs of long underwear she wore all winter, and then it would be too cold and she would have to finally find shelter. She shivered ever so slightly. She hated shelters, and then her mind slipped back momentarily to the desert and she wondered how winter would be on the sand.

Merna was driving fast and honking at the jerk that had just cut her off along I-25. The son-of-a-bitch knew the 6th Avenue turnoff was coming up. Those kind never plan ahead. Bastards! She flipped her hand in the air, middle finger raised in protest. She could feel the lingering value of the weekend's hot springs slide from her body. It was Tuesday, and back to work was the usual.

She arrived at the post office, parked behind in the employee lot and grabbed a soon-to-be shaded spot for her Subaru. As she got out of the car, she wondered what that little sawed-off son-of-a-bitch of a boss would have to say to her today. Probably something about her taking the previous day off. That little bastard. He could say *what* he wanted for as *long* as he wanted. It didn't matter in the least to her. She wasn't retiring.

She clocked in and grabbed the sacks of mail for her route and began the sorting process. She was almost finished when she came to a business envelope addressed as follows: TO SUNBONNET, WEST SIDE BENCH, SLOAN'S LAKE 80214.

"What the hell—" Merna looked up and around for that little sawed-off-son-of-a-bitch. What kind of test was he administering to her anyway? Her bastard of a boss was nowhere to be seen, and all others were busy sorting their mail. No one looked her way.

She started to toss the envelope aside as she mumbled to herself about the slops at the main sorting station downtown. How had they let that one slip past she asked herself? Merna went on, finishing her sorting, going to the bathroom, past

Accountables, all the while keeping her eye out for some prick practical joker with a sneer on his or her face.

She loaded her baskets into the van, and then went back to the sorting room, picked up the envelope and returning to the van, tossed the envelope onto the front seat. Her head was beginning to ache as fingers of pain crawled up the back of her neck. So much for the relief she had felt in the hot springs just the day before. She started the engine, backed from the parking space and headed for the beginning of her route. "Silly bastards," she said to herself, meaning no one in particular, but more or less everyone in general.

For his seventieth birthday, Jasper held a party for himself. It was a fancy catered affair, lavishly prepared in the offices of his Advertising Agency in the newly remodeled brick building on Blake Street. He invited all his associates, clients, the Denver Chief of Police and Mayor Wellington Webb, who, at the last minute, decided not to attend. The whole area of Lower Downtown Denver was vibrating with restoration. Lofts, businesses and crowds of young people buying real estate around his office had made sweeping changes in the district, and Jasper felt honored to be in the middle of it all.

It was during the cake cutting, which came after his blowing out the seventy candles (in only two breaths), that he made his announcement.

"I'm retiring and leaving it to you youngsters" he had said pointedly to his partners, the very ones that had purchased the agency from him two days before the party. A hearty round of applause followed, with the clinking of champagne glasses. Jasper felt his face flush, a blanket of warmth swept over his thin frame, making him feel warmer than he had felt since just before 1942 — before he had gone to France and crawled on his belly through the ice and snow.

Retirement? It took only a few months of it to make Jasper realize he didn't know what to do with retirement. He tried attending programs at the museums where he had long held memberships. He studied catalogues for college classes, but found none that really interested him. He thought about travel, maybe even Bermuda, but the travel brochures had just stacked up into tiny mountains around his apartment.

Some days, he just sat around, wrapped in a blanket and stared at his art collection, but the Pollacks, the Sargents, the Picassos, and the Teegardens gave him little enjoyment, although for years they had been his best friends. One evening, wandering the streets of Denver, he saw, in a sporting goods store window, a pair of skates, inline skates. He had roller-skated and ice-skated as a child, and the combined mechanics of the inlines excited him. The next morning, Jasper was waiting for the store to open, and he purchased the best pair of inline skates the store had to offer.

He drove to City Park, the skates still in the box resting lightly in the front seat of his Mercedes. Once parked, Jasper eagerly laced the skates on his feet, and immediately he had freedom *and* warmth even though it was late March and quite cold that particular day. It was if he had found his Bermuda right there in Denver. He couldn't remember how many laps he skated around the lake, then up around the adjacent museum, and back around the lake, until his legs were weary, and his shins hurting like the dickens, and his heart pounding in his ears.

He developed a routine of exploring new paths in unfamiliar parks in the Denver metropolitan area. He had not known there were so many places to skate. He soon developed a familiar pattern, Monday at City Park, Tuesdays and Thursdays around Sloan's Lake, and Wednesday, Washington Park. That left Friday and the weekend to explore Cherry Creek, or any other new and unfamiliar path he could find.

He was happy as his speed increased, and elated with the proficiency with which he was developing his turns. Braking was still a little problem, but how often did one really need to stop anyway? One day, early in his explorations of Sloan's lake, he had stopped by the supermarket on 20th to purchase some Band-Aids for a blister he was developing on the little toe of his right foot. A bold sign begging him to purchase some fancy chocolates for Mother's Day had caught his eye, and on the spur of the moment, by his old game, advertising, he had purchased them along with the Band-Aids.

He was on his second lap around Sloan's when, spontaneously, he decided to share his chocolates with the homeless lady he had seen in various places around the lake. Of course, his own mother was long ago buried in Massachusetts, and it wasn't as though the women reminded him of her. It was more a way to practice his stopping he had told himself later, trying to understand the rough rebuff of the shouted "No!" to his offer. Sure he had ended a little close to her, almost on top of her actually, being a little slow with the stop, but he had not meant to offend her. She had been very firm in her refusal, and in some way, as Jasper skated away, he was more than offended himself.

The poorly addressed letter lay on the front seat of the mail van, mostly forgotten, when Merna, eating her lunch at the lake, noticed a women sitting to her right, some distance away, wearing a sunbonnet. The bill of the bonnet was exceptionally long. The woman was very tan, and it looked like she was sewing something. There was a grocery cart full of junk parked behind the bench, and it was covered with a large piece of black plastic. Merna didn't think of the letter, busy as she was getting her lunch from the cooler.

Merna was sitting in her usual lunch spot at the lake, and she had been watching the clouds gathering over the mountains. She was hoping for rain, or at least some shade for the last part of her mail route. It had been a little bit of a tough go this morning when the Mason's dog nearly nailed her butt. They had apparently forgotten and left the beast in the yard and Merna hadn't seen the snarling, shaggy mutt lying under the shade of the lilacs. She got the gate slammed in the bastard's face just in the nick of time. Yep, it would be some time until the Masons saw their mail unless they came crawling in for it at the post office. She would keep their mail in the van "by mistake" so several trips would be needed before they would be able to pick it up.

"The pricks will remember next time," she'd said to herself.

She glanced once more at the woman to her right, got up, brushed the crumbs off her shorts, and headed for the van. "Time to wrap up the route," she mumbled to herself as a yellowed leaf from a nearby willow floated down and stuck to her cheek, just under her right eye. "Bastards!" she said as she rubbed the leaf away and opened the door to the van, noticing as if for the first time the letter lying in the front seat where she had hurriedly tossed it two days ago.

Jasper was losing weight which he attributed to all the inline skating he was doing. His usual thin frame was even thinner, boney even, and sometimes it was uncomfortable for him to sit. Finally, he began to feel exhausted, and he slowed his skating schedule down to two or three days a week. Still unusually tired, he made a doctor's appointment, his first in many years.

Ever since his Army days and the rough physicals (especially the rectal exams), Jasper had shied away from doctors whenever he could manage. With great reluctance, he dropped his drawers and pointed his rear toward the doctor. The exam was only mildly painful, causing Jasper to wonder what his fear had been all these years. The results of the exam would be more painful, but he wasn't to know that for five days when the PSA test results had returned.

He fidgeted in the waiting room for his scheduled test results consultation, and finally after forty-five minutes of waiting the doctor appeared. Oh, his cholesterol and triglycerides were great, nothing to worry there, and his blood count was normal. There was one matter they needed to talk about, and that was his prostate. The doctor suspected cancer, and it may be advanced.

Two specialists and several rectals, a biopsy, and a CT scan later, it was true, advanced prostate cancer had invaded his bones like a Nazi death squad. He was a doomed soldier with no foxhole in which to hide. He didn't inline skate again, but stayed wrapped like a mummy in a blanket, on the floor of his darkened apartment.

The first snow flakes settled like doves on Maggie's mittened hands. She watched as they slowly melted. She had replaced the sunbonnet with a scarf and a stocking cap, and she had pulled on her big winter coat. The days were much shorter now, but the nights were increasingly long. Unknowingly, her mind thought again as to how winter would feel in the sand, not just the desert sand, but any sand, anywhere where it might be warmer. She shook her head from side to side, watching the snow doves as they continued to land.

Merna usually finished her route near Colfax and drove back to the post office via Colfax and then north on Federal. She began her turn onto Colfax when an SUV as big as a bus cut her off and she had to turn right instead of left, pointing her van west towards the mountains.

"You dirty son-of-a-bitch," yelled Merna, raising her right hand as she smashed the horn with her left. She drove the short distance to Sheridan Boulevard and turned north, passing Sloan's Lake on her right. Stopped by the light on Twentieth, she noticed a woman, looking vaguely familiar, sitting on a bench just west of the lake, and Merna recognized her as the one she had seen sewing earlier in the fall on the other side of the lake.

Merna glanced at the empty front seat; the letter was gone. She drove to Twenty Fifth, turned right, and pulled into the north parking lot. She looked around for the poorly addressed letter that she had thrown there at least a month ago. Not finding it, she got out of the van and opened the passenger side door and began searching, finally finding the now smudged envelope under the seat.

"Dammit," she said as she scratched the back of her hand as she pulled the envelope from its hiding place. "Bastard," she grumbled.

TO SUNBONNET, WEST SIDE BENCH, SLOAN'S LAKE 80214, the envelope read. There was no return name or address. Merna glanced behind her, and the woman was still sitting on the bench, on the west side bench as a matter of fact. Sure, the sunbonnet was gone, but she was sure it was the same woman she had seen wearing a sunbonnet on the far side of the lake that fall day.

It began snowing harder now, and the flakes were stinging Merna's face as she began walking toward the sitting woman. She was about halfway there when the woman got to her feet, took hold of her grocery cart full of junk, and began walking away from Merna.

"Wait up, you old bitch," Merna said under her breath, quickening her pace. Catching up with the slow-moving woman was easy for mountain-climbing Merna, and in fact, she passed her, then turned to face her.

"Do you have a sunbonnet?" Merna shouted at the woman. The woman turned slightly away from her, and continued to push her cart past Merna without saying anything.

"Look, you old witch. I didn't beat my cheeks over here for you to walk past me without an answer," she shouted waving the envelope in the air with exasperation.

The woman stopped, looked at Merna, sizing her up, contemplating the uniform, then pulled back the black plastic covering the cart, and pulled out a faded, yellow-checkered sunbonnet with the longest bill Merna had ever seen.

She thrust the envelope towards the woman. "Delivered, US Postal Service employee Merna Stradovitch with your delivery." She snapped her heels together and stood at full attention.

The snow was falling heavily now, as the woman hesitantly

took the envelope from Merna, held it against her heavy coat, then looked at the face of the envelope slowly reading the typing, and held it tight again. Pushing her cart with one hand, Maggie began walking past Merna, and as she did, Merna heard a mumbled, "Thanks."

The woman moved on toward the south side of the lake, pushing her cart slowly, and Merna walked into the biting snowflakes to her van. Reaching the van, she looked back, but either due to the snow or the distance, she could no longer see the woman.

"Bastards," said Merna as she started the van and began again toward the post office, blowing on the fingers of her left hand to warm them.

Later that night, in a small space between two exterior walls of St. Anthony's hospital, in the dim glow from a security lamp and out of the wind that had come up since the snow had lessened, Sunbonnet slipped off her mittens. The bottoms of her feet began to burn as if she were standing on hot sand, and she began to shift from side to side as she gently tore open the envelope. She felt an urgent need to pee when she took from the inside of the envelope a plain sheet of paper with two handwritten words separated with a comma: Enjoy, Jasper. Folded within the sheet was a cashier's check with the amount typed in red flowing script: *Five hundred thousand dollars and no cents.*

Katherine & Marlene

Katherine is stuck at the curb. She has pushed her laden grocery cart through the deep snow, across the street, but can't get it up and over. An early morning jogger goes past, his shoes *schuss-schuss* in the snow.

Because of the bulk of her dress and the heavy hood on her head, she walks slowly to the front of the cart and wrestles the wheels out of the gutter and onto the buried grass. Walking back, she pushes mightily, and the cart lurches forward onto the grass. Ten more feet and the unwieldy cart is on the plowed pathway around the lake.

Rubbing her hands together in thick worn gloves, still adjusting to the cold, she straightens her possessions, the bulging, black plastic garbage bags sway and flop against the cart as she begins her slow march toward the street side of the lake.

Katherine meets several walkers, some with dogs, but she keeps her gaze down, her face hidden within the hood, her breath fogging around the edge. She feels lucky. This storm and cold were hard, but she had found a warm grate to sleep on behind the hospital across the street. It made the nights tolerable, and relieved her from going to a mission. She hates going to missions other than for food.

Always a solitary person and not enjoying the company of others, she sometimes thinks about school back in Boston, where she was called "Loner" and sometimes, "One." She stops pushing, pauses, straightens a bag that is lofting to the side.

"Boston?" she asks herself.

It could have been Boston, or it could have been Cleveland. Her family was always on the move. Whatever. No matter. Her "family" was always someone different: an aunt here, an uncle or cousin there.

Eventually Katherine reaches the bench near 20th Street. Maneuvering her cart precisely perpendicular to the bench, she pushes off the remaining snow, slowly spreads a thick cloth from the cart onto the iron seat of the bench and eventually sits down on the sun side of the cart. Turning and pushing back her hood ever so much, the slight warmth of the sun feels good on her face, but it will take awhile to penetrate the layers of clothing she is wearing.

Reaching to her side, she lifts a box from the cart. Sliding her rubber overshoes from side to side, she clears the snow from the cement pad anchoring the bench, places the box in the path, and puts her feet on the box. "Maybe now they'll warm up," she mumbles to herself as she brushes the snow from the rubber.

"Marlene. Maybe Marlene will be along."

Katherine has been on the streets for six years and only once before was she "friends" with anyone. She doesn't think about it much anymore. What good does it do anyway, except make time pass. That "friend" took her spot in the mission, and all her belongings too.

"No more 'friends' for me!"

Marlene has become her exception. Marlene is different somehow. They passed each other, pushing their carts in slow motion around the lake for the entire summer of 2000, never speaking, never looking directly at each other.

In October, Katherine was sitting on this very same bench looking out over the lake and watching the geese practice their landings.

"Got room?"

She looked up, and a woman with a terribly sunburned face was standing with her cart and nodding toward the other end of the bench. Katherine went back to looking over the lake, thinking to herself, "Get lost."

The woman, her reddish, gray-streaked hair falling over the shoulders of her faded orange coat, aligned her cart parallel to Katherine's and stood by the end of the bench, saying nothing.

"I'll be back. Watch my stuff," and with that the woman disappeared behind the bench and out of Katherine's peripheral vision.

Within five minutes, Katherine began to perspire. She wiggled, and stretched her legs, and finally had to stand up and look around. There was no sign of this woman, only her cart. Katherine wanted to leave, but couldn't tug herself away from the unwanted responsibility given to her.

Another five minutes passed, then ten, and Katherine could stand it no longer. She reached for the handle on the woman's cart and was just about to push when she heard from behind, "Coffee?"

Turning, Katherine faced the same women, a steaming cup in each of her hands. They stood looking at each other for one, maybe two minutes until Katherine took her hands from the cart, dropping them to her sides, unsure of what to do.

"Here," the woman thrust one cup in Katherine's direction.

Hesitantly, Katherine took the cup, and still feeling unsure said, "I wasn't taking off with your stuff. I just—," her voice trailing off as she smelled the thick black coffee steaming in her hand.

"Name's Marlene. Didn't mean to take your bench."

With one hand wiggling into a plastic bag in her cart, Katherine came out with two sugar packets. She offered one to Marlene.

"Thanks, but I take mine straight." She brushed her stringy hair back from her face and looked out over the lake, moistening her cracked lips with her tongue. Katherine returned to the bench and, tearing one packet open with her teeth, poured the sugar into the coffee. The hot thick liquid tasted good.

Marlene looked back, and gently sat on the other end of the bench next to the carts. They drank their coffee, silence bulging between them, surrounded by the rush of traffic on the street and the occasional honking of the geese that were still practicing landings and takeoffs on the lake.

And so it was for the rest of October, November and into December. The two would often meet on their slow treks around the lake, pushing their carts. Sometimes they would nod to each other, sometimes not. They never spoke. Occasionally the two would stand in the same vicinity for hours at a time watching the leaves fall from the trees or the children playing on the park equipment.

About once a week, or maybe less often, the two would sit on the bench on the west side of the lake and drink coffee that Marlene would always provide from the Sonic across the street. Rarely, words would pass between them. It was getting colder by the day, and the steam from the coffee would disappear into the graying sky, and the liquid would warm their often-empty bellies.

Just before Christmas, an unseasonably warm spell came that lasted for about a week. Katherine did not see Marlene all that week, and although she tried not to "look" for her, she couldn't help but wonder where she might be. As she walked around the lake, she glanced into the willows along the edge where she knew Marlene would sometimes sleep, but she did not see her cart, nor any evidence that she had been there.

The day before Christmas, winter returned with a very cold north wind and snow. It piled up ten inches before it blew out two days later. The willows along the lake were bent by the weight, and the frozen surface made a slide for the landing geese.

Now, even with the cloth under her, the cold begins sneaking like a snake through her sweaters and coats. Katherine's feet are still cold in spite of the sun. Trying not to think about how good a hot cup of coffee would taste right now, she gets up from the bench, shakes, then carefully folds the cloth and returns it to the bag on her cart. She picks up the box that serves as her footrest, lays it on top of the bags, and begins slowly pushing her cart around the lake. Her empty stomach growls with yearning. Pulling up her heavy hood, she hopes her feet will warm with the walk.

Near the other end of the lake where the path runs right along the shore through the bent willows, Katherine notes a grocery cart tipped and frozen into the surface of the lake. A plastic bag flutters as it lies partially on the surface, partially frozen in the ice, and in the ice, like a reflection in a mirror, she sees the contents: bits of colorful clothing, a stocking cap.

Pausing, she leaves her cart and walks to the edge for a better look. Geese are flying overhead, honking, and as she stops, under the clear of the ice, she sees orange, a jacket. Quickly sucking in her breath, she returns hastily to her cart. The image of strands of reddish hair streaked with gray frozen flowingly in the ice follow her as she pushes her cart over the curb and into the street and down the tracks made by the cars through the snow.

Never Be Afraid Again

"You see this? Go ahead, but your brains will be painting this neighborhood."

He pauses in his stride, sticks his pointing finger into the corner of his jacket pocket, the outline looking like a gun barrel.

"You scum-bag. (laughs) You silly bag of shit. Go ahead and try my patience."

This time he sticks fingers of both hands deep into the corners, double barrels forming in his pockets.

He walks on down the street softly whistling under his breath feeling all the world like no one is going to mess with him again. Never!

It wasn't late night, only about 9 PM and the summer was just fading, dropping long shadows across the path. As the small waves of the lake were slurping gently against the shore, Oscar came around a looping bend in the path and this punk stepped out from behind a tree, demanding his wallet, his watch. He was holding a gun steady at Oscar's stomach.

Fear swept through him like a lightning bolt on its way to the ground, the results more like thunder. He had soiled himself

43

so caught in fear. After the punk had taken his things, he had hit Oscar above the temple with his gun, knocking him flat on the path. He lay there for a long time, crying, until he heard someone coming. He got to his feet, a bit unsteady, and stepped off the path so anyone coming would not see his wet face, his wet and heavy pants.

It must have been a duck or some animal, for no one came along. Oscar cautiously started for home, a seemingly long walk around the last two-thirds of the lake path.

Over the next months, Oscar became more fearful. He had trouble sleeping, tossing and turning in his bed like a rock in a tumbler. He was losing weight as food didn't interest him, and he had to force himself to eat. He had trouble concentrating on his job at the food store, and was so jumpy that his manager called him in and asked him if he was on something.

He should have told his boss his problem, but he was too embarrassed. Ashamed. Still scared.

When six months had passed, Oscar began to calm down a little. He was beginning to sleep better. Food was more interesting, and by eating more, he looked less like a Halloween ghost. Oscar still avoided the path around the lake, and instead had taken to riding the bus downtown on Friday nights to cruise the art galleries, attend the openings. With lots of people around, he was feeling quite safe, although he always kept a wary eye open along the dark storefronts.

Oscar stepped off the bus after a rather late Friday night. The art openings had been wonderful, and as he started the two-block walk to his home, he was thinking about the great photographs he had seen at the Gallery Obscura.

"Hey, shit. Gimme"

Oscar froze in his tracks, a shearing pain shooting up his spine, the reflexes letting go. Limply, he stumbled on the sidewalk and went to his knees. He saw the flash of what looked like a gun, his wallet gone, watch still on his wrist, his heart pounding in his ears. He was now lying on the sidewalk, unable to get up.

It seemed like hours passed when he heard another voice: "Are you all right? Should I call 911?"

Some unknown person had come to catch the late bus and had found him on the sidewalk. Oscar rolled over and attempted to stand saying, "I've been robbed, but I think I'm in one piece."

A sudden calm blew across his mind as an advertisement he had recently cut from the newspaper came clearly in his mind: "*Never be afraid again.* Sign up now for training for a concealed weapons permit."

The bus person was standing near a tree as if needing the protection, repeating herself: "Should I call 911?"

"No," said Oscar, "I live close to here, and I'll call the police when I get home."

Hearing a siren in the distance, he started walking crookedly in the direction of home. "*Never be afraid again,*" he repeated under his breath.

Oscar didn't call the cops that night, but first thing the next morning he got on the computer and found the webpage listed in the advertisement: www.nbaa.net.

Welcome to Colorado Weapons Training!

We proudly offer firearm education and training to the public. Our courses meet Colorado State requirements for Concealed Carry permits. Students learn firearm safety and competence, proper handling, and when and where you can carry your firearm.

The classes feature both live instruction and graphic video to give you a meaningful classroom experience. Our many satisfied students are testament to our commitment to total course excellence.

This course meets Colorado State requirements

for a concealed carry permit. Make sure you take advantage of this great opportunity!

Why We Own Guns

Over 70 million Americans own firearms and enjoy their safe and positive uses. Guns provide us with the means to participate in a variety of recreational, competitive and educational pursuits. Approximately 18 million people in this country hunt. Millions more enjoy competition and recreational shooting, gun collecting, and historical reenactment. Guns are tools for personal protection, and they are the elements upon which popular collegiate and Olympic sports are centered. Guns offer American society a vast opportunity for shared experiences - as long as we share the responsibility to learn and diligently apply safe gun handling practices.

Oscar had begun to sweat. His lips were dry and as he ran his tongue over them for moisture he could feel a crack beginning to form in the center of his lower lip *and* he had to pee. He scrolled down the page.

NRA Basic Pistol Class.

This course meets Colorado State requirements for Concealed Carry.

Coarse Goals

To teach the basic knowledge, skills and attitude necessary for the safe and proper use of handguns, and to provide information on the U.S. citizen's right to self-defense.

Now he really had to pee but he couldn't quit. He read further.

Course Lessons

-the importance of avoiding confrontation

-alternatives to lethal force

-ammunition

-planning for confrontations which may occur

-proper attitude, thinking and safety necessary for self-defense

-the role of handguns in personal protection

Oscar sagged into his chair for a minute and then ran for the bathroom. His stream exploded into the water in the toilet bowel. He shivered for a minute, shook the last drop and zipped his pants as he walked back to the computer. It was all there, and just what he needed. Never again would he be afraid.

The next course wasn't until September, but that was only a month and a half away. He printed the application form, wrote out his check and placed a stamp on the envelope. Oscar sat back from his desk and let out a big sigh. He could hardly wait. In the meantime, he would be very careful; maybe even giving up his Friday night gallery trips.

September 15: Oscar knew he was early, but he was so excited. Fortunately there was a bathroom right inside the entrance to the building, so he was able to relieve his tension before entering the main hall. He had to show his ID and receipt for his payment to the course before he was allowed entry. Both sides of the hallway were lined with tables displaying guns and accessories. Oscar stopped at the first table and looked. Sleek small weapons, revolvers, very large guns that he didn't even think he could lift easily let alone hold steady.

Other tables held similar ware, different manufacturers. Then there were the accessories: holsters of various kinds, ammunition, cleaning supplies and lots of literature. By now, Oscar was tingling, his feet hardly touching the ground.

The morning began in the lecture hall when a drill-sergeant-type-of-guy called role, last names only. There were about fifteen people, many of whom were women. Mike, the sergeant, introduced himself. He talked a little about his youth and his service in the military in Vietnam and then as a police officer.

Oscar was fascinated. Mike had a small, black, leather holster that miraculously hung just under his left armpit. It held a small gun of which Oscar could only see the edge of the handle.

"Before we get into the meat of this program," Mike was saying, "I want to give you a few safety rules. I didn't make them up but a friend of mine, Jeff Cooper, did, and now they are my rules too. You will memorize these rules and they will be yours. And if you never forget them, you will be safe."

Mike looked each and every person seated directly in the eye, then cleared his throat.

"Rule 1: All guns are always loaded."

Mike cupped his right ear waiting for the group to repeat rule number one.

"*Rule 1: All guns are always loaded*," they echoed.

"Rule 2: Never let the muzzle cover anything you are not willing to destroy."

"*Rule 2: Never let the muzzle cover anything you are not willing to destroy.*"

"Rule 3: Keep your finger off the trigger until your sights are on the target."

"*Rule 3: Keep your finger off the trigger until your sights are on the target.*"

"And the last one is Rule 4," said Mike, "Be sure of your target!"

"*Be sure of your target*," they shouted back, all sitting on the front edge of their chairs. By now the women's voices were almost matching the depth of the men's.

The silence as Mike again looked each person directly in the eye was eventually broken by coughing as the participants, along with Oscar, tried to relax. Someone laughed only to be fixed in Mike's stare. The coughing ceased immediately.

Mike pulled his gun slowly from the holster, pulled something from the gun, clicked a latch and stared at the gun for a minute.

"There are three types of weapons: revolvers, semi-automatic and automatic. Revolvers come in two types: single action and double action. A semi-automatic weapon fires each time you pull the trigger as fast as you can pull the trigger. With an automatic, you only pull the trigger once and the weapon fires until you let go of the trigger or it runs out of ammunition. You will be interested in the first two. You cannot own an automatic firearm without a special federal permit which most probably includes your first-born child."

Mike paused a moment, turning the gun in his hand over very slowly. Oscar held his breath as he felt the sweat dripping from his armpits.

"This weapon is a nine-millimeter semiautomatic weapon made by Glock. This is the barrel, the trigger and guard, the grip. This," he held up his left hand, "is the magazine. It holds the ammunition and fits into the grip. And this important little button right here is the safety. When the safety is on correctly, you cannot pull the trigger. The nine-millimeter tells you the size of the bore of the barrel and also denotes the size of the ammunition."

One by one, Mike dropped bullets from the magazine into his hand. Oscar counted under his breath: one, two, three, four, five, six, seven, eight—. Mike paused, shook the magazine and one more bullet fell into his hand.

"Empty?" he asked looking at his audience. "How do I know the gun is empty? Do I know the magazine only holds nine bullets? Is there one still in the chamber? Know your weapon people, know your weapon. Know your weapon inside and out. How do you learn this? First, read the instruction manual on any weapon you might decide to purchase. Then practice, practice, practice. Eat and sleep thinking about your weapon.

"Now, back to my question. Is this weapon completely unloaded? No!" Mike pulled back the chamber slide, then flipped up the barrel exposing a shell in the chamber. He turned the gun and paraded back and forth for all to see.

The lectures continued. Oscar was distracted during the session about *Always Wear Ear and Eye Protection When Shooting*. He could see the necessity of this when practicing, but it was certainly not an important consideration during self protection. An inward smile formed as Oscar thought about first pulling ear plugs and protective glasses from his pocket before shooting some scum bag trying to rob him.

The morning raced by, and it was noon before Oscar noticed. The group broke for lunch after Mike led them through one more round of repeating the rules of safety. This time the chorus of attendees shouted back each rule as Mike smiled with satisfaction.

Lunch was served cafeteria-style allowing the group to further check out the tables of guns and accessories. Oscar returned to the Smith & Wesson table. He really liked the looks of a small short-barreled revolver, a Model 640. It felt good in his hand when he picked it up, the gun nestled there, comfortable. And it was light weight and certainly small enough to be carried in a holster. It was not automatic, but Oscar thought that under his circumstances, he would only need one shot anyway. He picked up some brochures about the weapon for more information he could read about later. He also bought a book called *Gun Facts*, by Guy Smith. The contents promised a wealth of information on guns and gun rights plus a section dispelling myths about guns and their use.

After the lunch break, the group was gathered and guided to the shooting range for further instruction. Mike was replaced with another Marine-type, Major Chet.

"Hi," Major Chet began, his voice a dead ringer for Clint

Eastwood's. "Major Chet is my name, but you can call me Chet."

He was looking over the top of the group as if expecting an attack from the rear at any time. He was smaller than Mike, maybe five foot ten, but obviously worked out on a regular basis. His biceps bulged beneath his tee-shirt sleeves and his thighs filled the cargo pants he was wearing. In spite of his graying beard, his movements were quick, cat-like. To Oscar, Chet didn't look like he would need a weapon in any kind of circumstances.

There were tables set up along the back wall of the firing range, and as they passed, each grabbed ear and eye protection from the boxes laid out on top. Chet stood at the end of the table and handed each a weapon, a magazine, and a box of ammunition. They took places, as per instruction, in pairs at a designated station. Oscar glanced down the alley-like range and noticed the black on white targets were in the shape of a man. A sudden chill shivered down his back as the entire area became very, very quiet.

"Men," Major Chet began, ignoring the fact that many were women, "Remember the safety rules we taught you this morning. Now, place the ear protection around your neck so you can hear me. Put on your safety glasses. This afternoon, you will be shooting a Beretta 87 target pistol, a .22 caliber, semiautomatic handgun. This weapon can fire up to eleven rounds. The magazine holds ten. Now, make sure your weapon is on safety."

Major Chet moved quickly from station to station to make sure all weapons were on safety, and then moved to a position behind and in the center of the line of shooting stations.

"Place your weapons and ammunition box on the stand in front of you and hold the magazine in preparation for loading." Major Chet held a magazine high in the air.

"Look at the magazine and see if you can tell which is the front and which is the back. You can tell by looking in the open end of the clip. The spring will be at the back." He waited a few minutes while all inspected their magazines.

"Place one bullet on top of the open end, point towards the front, and push it in. Repeat this nine more times."

Click, click as the shells were pushed into the magazines. Occasionally, a shell would fall to the floor and a muttered "shit" or "damn" could be heard: once, a short giggle, then silence.

"Good work, men," growled Major Chet in his "make my day" voice. When I count to three, one person in each pair will pick up a weapon. The other person in the pair will place his loaded magazine on the stand next to their weapon."

Chet was quietly gazing out over the group, side to side, then ambushed them by shouting: "*Watch where you are pointing the muzzle and keep your fucking fingers off the trigger!*"

Oscar heard someone drop their gun. He looked down quickly to make sure it wasn't his, but the gun remained in his shaking hand. He was sweating profusely, the chills gone from his spine.

"Re-check the safety and then take the magazine and firmly slide it into the grip of the weapon until it clicks. *And watch where you are pointing the muzzle,*" he ended with a shout as he demonstrated the maneuver high above his head for all to see.

Still looking over the group, Major Chet lowered his weapon and said in a very low voice, "Place your ear protection and position your weapon using the two-handed technique we have taught you."

He quickly moved from station to station making corrections when needed to anyone's stance and returned to his center position in the line.

"Ready on the left? Ready on the right? Fire!

The shots sounded muffled and distant in the ear protectors as Oscar fired at the black silhouette. He finished his rounds slowly, trying to be as accurate as he could, aiming at first for the midsection, then the last two rounds at the head of the silhouette.

When all was quite, Major Chet yelled: "Safety on! Place your weapon on the stand." Chet walked from station to station looking and reporting on each target. When he got to Oscar's, he paused.

"Very good for a first try. You have eight of ten well placed. Congratulations."

Oscar felt his face flush and an icy tingle began again along his spine as Chet moved on to the last station.

"Switch positions and *watch where you are pointing the muzzle*," he said as he prepared to demonstrate once again the loading of the magazine into the weapon.

Oscar arrived home totally beat. The course had lasted a full ten hours. He wearily threw all the literature he had collected onto the kitchen table, went to the bathroom, peeled off his clothes, then fell into bed without even thinking about his nightly shower. He dreamed of scumbags and Glocks and Smith and Wessons and Major Chet yelling *"watch where you are pointing the muzzle and keep your fucking fingers off the trigger."*

He awoke all sweaty from running down a dream-like stairs where eighteen black silhouettes of men were chasing him hard and rapidly gaining.

The next few weeks were very busy for Oscar. Every night after work he studied guns on the various manufacturers' Web sites. He read and re-read the literature he had picked up at the weapons training course. He read *Gun Facts* from cover to cover. There were so many choices for a weapon his head would spin, his dreams filled with details: Glock, Berretta, caliber, barrel length, Smith & Wesson, magazine capacity, weight, revolver, semi-automatic.

Late on Saturday morning, he took the bus down Broadway to a gun shop and after a long discussion with the seller, decided on a Smith & Wesson 340 revolver. In hindsight, he had fallen in love with this sweet little weapon when he had first seen it at the training course. It would fill his need perfectly. It was small and light weight at only twelve ounces when empty. It had a black finish, so would conceal well, held five rounds and had great hitting power with a .357 Magnum caliber round.

He purchased a box of ammunition, a black shoulder holster, and cleaning supplies. The bill was astounding, but it would be worth every penny. He left the shop walking with a purposeful stride to the bus stop across the street, feeling very good about himself. There was only one-step left to take before he was ready and he would go to the county offices on Monday to get his concealed carrying permit. Then, a few Saturdays of practice and he would never have to be afraid again

It had been months since Oscar had walked around the lake. He loved the light as it rippled off the changing autumn leaves of the large trees surrounding the lake. It was a beautiful evening. He began whistling a light tune and then said to himself: "You see this? Go ahead, but your brains will be painting this neighborhood."

He pauses in his stride, sticks his pointing finger into the corner of his jacket pocket, the outline looking like a gun barrel.

He laughs and says, "You scumbag. You silly bag of shit. Go ahead and try my patience."

This time he sticks fingers of both hands deep into the corners, double barrels forming in his pockets.

He walks on down the street from the lake toward his home, softly whistling under his breath feeling all the world like no one is going to mess with him again. Never!

There is a changing chill in the air as Oscar steps from the bus. He doesn't particularly like winter, but his new sport coat makes the walk toward home tolerable. His mind is wandering over the paintings he has just seen at the Friday night opening of the Sherrill Gallery. Although modern art isn't his greatest love, there had been some very interesting pieces. He smiles as he thinks about the one that reminded him of his recurring dream: the black silhouettes from the training gallery that often chase him down those dream-like stairs. At least in the painting, they were not gaining on him, but were being held in the background by wispy red cables or ropes. Or maybe they were spider webs. Whatever.

"Hey, bullshit. Gimme."

Oscar freezes in his tracks, a shearing pain shoots up his spine, his reflexes tense. He slides his right hand into his coat and feels for the grip of his revolver in the shoulder holster sitting under his left armpit.

"I said gimme. Wallet and watch, *now* damn it!"

In spite of the chill, the young man is dressed in a dark tee-shirt and black trousers. He is wearing a red bandanna on his head, and Oscar doesn't see any weapon in his hand.

"All right," Oscar tells the young man as he feels the grip of the revolver slip easily and comfortably into his hand. They hear a siren in the distance and both glance in its direction, a strange thing for either of them to do given the circumstances. Oscar's gun is just clearing his jacket when he hears a loud *pop-pop-pop* from behind. Suddenly Oscar cannot get his breath and, limply, he stumbles to the sidewalk onto his knees.

"*Keep your finger off the trigger until your sights are on the target,*" instructor Mike's forgotten voice shouts from somewhere. Now there are two men pawing him for his wallet and watch and as he is pushed onto his side he hears Mike again: "*Be sure of your target.*"

Oscar pulls the trigger on the Smith & Wesson, but he is already too weak to bring either man into the sights, and the round zings off the sidewalk whistling like a jet engine starting up on the concourse.

"*Never let the muzzle cover anything you are not willing to destroy,*" Mike whispers loudly into Oscar's left ear.

Oscar's heart is pounding in his ears. His breathing is shallow and quick with little air moving in his throat. There is a hissing sound in the front of his chest with every attempted breath. He is lying on the sidewalk and hears the men race down the street.

He tries to keep his eyes open, but the red spider webs forming around his eye lids make it difficult, and the black silhouettes are desperately forcing themselves through to where they are standing on his chest making it quite impossible to breathe. From somewhere, Mike leans in closer to his ear and says quietly, "Remember, all guns are always loaded."

"Are you all right? Should I call 911?" someone beside him is asking, her voice sounds distant and hollow as if in a long tunnel.

Oscar tries, but is unable to tell her, "No, I'm all right, thank you, because I'll never be afraid again."

Balby, England

She was beautiful, really, and she was walking down the train aisle exactly toward him. Her dark-rimmed glasses accentuated the high cheekbones and the darkness of her hair. She was dressed very smartly: a two-piece suit, beige blouse and a brightly colored scarf thrown casually around her neck, untied. Her heeled shoes were tapping the rhythm of her steps.

She smiled; warm, open, engaging and now she was looking directly at Harvey, who cleared his throat and quickly glanced behind to see who might be the recipient of that wonderful smile, but no one was seated near.

"May I?" she said to Harvey, indicating the empty seat where Harvey had placed his camera bag.

"Uh, sure," he replied as he swept the camera from the seat. She sat down as if exhausted, unloaded a small leather briefcase from her shoulder, snapped it open, removed a make-up kit and began applying fresh lipstick, puckering into the refection of the tiny mirror.

A slight scent of honeysuckle passed Harvey's way, and feeling slightly uncomfortable, he watched with fascination out of the corner of his eye.

"Lovely day," the young woman said, taking a deep breath as if to savor every minute. The train began pulling from the station and Harvey could feel his body push back into the seat. He looked across the small table to his wife of forty-one years. There was a slight crease in her brow as she turned a page in the book she was reading. She looked up and winked at Harvey as his face immediately flushed.

Two Americans, Harvey and June, were on vacation in England for the first time. And the weather! They had been prepared for rain and more rain. That's what everyone always said, but in the summer of 2003, England was having a drought and the weather was extraordinary. Blue skies had been the rule, and the crispness of the air was delightful.

Harvey cleared his throat again and said to his new seatmate, "Going far?" Though flattered, in the back of his mind was the thought: "I wonder why she chose to sit next to me? The train is not very crowded and there are plenty of empty seats."

"Not far," the young woman turned, facing him, "Just to Station Nuneaton. I'll catch another train for a bit to Leicester. My mum lives near there. And you?"

"My wife and I," Harvey nodded toward June, "are going to Chester. Do you know anything about Chester?"

"Medieval setting, they say, although I have never been." Another glorious smile. "I'm Madeleine," she said as she opened her case and started looking for something apparently not easily found.

A food porter was passing through the car and Madeleine ordered something, maybe a coffee, although it was hard for Harvey to understand. It was surprising to him how hard the English language could be at times. Again to himself, wondering: "Maybe she just likes company, likes to talk to foreigners." And with that, further questions were melted by her engaging smile and especially the honeysuckle perfume.

"You work in London?" Harvey asked, watching the

countryside flash by the windows behind his new friend who was still looking in the case. They had left London quickly behind.

Madeleine chuckled. "I'm going to college there, getting my advanced degree for teaching, which I do part time. I'm on my way home for a short visit with Mum. And do you have business in Chester?"

"We were supposed to attend a meeting there, but it was cancelled." Harvey began thinking about the circumstances that had brought them to England. Harvey was a surgical technologist, the person in the operating room that hands the instruments to the surgeon. That is, after being sure that all equipment and instrumentation needed for that particular surgery was in place and properly prepared prior to the actual surgery being performed.

Surgical technology had been a second career for Harvey, who started training after he had become tired of teaching biological science to restless junior high students. He had been working at University Hospital in Denver for over ten years now. There was a world conference for technologists scheduled in Chester, and the hospital was willing to pay part of the tuition. He and June had thought this would be a great opportunity: attend the conference and then spend time looking around England. Then, at the last minute, the conference had been cancelled, but they had decided "what the heck" and went anyway.

They had spent their first four days in London, walking Hyde Park, sampling Piccadilly Square, taking a river cruise on the Thames. They had visited Westminster Abbey, ate lunch in the shadow of Big Ben, rode the Millennium Wheel, and visited the Tower of London. They had ridden the underground and had gotten terribly lost late one night and were just lucky enough to catch the last train back to Paddington Station, which was near their hotel.

Madeleine finished searching through her briefcase, but she really wasn't searching for anything. She was observing and evaluating Harvey and his wife, June. They appeared to be a perfect couple. She had her criteria: elderly, but not too elderly, sweet, but not too sweet, wealthy, but not too wealthy. And trusting. They had to be trusting.

For you see, Madeleine was not really a student, nor was she a part-time teacher. She was from a little town near Leicester, Blaby to be exact, and she wasn't going to meet her mum, but her boyfriend, Carl. It should be a great weekend away from the city, and she was very excited and was much looking forward to it.

The food porter returned with a small tray. A napkin covered the sandwich Madeleine had ordered. The covered cup held coffee.

"£5.85, Miss," the porter said. Madeleine began another search of the briefcase producing some bills and coins. The porter stood impatiently waiting as the search for more money continued.

"I am so sorry," she looked up briefly and smiled at the porter. "I know I have more money here somewhere. It must have fallen from my purse."

"May I help?" Harvey said reaching for his wallet in his back left hip pocket.

Her long, slender fingers were still leafing through the case. "I'm sure I have some bills right here. They must have fallen out."

"Go ahead and help her, Harvey. She can pay you back when she finds her money." It was June, who had set her book on the table and was speaking.

"Oh, please, I'm so embarrassed," said Madeleine as one of her hands flew from the case and came to rest on top of Harvey's just as he opened his thick wallet. Madeleine's hand paused fleetingly as she estimated around £200 in notes open to her view. There may have been a few American bills pressed to the back of the notes, but she couldn't tell for sure. Harvey's passport was stuck in one of the smaller compartments as were various credit cards. The passport fell onto the table as Harvey started pulling at the notes.

Her hand fled from Harvey's back to the innards of her case. "Just give me a moment."

"Well I'll be," began Madeleine as her fingers floated to the surface with a £20 note, handing it to the porter, who quickly made change, and after Madeleine handed him an even broader smile and a tip, hurried down the aisle and left the car.

Harvey gathered his fallen passport and folded his wallet, replacing it back into his pocket.

"This is a brand new purse," said Madeleine with a very stern voice, and she produced a new-looking purse which was smaller than Harvey's wallet. The shiny silver clasp at the top appeared intact and closed. She snapped it open and stuffed in the change. The small purse now appeared bloated as the sides were pushed out in an awkward shape.

The purse disappeared into the briefcase, whose latch was secured in a flurry by Madeleine's fast-moving fingers.

"There," Madeleine began, "Do you mind if I eat a bite? I seem to be rather famished."

She unwrapped the sandwich from its papered cell and took a dainty bite.

"I'm sorry. How ill-mannered of me. May I cut this and share with you?" She looked first at Harvey and then at June.

"Oh, we ate just before we boarded, but thanks anyway," said Harvey as he leaned back against his seat. June picked up her June Austin book, *Mansfield Park*, that she had purchased in London after walking by a park dedicated to the author, and began reading.

While Madeleine ate her sandwich, Harvey told her about their first day in London: "You should have seen us. I'm sure you would have laughed yourself silly. We took The Tube in from Heathrow to the Paddington Station terminal. Our hotel, a Comfort Inn, was supposed to be within walking distance of the station. I bought a street map in the bookstore in the station and found our street right away.

"So here we go, dragging our loaded suitcases along— well, they do have rollers if you know what I mean."

Madeleine shook her head in agreement as she was finishing her sandwich.

"It didn't take us long to get to the street, Craven Hill something or other, I believe, but there was no corresponding number for the 18 or 19 we were looking for. And, I might add, no hotel in sight either. So, we tried to walk around the block, but that put us quite a way away from the street we needed, so back we went. And then again. We came upon a mailman— a postman I guess you would call him, and we asked him where our hotel might be. He hadn't a clue.

"About our third trip of trying to get around the block, we both, June and I, realized that we were meeting a women pulling her suitcase obviously also looking for her lodging, so we stopped her thinking we might be looking for the same site. No such luck, but in hindsight she was just as lost as we were, so what help could she have been?

"We finally walked back toward Paddington Station until we found a store that had a telephone and they tried to look up the hotel's number which, of course, we hadn't brought with us, but they couldn't find it in the book."

June had set her book down again and joined in. "We had our umbrellas along prepared for rain, and all they did was provide extra weight as it was sunny and hot. I began to sweat like a pig, and my good-natured disposition was beginning to fade."

Madeleine seemed to be enjoying their adventure and had been laughing as the story unfolded saying, "'Lost in London.' Sounds like a good title for a book I'm going to get busy and write one of these days."

"We got out our map again, and these women in the store finally solved our problem. There were actually two streets by the same name, about one block apart, but the one we needed was a dead end and you had to enter it from another cross street."

"It does sound rather confusing, and I thought I knew

London pretty well," said Madeleine as she folded up the throw-a-way tray preparing it for the trash bin.

"We started out again, and this time we walked right to the hotel. The crazy thing was, it turned out to be just one block from where we had asked the postman. Can you believe that?"

"Excuse me for interrupting— " began Madeleine.

"Oh, that's really all there is to the story. We had finally arrived, albeit a little tired in the legs and a little grimy," June said as she smiled in recollection.

"My stop is coming up soon, and I just wanted to point out a very beautiful farm." Madeleine leaned past Harvey toward the window, looking sharply at the landscape. "Here it comes now."

Madeleine leaned back into her seat so Harvey could turn and lean to the window for the view. June pressed her face close to the window and there was a thatched roofed barn and house framed beautifully by huge trees and a stone fence with a slightly askew wooden gate. Sheep were grazing just beyond the barn.

Madeleine's fingers were resting lightly on the top of Harvey's wallet as he was admiring the outside view, and with a wispy twist of her lithe fingers, she popped the top of the wallet above the edge of the pocket. One quick flip and it would be in her hand.

"And we thought Colorado had all the scenery," said Harvey as he turned more toward his wife, June, and he reached across the table and took her hand.

"It is truly beautiful," June replied as the train began to slow.

"This is my stop," said Madeleine as she shouldered her briefcase and picked up her folded tray from the table. "It's been my pleasure to have met you and I hope you enjoy Chester."

She gave them another fabulous smile, straightened her suit jacket, and turned up the aisle to the train exit.

Later that evening as they were snuggling under the covers in their bed at the Dene Hotel in Chester listening to the rain splattering on the trees outside the window, Harvey said, "You really have to wonder why a charming girl like Madeleine would take up with us. There were plenty of empty seats on that train, yet she chose to sit with us." He really meant "Why would she choose to sit next to *me*," but he had said "us" to avoid an argument.

"I'm sure it was your magnetic personality," said June as she placed her freezing toes against Harvey's warm legs.

"I'm sure," he replied, yet he still wondered.

It wasn't raining in Blaby but Madeleine felt cold and isolated. She was in bed and was trying to get up enough nerve to put her arms around Carl. She needed him to comfort her, but he was distant, "being Carl" she would say had she enough strength to confront him. Carl was pissed that she had come home empty-handed. She tried to explain what had happened, but she had broken down in tears because in reality, she didn't know what had happened.

She was a finger flip away from a decent take and she couldn't take it. It was the first time this had happened, and she didn't understand what or why she couldn't go through with it. Everything had been perfect. She'd done the same thing on the same train at the same place on the same schedule many times.

She lay there and rationalized to herself. But she hadn't felt suspicion from Harvey. June had not caught her eye. She turned her back to Carl and tried to sleep. She closed her eyes and took a deep breath, letting it out slowly. In her mind she saw, like a movie re-run, Harvey reach lovingly across and take June's hand. The tears spilled from her eyes and rolled toward her pillow as a broad smile spread across her beautiful face.

Death and Taxes

Someone once said: "There are only two things you have to do in life, die and pay your taxes." But why should a man have to pay taxes if he is dead? I mean, one or the other seems a just penalty, so I think we should change the statement to read: "There is only one thing you have to do in life, die *or* pay your taxes." And if you had a choice, which one would you choose?

Eighty-five year old Loomis stood on his brick patio watching the workman putting tiles onto the roof of the house being built next door. After about ten minutes of observation, his slippered feet began to tire, and he could feel, through the worn soles, the rough texture of the bricks on the bottom of his feet. Uncomfortable as he was, it pained him more to see the house so close to his own, and he wondered why, with a lot size of five acres, they had chosen to place the house there.

He watched the workman heave and place tiles for another two or three minutes, all the while shifting his weight from foot to foot, hoping to relieve some of the pressure on his tender soles. Finally, he turned, his blue- and gray-colored bathrobe fanning in the breeze, and he walked haltingly though the back door and into the house. Rangy, a small mixed-breed terrier, woke from his morning nap and began wagging his tail at the sight of the old man.

"What do you think, Rangy? Think that house is too close to us?"

Rangy's tail accelerated in motion as if the only answer to the questions posed to him by his master was affirmative.

"The neighborhood has gone to the dogs, Rangy. Now, no offense—I mean that in the most generic way—you understand, Rangy?"

Showing no affront to Loomis's comment, Rangy got up from his place, tail beating rapidly, and walked slowly past the kitchen table where the loose sash of Loomis's robe had sent a sheet of paper spiraling to the floor like a dead pigeon from a barn roof. Rangy followed the old man, stepping squarely on the fallen paper, the main copy of Loomis's property tax form, due in full tomorrow. Loomis sat down on a kitchen chair, and Rangy moved in front of him, sat down and cocked his shaggy, brown head, hoping for a treat.

Without getting up, Loomis scooted the chair inch by inch toward the kitchen counter where a small TV held its place among the trinkets and artifacts collected on numerous trips to the Southwest. Rangy kept changing his position to avoid being stepped on or pinched by a chair leg. Finally, giving up on an early morning treat, Rangy passed gas, let out an audible sigh and went back to napping in the sunlit corner of the room.

Loomis turned on the TV to see what was going on in the world. Having no remote control, he had to reach forward to punch the channel buttons on the front of the TV set.

"Only soaps, Rangy. Just the dag-burned soaps!"

Rangy ignored him.

"Please turn the TV down, Loomis," shouted Franny above the extreme din of the TV. Her hearing, although not good, was far better than Loomis's. He was almost deaf without his hearing aid, and he always forgot to put in his aid until she reminded him of it as she did now.

"Where's your hearing aid, honey?"

"What?" Loomis shouted back to her even though she was standing right next to him. He did not take his eyes off Howie Mandel, who was interviewing some troubled, short-skirted teenager with tattoos clearly evident on both arms.

"Your hearing aid. Where's your hearing aid?" She put her hand lovingly on his shoulder and leaned closer to his left ear as she spoke.

Loomis automatically reached to his right ear, searching for the hearing aid. He was supposed to wear one in each ear for optimum effect, but Rangy had eaten the left one almost two years ago, thinking it a treat when it tumbled from Loomis's shaky hand.

"I guess I left it in the bedroom," Loomis said, as he leaned forward and pushed "up" on the TV sound button. Howie's voice boomed though the house.

Franny turned and walked toward the bedroom to search for the missing hearing aid. Rangy jumped up from his nap as she passed, and he dogged her heals into the other room and out of sight from the kitchen. Loomis punched the "up" button once more and leaned back in the straight chair as a Chevrolet truck commercial filled the screen in front of him.

The sharp, screeching sound of the roof tile saw next door coincided with the sliding halt of the truck, ending the commercial. Howie was through with his interview, and some tall, thin fellow was shaking Howie's hand. It might have been Ian Flyn, the famous author, although the previously interviewed teenager ignored him and busied herself by examining her fingernails.

Rangy returned to the kitchen without Franny and stood looking up at Loomis, still half-expecting a treat. Looking down at the scruffy dog, Loomis said, "Guess I'd better get dressed so we can go down and feed the horses, Rangy. Would you like to do that? Huh, Rangy?"

Loomis reached down, almost falling off the chair, and

scratched Rangy behind the ears. Rangy's tail beat lightly on the tile floor, indicating he was already dressed and ready to go.

Things were a lot different back in 1934. While attending the University of Colorado in Boulder, Loomis was big on the polo team. Loomis loved polo, the skill it required and the teamwork between horse and rider. He was the team's top scorer, and in fact, his scoring was unsurpassed until 1952 when Eric Schneider toppled Loomis's record by one goal. No one had come close to either score since.

Francis Louise Bacon loved horses. She was ranch-born and horse-wise, having started riding horses on her father's lap at the age of two. At three, she was riding her own pony, and by five could outride any white man or Indian along the White River. Although it was her interest in art that brought her to the university, it was her love of horses that brought her to the polo games. She desperately wanted to play, but in 1934, it was not considered lady-like. Thinking this was totally unfair, she challenged the rules, but in the end, watching from the sidelines was all she could do.

It wasn't long until she noticed the strong, sandy-haired player on the big chestnut horse. He was a very aggressive player, and she admired his skill and watched him rack up scores. Loomis had noticed her, a slight dark-haired beauty, sitting in the front row of the small set of bleachers. He liked the way the sun glistened on her hair and caught the reflections of her silver and turquoise jewelry. He also liked the way she shouted encouragement to him even though he hadn't the faintest idea who she was.

Mysteriously, when a match would end, she would vanish. One day, during a break in the game, he walked his horse directly toward the bleachers where she was sitting dressed in a white shirt and pants amid the small crowd of spectators. As he rode closer, he noticed she had tucked her pants' legs neatly into the tops of her fine leather boots. The boots themselves were ornate, and the tops were overlaid with green leather trim.

"Like polo?" Loomis inquired.

"I like the horse you're sitting better," she replied.

"I'm Loomis, captain of the team," he said as his horse turned away from the fans, looking back to the field for action to begin again.

Today Francis wore a wide-brimmed western hat, and she pushed it back slightly, silver bracelets jangling, as she dazzled Loomis with her best smile.

"And your horse's name?"

So dazzled by her smile, Loomis had to think a minute before he replied. "Chad. Chad is the horse's name."

Somewhere on the field a horn blew, and Loomis turned Chad and loped back to the center of the grass expanse. When the game was finally over, Francis was still sitting on the bleacher looking radiant. Loomis was not the top-scorer of the game that day!

For their first date, Loomis picked up Franny at her boarding house, and escorted her to the polo team's picnic out by the lake. The fact that he came in a fringed surrey propelled by a beautiful black gelding seemed normal to Francis, and the gelding's pacing gait was as smooth and soft as the mid-spring breeze. Nearing the lake, Francis leaned against Loomis's shoulder and let out a deep, silent breath. Loomis was definitely her kind of man.

Loomis, clucking to the horse as he turned down the narrow road to the lake, felt Francis's head against his shoulder, light as a breast feather from a sparrow hawk. He could hear her humming a lilting tune beneath her breath, and it reminded him of Ireland. He looked at her capable hands, gloved in fine leather, crossed, and resting lightly on her knee. Her boots, the same ones he had seen at the polo field, perfectly polished, had horse manure stuck to the edges of the high heels. Francis, he knew, was his kind of woman.

After a courtship that balanced two egos as spirited as the horses they rode and as soft as minute-eggs, Francis Louise Bacon and Loomis Bradley Tomes were married in a quick ceremony at the county courthouse in Boulder. No one, other than the judge and his wife, was in attendance. Fearing criticism, they decided not to inform their parents until sometime later, much later, in fact. Their ten-day honeymoon was a horse pack trip to Indian Peaks, late in the summer of 1935, where they explored the country, their goals in life and each other. The third night out, snug in their bedrolls laid out under a million stars, Francis's joy spilled, and as Loomis held her, tears rolled down her face and splashed on his strong and hairy chest.

She dazzled him with her horsemanship and her pancakes, and he swept her away tying knots that held the pack saddle securely, and tied her heart permanently to his. He raved about her pancakes and proved he meant it by eating, without stopping, twenty-six pancakes their fourth morning on the mountain, although the fact that Loomis ate no lunch or supper that day did not go unnoticed by Francis or the horses! So involved in love, they were four days late getting back from their honeymoon. They caused worry at the stables and set a pattern that would follow them forever.

That fall at the university, only Loomis returned as a student, continuing his engineering track. Francis would train horses, supporting their meager income until Loomis could finish his degree sometime within the next year. It was December 1936 when graduation occurred, and Loomis immediately accepted a job with Mead and Mount Construction Company. He would be a junior supervisor for the Albany Hotel project on Seventeenth Street. His starting pay was one dollar and fifty cents an hour.

Franny found a delightful little apartment on West Grove and began decorating before the ink was dry on the contract. The only problem with the little place was that there was no stable for their horses, Chad and Ren. They would have to find accommodations elsewhere for them.

After boarding the horses for the winter, it was during their search for pasture in the spring of 1937 that Loomis, one evening just at dusk, spotted a small, poorly handwritten "FOR SALE" sign stuck to a stick along the edge of a large piece of ground. He had to get out of the old Chevrolet and walk about twenty paces through the sandy soil to read the rest of the sign.

"One hundert acres, no water, $6,000. See me at Ed's"

The next day, after work, Loomis drove Franny out to see the property. The land lay several miles south and east, beyond the boundaries of Denver, even past the cherry orchards of Englewood. It was scrubby land, with sagebrush growing in huge clumps. The parcel was slightly rolling, falling off to the west giving them a fabulous view of the entire mountain range. South they could see Pikes Peak and to the north, Long's. Directly west, Mt. Evans shimmered in the evening light as streaks from the lowered sun mirrored across the presence of snow.

They were holding hands, gazing out across the piece of land. They walked most of the entire acreage that soft early summer evening, deciding that the house should go here, or maybe there. The corral and barn should go here, or perhaps there, or maybe even clear over there! Finally, they both agreed the house should go by the one small tree present, which was about two hundred yards from the moist but basically dry wash running diagonally through the property. Loomis found an old tree branch and stuck it in the ground, marking the spot.

By then it was dark and the cries from the Meadowlark gave way to coyote howls. Behind them, a near full moon was rising, casting eerie shadows from the silvery sage. In the distance, a few lights from Denver flickered against the deepening darkness. Loomis took Francis gently in his huge arms and held her against him, smelling her hair, loving her with all his heart. She held him back, very tightly, and for only the second time in her life, tears spilled down her beautifully tanned face.

Two weeks later, on a hot evening early in July, they managed to get the banker to drive out and look at the property. Loomis and Franny needed the huge sum of one-thousand five hundred dollars for a down payment. They were already at the property, making drawings in the dirt, outlining the size and shape of the house they would build when they heard the purr of a car coming. They saw the dust from the road before they could actually see the big black car pull over the nearest hill. Jess Franklin, the president of Mountain States Trust, brought the big Buick to a dusty halt. After waiting for the dust to blow away, Jess rolled the window down all the way, shut down the engine, took two puffs on his Havana cigar and said, "You brought me all the way out here to see this? No offense, Loomis, but what in the world made you think I'd loan you even a dollar on a piece of ground as worthless as this? Look at it. All dry and nothing but sage brush!"

"Well," Loomis started, "since you did come all this way, Mr. Franklin, why don't you get out and have a better look. I'll show you where we plan to drill a well and where the house will sit. I think you'll like it a whole lot more if you just get out and look."

Jess turned the key in the ignition and stepped on the starter button, the Buick roared to life as if anxious to leave. "And it's too damn far from town!" he hollered, and with that, he rolled up the window to keep the dust from coming in, backed up the Buick, made a wide circle turn and faded into the setting sun as he drove off in the direction of Denver.

Rangy followed Loomis through the old part of the house: the rest of the kitchen, the den, and into the new part of the house which consisted of the living room, the master bedroom, and finally, into the bathroom. He watched as Loomis looked at his reflection in the mirror, stroked his face with his hand, decided he didn't need a shave, and dropped his robe to the floor. Standing in his flowered boxer shorts, Loomis continued to look at his mirror image: the sagging flesh, the wrinkled skin, the sandy red hair now mostly gray and thinning.

Rangy, sitting to Loomis's side, suddenly sneezed, almost falling over backward from the force.

"Gesundheit!" soothed Loomis. "Bless you."

He reached down and scratched Rangy along his back,

and Rangy quickly rolled tummy up waiting for more. Loomis obliged, then dropped his boxers and sat on the toilet all the while still scratching Rangy's tummy.

"It's better to sit even for number one," Loomis said to himself. Then to Rangy, "Never stand when you can sit, I always say."

Loomis got up from the toilet on the second try, pulled up his shorts, and walked back into the bedroom where he began to put on a pair of work pants. He had one leg in and was balancing against the overstuffed chair along side of the king-sized bed when Franny appeared in the doorway.

"I found it by the blender," she shouted.

"What?" answered Loomis.

"I found your hearing aid in the kitchen alongside the blender."

Not hearing her, Loomis was just about to say "what" again when he recognized the aid in her outstretched hand. Still balancing against the chair, he reached out and took the aid and placed it in his right ear. He fiddled with the adjustment.

"The battery must be dead." He took the aid from his ear and placed it on the back of the chair and continued with his pant dressing.

Franny took the aid and disappeared into the bathroom. Loomis was attempting to button his shirt when she reappeared with the aid in her outstretched hand. He stopped and took the aid, placed it and began pushing on the adjustment. A high shrieking sound bounced from the walls. Rangy let out two sharp yips, turning his head from side to side as he did so. Franny helped Loomis with his shirt buttons. Loomis made another adjustment, and Rangy, forgetting he was waiting to have his tummy scratched again, bolted from the room, his ears unable to take the pain from the piercing sound.

"Where are you going?" shouted Franny, finishing with the last button.

"You don't have to shout. I'm right here!" said Loomis as

he reached up to his hearing aid and turned down the volume. "Rangy and I are going down to feed the horses."

He looked around for Rangy, but he was nowhere to be seen.

"Rangy! Where the heck are you, Rangy?"

Rangy appeared at the bedroom door, his ears pressed flat against his head making him look a little like a very young coyote. That is, if young coyotes had long scraggly hair.

"There you are. Let's go and feed those hay-burners before they starve to death."

Loomis started for the door, taking a pair of leather gloves off the dresser top on his way by. Rangy took a chance and pricked up his ears as he followed Loomis around the corner and into the living room, or, as Franny called it, the great room. The room had high cathedral ceilings, very high in fact, and the huge window allowed a terrific panoramic view to the west. Except for a humongous evergreen blocking the northern portion, the mountains could be seen for their entire length.

Rangy and Loomis crossed the great room, angled through the den, and brushed past the tax papers on the kitchen table causing one more "pigeon" to spiral to the floor. The screech of the tile saw being used next door greeted their arrival into the sunshine. Loomis paused causing Rangy, who was not expecting such a sudden stop, to plow into the back of Loomis's legs, almost causing him to fall.

"What the heck are you doing?" Loomis spoke to Rangy, who had already recovered enough to move to the side. He sat and perked up his ears wondering whether to roll over and get his tummy scratched. While he was thinking this over, Loomis moved on across the lawn toward the corrals. The corrals, which Loomis had made out of four-inch pipe and metal posts to keep the horses from chewing, were located south of the house, down the steepest part of their land. The wooden barn, large enough for four horses, was located east of the north corral.

Loomis took his time walking down the path, past the clump

of aspen and the elderberry tree, past the enclosure where peacocks had once screeched their song, past the rotting trampoline and the remains of a croquet court, past the small orchard of one pear and six apple trees, to the gate of the corral. He unsnapped the chain and let himself into the corral, closing the gate behind him. Rangy scooted under the gate. He was small enough that he hardly had to lower his back to clear the lower gate bar. One of the horses whinnied a greeting.

The sun was intense, and it seemed to Loomis that it was unseasonably hot for so early in the spring. Denver was always unpredictable about snow, but this winter had been very mild, warm and dry. It wouldn't be long until the trees and bushes would start their spring leafing. It was probably Loomis's favorite time of the year. Franny, on the other had, liked all the seasons equally well, and went easily from gardening to leaf raking, from skiing to planting. For both, every time of the year was good for horse trips, even the winter. At least that is the way it used to be, when they were younger.

He leaned against the top rail of the corral and waited for the horses to come up from the small pasture. Yesterday he had turned them out for a little exercise. Today, when they came for their hay, he would close the gate again, allowing the pasture to green and grow before turning them out for the summer. Loomis looked southwest across the old cattails of last year's crop. Many were "fuzzing," and the gentle morning breeze was busy scattering the seed. It was interesting to Loomis that the "creek" that cut through the property ran more water now that it ever had in the early years. He guessed it was runoff from everyone above watering their huge lawns. Besides, with all the paving, there was no place else for the water to go.

He noticed the people in the house on the land just past the cattails had finished their addition. The house had been huge before, now it was hotel size.

"Must be expecting a whole lot of company, don't you think, Rangy?"

Rangy was busy sniffing along the base of the barn, hoping he might find a mouse or a rat to chase. He began digging near the corner of the barn where he was sure some creature was lurking.

"Hey, I told you before. Stop your digging, Rangy. All you do is stir up the dust and you know you've never dug up anything worth looking at."

Rangy ignored Loomis, but soon tired of digging. The ground was very hard from the constant trampling of the horses, and besides, the horses were coming into the corral, and Rangy had to be wary. The big black horse liked to chase him from the corral, and the old bay mare had been known to kick if he got too close.

Loomis was entering the barn to get a pitchfork, and Rangy watched for his return out of the corner of his eyes. Mostly, he kept his gaze on the horses as he edged a little closer to the corral fence just in case he needed to make a quick getaway. The horses were snorting, blowing dust in little swirls as they put their noses close to the ground waiting for their hay. Loomis came out with the fork, stepped through the iron rails to the bales and forked some hay into the bin.

Realizing he was being ignored by the horses, Rangy went back to his sniffing along the barn. He still kept the horses in his corner vision just in case as he knew he had to be careful. Loomis finished with the hay, replaced the fork and walked between the horses.

"How you doing, big boy?" He stroked the big black horse and then turned his attention to the bay. He worked for a few minutes on a knot in the mare's mane, but gave up without making much progress. All the while, he spoke quietly and gently to the horses. They, in turn, nuzzled him and blew friendly, blowing noises from their noses between bites of hay.

Loomis bent down and picked up one of the mare's front feet. The edges of the hoof were long and ragged.

"Remind me to call the horseshoer, Rangy. Did you hear me, Rangy?" Loomis had raised his voice and was now looking between the horses to see what Rangy was up to. Hearing Loomis's voice, Rangy came around from behind the barn and stood looking at him, his tail making brush strokes in the air. Loomis dropped the foot and came from between the horses. He moved to the side and leaned again on the rail and looked at the hotel house.

"You should have seen this place in '45—nothing but sage brush and dust." Rangy didn't know whether the remark was directed to him or to the horses. The horses were busy eating and didn't really seem to care.

A lot of things happened between 1937 and 1945. Loomis worked on a variety of satisfying building projects in Denver. He and Franny lived in various houses and apartments: on South Marian Street, downtown across from the YMCA, and in a cute, little, white house on South Emerson. They had made many pack trips through most of the surrounding areas, particularly into the mountains that they loved so dearly. Their favorite trip had been to the Never Summer Range, rugged big peaks named after the very clouds that often obscured them: Mount Stratus and Cirrus, Nimbus and Cumulus. The glacial bells were fragile, blue and beautiful even in late July, the waters icy cold, and in their bed rolls, the stars at their fingertips.

Three children were born, two girls and a boy. The first of the girls, Julie Ann, died shortly after being born, in 1937. Rick was born at home in 1938, an easy delivery with a mid-wife, and Sandra Viola arrived after a harrowing trip down from the mountains in a '39 Ford pickup in 1941. She was delivered in Denver's Presbyterian Hospital, although Franny would always say she was actually born on the top of Berthoud Pass.

During this last pregnancy with Sandra Viola, Franny became extremely heavy with child, forcing her to give in to Loomis's wisdom and forgo a summer pack trip to the Ragged Mountains, one they had planned for several years. Her pregnancy with Rick had been so routine, but not this one. Although she never complained, she felt nauseous almost the entire length of term.

Nothing seemed to help, and in the latter two months, she had lots of swelling in her legs making her feel bloated and looking like a beached whale, and she was immensely fatigued.

It was two weeks until the baby was due, and Loomis, tuned to Franny's disappointment over the cancelled pack trip earlier in the summer and her feelings of fatigue, thought a car day-trip to the mountains would be a nice treat. They decided on Hideaway Park, a picturesque little town nestled below the combining of Jim Creek and Parry Creek, which formed the Fraser River. The aspen were in full color and both thought it should be an exciting and colorful trip. How exciting, they would find out later.

Loomis carefully loaded the pickup bed with a few supplies just in case they had car trouble: tire pump, tire patches, a couple of blankets stuffed in a fruit basket, some crackers and a jug of water. Bart, a part-shepherd, part-anything dog Franny had found lost on the streets of Denver over a year ago, jumped into the back ready to go. Loomis placed Rick in the center of the seat on a folded blanket so he could see out the windshield, and helped the smiling, bloated Franny into the cab.

The aspen were even more spectacular this year than usual, especially in the avalanche chutes streaking down along the road on the way up Berthoud Pass. Miles of golden leaves contrasted against the clear blue sky. It was a perfect day. The pass topped out at eleven thousand three hundred fifteen feet where they stopped for a rest from the driving. Franny had a few crackers and a good drink of water thinking that her shortness of breath was only from the altitude. Otherwise, she felt better than she had for days, and was surprised she felt no nausea whatsoever. Bart busied himself chasing chipmunks, and Rick entertained them by throwing rocks into the trees lining the roadway.

They all piled back into the dark, green pickup and made an uneventful trip down the pass into Hideaway. They lunched at the Rainbow Café, a little local spot, and listened as the locals gossiped about a proposed ski area.

"Seems like a good idea to me," Loomis said to Franny in

a lowered tone. "Ought to make some use of all the snow up here besides freezing your backside." Hideaway and neighboring Fraser were widely known for their great depths of snow and extremely cold winters.

"How are they going to get people to drive this far just to ski?" Franny asked.

Loomis thought a minute. "They won't have to drive. Passenger trains through the Moffat Tunnel will bring all the skiers they can handle."

The locals, stopping their own speculations in midbreath, pricked up their ears when they overheard that new information.

Soon, Rick became restless, so they hurriedly finished their lunch and went back to the pickup for the ride home. Bart was no where to be seen.

"Now that's strange." Loomis said as he picked Rick up and put him in the seat on the folded blanket.

Franny, sway-backed and holding her huge stomach, looked up and down the street replying, "He never runs off like that. Where in the world could he be?" A frown of worry creased her pleasant, swollen face.

"Here, let me help you in. We'll drive up and down the street and see if we can find him. He must have found some girl dog in heat. That's the only thing I can think of that would make him leave the truck."

With that Loomis gave Franny a boost into the cab of the pickup.

"Oh!" she said with a slight groan. Loomis was so intent on finding that darn dog that he missed hearing the groan. Had he heard it, he might have done things differently, but instead, he started up the motor and began searching the streets of Hideaway, one by one. Although it was a very small town and the streets were short, it still took them thirty minutes of looking before they completely covered the town.

"Here, Bart!" Loomis would holler out his window.

"Bart! Come on Bart!" Franny would sing out her window, still holding her stomach.

"Barr, here, Barr," Rick chimed in with his high-pitched little voice.

Bart was nowhere to be found.

"Guess we'll have to leave without him," Loomis said rather gruffly.

"Oh, Loomis, we can't!"

Loomis looked at Franny and thought he saw a tear coming in her eye.

"Oh!" she said again, wiggling to a new position on the seat, but Loomis was busy turning the truck around for one more pass through town before heading home. They were about halfway through the little town when Franny said, quite loudly, "Oh! Oh my!"

This time Loomis heard her cry, and turning toward her saw the wrinkles on her forehead and the sallow color to her usual robust cheeks. A shiver of fear nibbled darkly at his heart.

"What's the matter, Franny? Are you hurting? What's happening?" He had taken his eyes off the street, and as he looked up he had to brake very suddenly to keep from hitting Bart who was standing in the middle of the street looking more than a little sheepish. The sudden stop threw Rick against the dashboard where he bumped his head. He, of course, immediately began to cry in a shrill, piercing voice. Franny was pushed forward, but because of her large stomach, did not hit heavily since she had only a little way to go before she contacted the dashboard.

"Oh my!" she said again, and took her hands away from her stomach to help Loomis get Rick back in his position on the folded blanket. She turned as best she could and comforted the child as his sobs lowered about thirty decibels. Loomis jumped from the pickup with shear malice in mind, but Bart jumped so quickly and artfully into the back of the pickup, he didn't have a chance to lay a hand on him. Bart was facing forward as if the wind was already in his face, and was looking out of the corner of his eye at Loomis to see if he was still in immediate danger.

"Darn dog!" said Loomis as he re-entered the pickup. He had killed the engine in all the commotion and had to restart it.

"OH!" said Franny, letting go of Rick and grabbing her stomach.

"What?" asked Loomis as the engine took and the pickup started rolling down the street.

Francis Louise Bacon Tomes said in a quiet, calming voice, "The baby's coming, Loomis. Please hurry home."

Loomis took one quick glance at his pale wife, and pushed the accelerator to the floor. The pickup slowly gathered speed, working its way up the twisting curves of Berthoud Pass. Somewhere during the curviest part of the downhill run from the summit of the pass to Empire, Loomis glanced in the rear view mirror. At that moment, the tires were screeching around a curve, and in the mirror he saw Bart struggling to stay in the bed of the pickup. His feet were braced in the front corner and, swear to God, his lips were parted, and he was gritting his teeth! His eyes were wild with fear, which, when Loomis caught a glimpse of his own eyes in the reflection of the side window, mirrored the very same expression.

They sped through Empire, Georgetown, and even though they did, Loomis didn't remember going through Idaho Springs. He raced down Colfax Avenue. In those days there were no traffic lights to contend with, only a few stop signs, which Loomis ignored. When he reached Glenarm Place, he turned left reaching 19th Street just as the one traffic light turned red. He sped through the light, hoping against hope that no one was coming. Fortunately, the one car that was coming screeched to a halt missing them by no more than six inches. As Loomis sped on, he saw out of the corner of his eye, the car's driver shaking his fist wildly.

Speeding east on 19th brought them past Children's Hospital, St. Luke's, St. Joseph's, to the front entrance of Presbyterian

Hospital. Looking like a wet noodle, Franny had her head on the dashboard. Little rivulets of perspiration were running down the sides of her face. Rick was whimpering, tears painting his little, round face. Loomis, shirt wet thorough the back, lurched to a stop, the pickup coughing, dying, like a totally spent horse. He leaped from the cab, ran around to open the door for Franny.

"Get the doctor, Loomis. I can't move," her voice a whisper in the wind.

Loomis stood immobilized for what seemed like ten minutes, but within seconds, he was bounding through the front door of the hospital. In minutes, two nurses, dressed in white, one pushing a wooden wheelchair, came dashing out the front door, Loomis immediately behind. The nurse not pushing the wheelchair won the race to the pickup, reached in the open door and jerked Franny's skirt up for a professional look-see. Whether it was because of what she saw or whether she hit her cap on the top of the doorframe, no one knew, but her spiffily, starched cap went flying, spiraling into the street; a powdered donut on the run.

The two nurses, with Loomis's fumbling help, managed to get Franny into the wheelchair, and they charged full speed ahead, a chariot and two horses, into the hospital. Loomis threatened the thoroughly-shaken Bart with an early demise if he even thought about leaving the truck, reached in and scooped up Rick, and ran after the nurses. By the time he reached the information desk, Franny was nowhere to be seen. He was instructed to go up one floor to the maternity ward, and sit in the waiting room until the doctor came to talk to him.

Reaching the designated room, Loomis began an eternity of pacing, first with Rick in his arms until he fell asleep and he was able to lay him gently down on the floor in a cozy corner, and then by himself until, finally, the doctor appeared at the door.

"Congratulations! She's a brave woman, but I guess you already knew that. Well, Mr. Tomes, you are the father of a seven-pound five-ounce baby girl. Both the mother and the baby are doing just fine. The little one has quite a set of lungs, I might add."

The doctor reached out and shook Loomis's hand with vigorous shake.

The doctor was studying Loomis, who was yet to utter a word.

"The nurse will come for you in about fifteen minutes, and then you can see your wife and baby girl. Have you decided what to name her?"

Again the doctor waited for Loomis to speak, and was just about to say something else when Loomis said, his voice so very low and quiet the doctor had to lean forward to hear, "Sandra Viola, but we'll call her Viola."

Another pause as the two men looked at each other. Then Loomis turned, went to the corner of the room and lifted the sleeping form of Rick, holding him close to his chest.

"Thanks, Doc."

The doctor shook his head in acknowledgement and left the room. Loomis sat in a chair, pressing Rick even closer to his chest as a tear rolled a squiggly journey over Loomis's cheek, and fell across the little boy's face.

"Yip! Yip! Yip, yip, yip!"

Loomis turned from his place at the fence rail and looked toward the barn where Rangy had obviously found some creature in one of the holes under the foundation. Rangy stuck his nose back in the hole and this time said, "YIPPPPPPPPPPP!!!!!!"

He jetted back quickly from the hole, and Loomis could see blood coming from the side of Rangy's little black nose, evidence that someone was objecting to being disturbed. Rangy began to dig furiously, dirt flying by like dust in a furious wind, enlarging the hole big enough to stick his whole head in after whatever was in the hole.

Loomis began walking toward the barn, reached in the door on his way by for the pitchfork, and went to see what help he could give Rangy. Just as he reached Rangy's side, the little dog flew from the hole like a cork from a champagne bottle sitting in the afternoon sun. Clenched in his teeth was a rodent of some kind, his eyes bulging from the pressure of Rangy's grip.

"Get him, Rangy! Good dog! That-a-boy!"

Rangy gave one quick shake, and became so excited and flattered from the praise heaped on him by Loomis that he tried to wag his tail and grin at the same time. The forces of physics, being what they were, caused a loosening of the jaw and the rodent skittered from Rangy's mouth, and he or she made his or her hasty escape back into the dark, dank hole.

Rangy was stunned, to say the least. He looked sheepishly at Loomis, his face one big question mark, which quickly faded to disappointment. Loomis didn't know what to say.

"Sorry, Rangy. The darn thing got away from you, didn't he? Well, that's all right, you were right on top of him when it really mattered."

Rangy turned and re-attacked the hole with renewed vigor, but the dirt proved too hard, and the hole too deep. Loomis stood in the hot sun and watched, leaning on the pitchfork handle. Soon, Rangy gave it up, his nose adobed with dirt and blood; his fur disheveled and caked heavily with the remains from the diggings. He started to scout another hole, but Loomis said, "Let's go to the house, Rangy. I'll bet Franny has some biscuits for you, and she probably has my lunch ready."

Just as he spoke, the sound of a loud bell, not unlike a large church bell, came rolling down the hill from the house.

Loomis adjusted the hearing aid in his right ear. "See there, Rangy. Just like I said. Our numers are ready."

He reached down and dusted clots of dirt from Rangy's hair with the back of his hand.

"Besides, we've got to let Franny check that nose of yours."

Loomis looked toward the horses one last time, and seeing them still feeding, he walked slowly toward the gate of the corral. He released the chain and let himself through, waiting a minute for Rangy, and closed the gate. Small beads of sweat formed on his forehead. He stopped for a minute, took out a large red bandana, and wiped his brow.

"It's warming up, Rangy," he said as leaned on the gate. Again, he looked south, past the feeding horses, to the hotel house, then west through the distance to the snow on Mount Evans. "Pretty as a picture," he said to himself, still wiping the sweat from his brow. "Pretty as Viola."

Viola was just seven weeks old when the Japanese bombed Pearl Harbor. President Roosevelt declared war, and suddenly the United States was in the middle of World War II. Pushing Franny's protests aside, Loomis went directly to the recruiting office and signed up for the infantry. Only trouble was, he didn't pass his physical. An old polo injury to his left knee kept him at home, 4-F.

Wanting to do something to help the war effort, Loomis put his engineering skills to work building barracks at Lowry Air Base, Camp Hale between Leadville and Minturn, and other bases, some as far away as Kansas. He built airplane hangers in Cheyenne, and internment housing in the Arkansas Valley. Although Franny was proud of him, she and the children missed him greatly during his many out-of-town assignments. When she could get enough gasoline by saving up her rationing stamps, she would load the children into the old pickup and visit for a day or two, military permitting and the destination not too far away.

The war ended in 1945, and Loomis and Franny were optimistic, as was all of the United States of America. This had been the war to end all wars, and nothing but prosperity could be seen in the future.

"Now is the time to stretch and buy that piece of land if it is still for sale," Loomis told Franny one evening after supper.

The children were already in bed, and the evening was soft and sweet. The two were sitting on the front porch steps of the little, white house. The nighthawks were skimming bugs from the sky: diving, twisting, daring. They sat, leaning against each other, feeling each other's hearts, and listening to the birds settling in for the night.

"Yes," said Franny, softly, "now is the time."

Although not an easy task with two small children, Franny had been able to put a little something aside from each of Loomis's paychecks. Loomis sought out Ed, only to find that there were only fifty of the original one hundred acres available. Ed wanted five thousand dollars. Eventually able to borrow a little from a friend to go along with Franny's nest egg, they had to settle for twenty acres. It cost them two thousand one hundred dollars.

After signing the papers, Loomis drove Franny, Rick, and Viola out to the property, and while Franny and Loomis stood holding hands, the kids raced through the sagebrush filling their shoes with sand. The western sky was hanging heavy with thick black clouds, and they could see a squall line of rain coming down over Mount Morrison on to the hogback. Lightning was splitting the air, making way for the sheets of rain as the clouds moved out over the plains.

They stood there, watching, until the first drops reached them, spilling on their faces, plinging in the dust and crashing on the leaves of the sage.

"Get in the car!" Loomis yelled to the children who by now were down by the wash in a small clump of willows.

Rick, leading the run, dashed for the car. Viola, always the swiftest, raced past him amid the giggles and laughter, and was first to the car.

"Just in time," said Franny, her eyes shining with excitement for the evening.

The rain pelted the car, coming in waves, until they could no longer see out of the windows, partially due to the rapidly forming fog from the heat of their bodies and the quick breaths from the excited children. But the rain was too hard and too steady to roll down a window. Lightning continued to crash around them and the wind violently rocked the car.

"It's a sign," laughed Loomis, who was never one to think about anything spiritual.

Franny replied, "Now don't mock what you don't understand."

They could hear water running in the wash, the sound growing louder each minute.

As suddenly as it had started, it was over, the thunder growing more distant to the east. The sun pushed through the clouds as the rain stopped, and instantaneously a golden glow magically illuminated the land. Loomis opened the car door and the children, Viola first, piled out into the wet sand and mud. The wash was running full with water, and behind them, a brilliant rainbow arched completely across the sky.

"Look," cried Viola, "it's a double rainbow!"

"Wow!" said Rick.

Loomis put his arm around Franny's waist and said in his quiet voice, "See, I told you it was a sign."

She reached up, arms around his neck, and pulled down his head, his sandy hair damp from the rain, and kissed him softly for a very long time.

Feeling a little cooler, Loomis mopped his forehead once more, placed the bandana into his hip pocket and started up the path to the house. He didn't get very far when he began to feel a little dizzy, faint. He turned off the path to stand under what little shade the budding apple tree could afford. It wasn't much, and Loomis slowly took the bandana from his pocket and wiped his forehead several times.

"Whew. I feel strange, Rangy," he said to the little dog, who also stopped and was trying to scratch his sore nose with a front paw. "What do you think is wrong with me? I don't hurt anywhere; it's just strange —like I've completely run out of gas."

Rangy was not paying the least bit of attention to Loomis. He was still busy trying to find a way to scratch his sore nose without it hurting.

Loomis looked toward the house and knew Franny would be coming looking for him. He'd best get on up to the house as he certainly didn't want to worry her. The house, white brick, stood as a beacon. He looked at the old part, which was facing him, then the new addition, finished in the early '80s rising above and behind the old, a completion of their dream.

Standing in the faint shade the tree offered, and looking at the house caused Loomis to remember its original construction. Because of his work, Loomis had a lot of friends in the building business, and that helped get them started. Within a month of buying the property, he had a friend excavate for the basement and work began in earnest. Before the snow flew that fall and winter, the basement was finished, enough to be livable, and Loomis moved the family into the finished portion. The biggest hardship was water. They couldn't afford to drill the well until the following year, so hauling water became part of their routine.

The second thing he did, with Franny's help, was build a corral so their horses could be with them. They turned the horses into the corral and watched as they ran, tails up, ears forward, snorting as they explored their new place. Every minute of spare time away from work, Loomis would build on the house, many times until midnight or even later, yet be up early the next morning for his regular job. After the children were put to bed, Franny would often help, holding boards, driving nails and fixing pot after pot of very black coffee.

It made Loomis even more tired now to think about it: God, the work, the long hours. The new part had been easier, added after the children were through college, gone on to lives and families of their own. The years had been hard, desperate at times, but it had been worth every nail and brick and energy spent.

"It was worth every drop of sweat, Rangy," Loomis said, his voice sounding dispirited in spite of his conviction of the truth to the words.

Still feeling weak, Loomis left the meager shade, and took a few steps toward the path. Slowly, with Rangy following, he began walking in earnest. He reached the trampoline and felt so weak he had to sit down in an old, decrepit, lawn chair that he had forgotten to put away last fall.

"Remember what I told you Rangy, never stand when you can sit. It feels darn good right now to take my own advice," he said to the dog, and Rangy, starting to whine, immediately wanted up on Loomis's lap.

"You know, Rangy, the trouble began in the '60s. First, the darn neighbors went and got this area christened 'Cherry Hills Village'. Then everyone and his dog—sorry Rangy, no offense, wanted to live out here. First thing that happened, land prices went through the sky. Then before you knew it, taxes went even higher, like a weather balloon that lost its tether. It was foolish, just foolish, that's what it was!"

A wave of nausea swept over Loomis.

"I must have eaten something that didn't agree with me, Rangy," he said as he bent forward and held his head, trying to keep the world from spinning. Rangy was sitting on the ground right in front of Loomis, hip cock-eyed to the ground, still hoping to get on Loomis's lap, or, second best, get his tummy scratched. Rangy licked Loomis's fingers, hoping the additional attention would bring him one of his wishes.

Feeling a little better, Loomis looked at the ragged dog.

"Taxes got so high, that the only way I could pay ours was to sell off a few acres here and there. And look what they've done with it!"

He waved a feeble hand toward the hotel house. Not being interested in hotel houses, Rangy took a chance and jumped for Loomis's lap.

Loomis pushed him off. "Not now, Rangy, I'm not feeling so good."

Loomis leaned back in the chair and shut his eyes.

In the early '60s, Loomis interviewed for a position with a new engineering firm. This job became his introduction to computers; quickly they became his fascination. Early to recognize the work and versatility computers were capable of doing in cost analysis, Loomis, after a few months, left the firm, and began his own business designed to analyze construction costs, day by day or minute by minute, for large construction firms. Burning the midnight lamp, he wrote his own programs, and tailored computers to do the work. In between, he fought with the finicky, often unpredictable computers and bent them to do the finite work he wanted.

During the day he called in person, or telephoned out-of-state firms with his ideas. Slowly, very slowly, the new business grew roots through the construction trade, and even though computers were very expensive, the business began to show a profit. But not enough profit to keep up with Cherry Hills Village.

Then came the construction crash of the '70s. Savings and Loan Institutions went broke causing a domino effect on many other businesses. The oil industry, many businesses of which were headquartered in Denver, dissolved, and suddenly the city was awash in overbuilt structures. The economy slid to a grinding halt, but taxes on his property and house didn't go down! In fact, as cities felt the lack of tax revenues, property taxes went up, and that's when Loomis had to sell the second parcel of land.

Loomis was feeling a little better. Rangy had crawled under the chair to take advantage of the shade, and tired from all the earlier excitement, had fallen asleep.

"Let's go," said Loomis, and startling Rangy awake by the movement of the chair as he got to his feet, together, they began a slow trek up the path. Eventually reaching the small aspen grove, he could hear the shrill of the roof tile saw.

"Why did they have to put that house so close?" he said to himself.

Loomis had retired in the early '80s, passing the business to Rick. The only problem was, retiring in the '80s did not keep up with the '90s. His and Franny's property was now evaluated for over one and one-half million dollars. The taxes were outrageous! Huge trophy homes dotted the surrounding hills, with more new hotel houses and new additions springing up like sprouts on a sun warmed willow.

"I should have hung on to it," he said to no one in particular, under the aspen, looking up at a few fluffy white clouds meandering by. To keep up with the escalation of inflation and the continued increase in taxes, he had sold the last parcel that they could sell early in 1992; the ground on which the house next door was now being built.

"I should have hung on," he said slowly, his steps slowing. "That two-acre lot down the street sold yesterday for eight hundred thousand dollars. Did you hear that, Rangy, eight hundred thousand dollars! Think how much dog food you could buy with that!"

Rangy cocked his head, sitting in that crooked style that so endeared him to Loomis. Loomis took a few more wobbly, plodding steps. In spite of the heaviness to his feet, his body was feeling surprisingly light, almost ethereal.

"I can't make it, Rangy, I've got to lie down a minute and rest."

Loomis gently folded onto the ground, and looking up, noticed the intricate pattern of the branches contrasting against the blue of the sky. He felt weary and cold, and although he was lying on the ground looking up, he felt like he was evanescent, floating in some pond, the waves swishing his body gently to and fro. Rangy began licking Loomis's face. To Loomis, it felt like rose petals being pressed against his face, and when he looked up, it was Viola, kneeling beside him, pressing the rose petals gently and lovingly to his face. Behind Viola, Rick was holding a bouquet of computer discs. He was smiling, looking down at Loomis.

"Now that's a silly thing to be holding," thought Loomis to himself, but then, remembering that Rick loved computers as much as he did, decided it was quite appropriate. Loomis rolled more fully onto his back, and the tree branches began weaving their tips together forming a ladder. He thought about climbing to get a better view of the new house next door, and possibly the mountains north, especially, but remembering how weary he was, decided against it.

Rangy didn't know what to think. He stopped licking Loomis's face and walked around his crumbled body. He stopped near Loomis's head and started whining. He looked toward the house and then back at Loomis. Loomis heard his whimpering, and it echoed in his head like a drop of water in an empty barrel.

"It's all right, Rangy. We'll be at the house in a minute, and you can have your dinner. You heard the bell. Franny has it all fixed, and she is waiting for us."

Suddenly, as if she had heard her name, Franny was kneeling beside him, and she was cradling his head on her lap. She was rocking back and forth, and Viola was pressing fresh rose petals to his eyelids. He wanted to open his eyes and see what Rick had done with the bouquet, but he was too weary; it was just too much trouble. He wondered if the ladder was still there, woven among the trees, and if he had gained enough strength to climb, because he knew the view would be wonderful, magnificent.

Beside him, on large black wheels, was some kind of a monitor, possibly a computer terminal. In the center, seated in a straight-backed chair was Ian Flyn, author of *Cube, I Cube, Millennium Games, Quandary,* and other works, and certainly Loomis's favorite writer. He was tilted back, his head at a jaunty angle, and there was quite a stern look on his pale face. It was rather nice of him, it seemed to Loomis, to be there after the rush of being a guest on the Howie Mandel Show Loomis had been watching just an hour ago.

Suddenly, the monitor was filled with hundreds of young people, some wearing white trench coats, some in graduation gowns, and a few in big, bulky, padded suits looking like stuffed scarecrows. They pressed to the center of the screen, and Loomis could feel them pushing against him, jockeying for a spot, and before he could protest, someone in the crowd began to peel away the rose petals that had been placed so tenderly by Viola.

Ian had moved to the upper left corner of the screen, and he was tilting even further in his chair. Replacing him in the center was a singular light source. Someone in the crowd, Loomis couldn't see who, hooked a large metal alligator clip to the second toe of his right foot; the one he had broken in his first college polo game. He could immediately feel a heart beat, strong and regular, and he knew instantly that it must be Franny's.

An excited, high-pitched voice from the group urgently shouted "clear", and Loomis could see the crowd scatter to the fringes of the monitor—all but Ian, who remained seated in the corner, staring intently at the light. The centered light blinked weakly a few times, and then returned to a steady intensity. The multitude came surging back to the center of the screen, and Loomis could feel them approaching, pressing, closing in. Rangy was sticking his head between the legs of one of the on-lookers to get a better view of the proceedings, and Loomis called for him to come so he could observe whether the bleeding had stopped on the scraggly, little dog's nose. But Rangy wouldn't budge, remaining, peeking from behind the legs. It didn't matter anyway, Loomis decided. He had observed the monitor was not in color, and he wouldn't be able to tell if there was blood present even if Rangy had obeyed.

"Clear!" the signal came, suddenly, unexpectedly, and Loomis witnessed the same result: the scattering of onlookers to the periphery of the screen, the central light blinking a few times and then steadying. Ian remained detached from the whole affair, looking lofty and arrogant, tilting even further in his chair, defying gravity, ignoring the workings of the light.

A third cry for "clear", and the same astounding outcome transpired, except this time, the light in the center remained fixed and then faded slowly from the screen; a candle extinguished in the blackest night. The heartbeat, known by Loomis to be

Franny's, was getting weaker, less intense by the second, until a withered, wrinkled, blue-veined hand reached forth from the gathering and removed the clip from his toe. The heartbeat stopped.

"No!" shouted Loomis, "Put it back!"

But his cry was unattended, and one by one, the crowd of young people disappeared from the screen, leaving only Ian. Ian had stealthily moved his chair back to the center of the screen, and instead of tilting, he was leaning forward, elbow on his knee, his hand under his chin. There was a faint smile on his paled face, and he was shaking his head slowly back and forth as his image began to dim, receding slowly from the screen.

Loomis wearily closed his eyes. He was cold and spent: tired of the whole thing. All he wanted to do was get home to Franny and Rangy and have a little soup for lunch. Maybe Viola and Rick would join them at the table. But someone, everyone, had pinned him to the ground, and he could not move, and he could feel his electrons oozing from his body, slowly, one by one—one by one, into the ground from the wound left by the alligator clip that had been removed from his second toe.

Honest to God

Honest to God's truth. This is how I got my first motorcycle, swear by it. I had this old beat-up, upright piano for sale. The old piano didn't look like much, as I already said, but it sure held its tune well, and the action was better than great.

So why was I selling it? I didn't need two pianos, that was all, and the one I'd inherited from my mother had been with our family a long, long time.

Anyway, this guy, a really funny-looking dude, dropped by to see the piano. He stood looking at it, running his hands over the beat up wood, and then he hit one key and then another and the next thing I knew he was playing a few rifts. Seems he needed a piano bad 'cause his ex had signed up the kids for piano lessons. His job was to come up with a piano for them to practice on. Only trouble was, he didn't have the bucks, and I was only asking six hundred fifty.

"Want a motorcycle?" he asked, still tinkering with the keys. Before I could answer, he had the front of the piano open, you know, dropped down the front, and was putting his hands on the sounding board. At least that's what he said he was doing, and satisfied, he soon had the front back in place.

I hadn't been on a bike for lots of years, and, in fact, the motorcycle I once rode belonged to a friend who managed to hit a car head-on late one night, actually it was very early morning, and, after that, the bike wasn't worth the metal it was made from. He managed to live through the accident, but he walked with a mighty, peculiar limp for the rest of his life. The driver of the car was drunk, or at least that's what they said, but it was hard to ask him since he died at the site of the crash.

Anyway, after that, I kind of stayed away from the noisy things.

"Why not?" I heard the words drop from my open mouth.

The dude turned from the piano and shook my hand, and that's how I became the proud owner of a 1972 Honda 500. It looked pretty good in a funny green sort of color, the tires were almost new, and it started right up as soon as I put in a battery. The only thing a little different were the handlebars. They were after-market, and maybe even an after-thought, who knows, but they shot up into the air like horns on a gazelle.

It took me a few practice runs to get the hang of riding again, particularly with those handlebars. All I needed now was to pass the motorcycle driving test and I'd be King of the Road.

I have to say I passed the written part of the test with no problem: the driving part was a little trickier. With those gazelle bars, it was most impossible to get that piece of metal through the cones, them being set so close together.

I was down to my third and last try, the sweat pouring down my back, when the engine died. It sure took me awhile to get it running again, and the lady with the clipboard was snapping her pencil pretty sharply by that time.

"Well, here goes nothing," I said under my breath and really, I was doing great until the last cone. Danged if someone had put it right in my way. I stopped and looked at the lady and I could see she was sweating too as she scribbled on the papers on her clipboard.

She ripped off the top sheet and handed it to me and looked

me straight in the eye saying: "I passed you, but don't you dare give anyone a ride on that thing. My only hope is you'll just kill yourself."

King of the Road. That was me. And I was off in a cloud of dust after another fifteen minutes to get the metal beast started.

Me and that metal beast had a love-hate relationship for the next two years, until one day it tried to kill me twice. Now I'm not that stupid: that was enough for me. The first time on that day began so easy, looking back, I couldn't imagine. We were out for a spin south of the city when we came to a road construction site. I slowed way down 'cause one of the things I had learned during the last two years was the Beast did not like dirt or gravel of any kind.

Suddenly we were on gravel and looking into my mirrors, I saw this black pickup bearing down on me at incredible speed. There is something about me and my vision of life that would just hate to get hit full throttle from behind while sitting on a motorcycle, so I took off to the right down the road embankment. The Beast objected, slipped to a halt and fell over on my leg. The guy in the pickup didn't even stop to help me lift.

It was quite a struggle between me and the Beast as we were lying on a downhill slope. That made lifting the thing off my leg particularly difficult, but after thrashing around some, I finally made it. Nothing broken, I decided after limping around in circles, swearing loudly. The Beast overstated its hurt feelings by not starting until the battery was almost run to nothing.

Later that same day, on the winding mountain road toward home, we were zooming around a corner when suddenly we were staring face to face with a white pickup coming down across the center line and half in our lane. It was coming on strong.

The pickup driver, his face turned white as the truck, hit the brakes and started to skid further into our lane. I shot the Beast to the right toward a stone wall. Somehow we missed the wall as we slid in the roadside gravel and now the beast was lying on my other leg, wheels spinning, with the manifold getting mighty hot on my tender parts.

Faced with the prospect of personal Rocky Mountain Oysters, it didn't take me long to get the Beast off my leg and into an upright position. Damn! The handlebars were no longer gazelle-like, but were drooping like a rabbit sick with Tularemia.

The pickup was gone and I could hear his tires squealing around the curves further down. Not knowing what else to do, I kicked the Beast and then started to hobble toward the nearest house. A kindly man helped me haul that pile of metal home and into my garage where, after draining the carbs of gasoline, it sat silently waiting, unused; a daily reminder of our torturous times together.

Searching for greater rewards, in 2000 I moved from my mountain castle to the great city of the plains. What to do with the Beast. Plan A: leave it sitting in the garage with the signed title on the seat and let the new owner deal with it. And Plan B?

I made the mistake of mentioning the Beast to a coworker. When he found out the year and model, he impressed me with the possible value of this "vintage" bike. Now I'm the kind of guy that thinks loving your work should come before monetary rewards, and I have always tried to live a simple, clean life. But darn it, if I was sitting in a confession booth, I'd have to tell you that I love to make a quick, easy buck.

So, I advertised the Beast for sale, and no faster than the ad came out in print, I had a possible buyer on the phone. The problem was I had to get the thing to town for show-and-sell.

I bought a battery, grabbed the lawn mower gas can, and headed up the hill. What startled me most was how easily the Beast came to life after sitting for four years. That eagerness should have been a warning, but I was joyously anticipating the sale and could not be bothered. We started down the gravel lane. To add drama, there were slick streaks of ice like little frozen rivers from the melting spring snow crisscrossing the road in shadowed areas.

We crossed the first three ice patches without a hitch. We slipped on the fourth, so quickly down that my breath was gone for a full five minutes. Have you ever tried to right a motorcycle from off your leg while on a sheet of ice? To say it got nasty is a nano-statement. Swear words didn't help. Neither did yelling or screaming, and I forgot about prayer. We finally slid on down to the gravel. We got up and there were more dents and scratches on me than on the "vintage" cycle. I'm sure it was an omen.

The Beast and I finally made it to town in one piece. The buyer liked the machine, and we shook hands as he handed me cash. "Oh, yes, I said, please take the helmet and the chaps too. They are part of the deal."

Now what made me tell you this story? Last week I renewed my driver's license. Music, a piano concerto, was playing softly in the background when the clerk asked me if I wanted to keep the motorcycle privilege on my license.

Privilege? Suddenly, in my mind, I could see that dude at my old piano, his fingers keeping up with the music floating out from behind the clerk, his head rocking back and forth like Ray Charles. Then I saw the Beast, the gazelle bars, the awful green color.

"Sir?" the clerk spoke.

"Sure, why not?"

Growing Up Ordinary in Idaho

I grew up ordinary in Idaho. I had an ordinary parent, and two ordinary sisters whose only friend was Mariel Hemingway. Yeah, she was at our house lots.

I don't know whether you've ever been to Idaho, but it's pretty ordinary too, except they say up around Coeur d'Alene it's different, but I've never had the privilege to see it. Anyway, I was born in 1970, and I wasn't even dry when my Momma slapped me with the name Havel Joe Wickers. Now if that wasn't enough of a handicap from the start, I was a middle child, squashed between two sisters; one beautiful, one smart as a whip.

I know what you're thinking. I know I said I grew up ordinary, and then I tell you about my sisters which don't sound very ordinary at all, one being beautiful and one so smart. It was the way they pulled it off, either one, without offending anyone, that made others think of them as ordinary. Besides, they were, after all, just my sisters.

My early childhood was ordinary unless you consider the fact that I wasn't weaned until I was almost three, and I still wet my pants on occasion at four. Some child raising authorities would have probably taken fault with my Momma about my nursing habits had they known. I know she would have just shucked them off and continued to pull up her blouse whenever I was hungry or needed comfort of some sort. As for me, nobody ever asked what I thought, but dang it, it just felt good to take that tit in my mouth and wait for the milk to flow warm and slow.

As I was saying, Idaho was ordinary for the most part, and Free Fall, Idaho, was your typical ordinary, as was the little trailer we called home. The thing I liked about the trailer was the way it was tucked back in with all the other trailers in town down along Free Fall Creek, under the shade of big willow trees and close to the bluff so the winter winds would rock the trailer less than had they been standing on that bluff. The view of the Tetons was comforting too, even if it was their less famous backside.

The trailer was small as I found out upon returning to Idaho for a visit later down my ordinary road of life, but at the time it seemed big. There were two bedrooms, a living room of sorts stacked with books, and the kitchen, efficient as hell. My sisters shared one of the bedrooms and my Momma and I the other, except on the occasional night the trucker stayed over. Then I'd get to make up my own bed on the couch, or, if sleep wouldn't come due to the wind or the occasional groan from the bedroom, I'd sneak into my sister's room and crawl up in bed between them, hoping they were asleep and would not notice me.

The willows would spread their narrow leaves and fan the trailer cool in the summer. In the winter, wind howling, trailer rocking, night black as coal, they would become wildcat claws on the metal sides and roof of the trailer, scaring the bejesus out of me. It was times like that I would roll over and reach for that tit. See what I mean about comfort?

When I reached five, I was the best road builder for toy trucks along the creek bank in Free Fall. I had a definite knack for taking the old yellow grader and grooming that dirt into the most magnificent structures. I had overpasses and underpasses and traffic circles even though I'd never seen any of them. Jack Longnecker, our closest neighbor, said I was just a natural, near as he could tell: the Michelangelo of Free Fall, Idaho, when it came to toy roads. I didn't know who Michelangelo was, but I could tell by Jack's voice that it was something to be proud of, so I was.

My older sister didn't like playing cars and trucks, especially when she hit her teens. She was too busy looking beautiful and trying to emulate Lauren Bacall, cigarettes and all. She would take long Pall-Malls she'd snuck from her best friend's mother's purse, and suck long and slow, letting the smoke drift from her nostrils. She'd half close her eyes, and slowly blink. She told me this was sexy, but not really understanding sexy, I thought it was just due to all that smoke in her eyes. They just looked watery to me, and that's what I told her, not intending to make her mean.

When my younger sister got a little older, she would play with me some of the time, but she didn't like getting down on her knees to push the cars and trucks. I would see her mind start to wonder, get lost, as she would try and invent some way to make them go without being on her knees.

But let's get back to when I was five, because that's when I made a startling discovery: rubbing my pecker in a certain way caused a funny feeling inside, and the more I practiced, the better the feeling. I learned that practice doesn't always make perfect, but it sure will give you sores and scabs to follow. I also found out that spit helped to keep the irritation down and the scabs small, but when my Momma took me to the doctor thinking I had some rare illness, the doctor explained that even though I was an ordinary kid, I was probably just a little ahead of my time. So why did she, my Momma, not the doctor, make me promise to stop? Well, of course I didn't want to go blind.

No matter how I promised myself, I couldn't keep from practicing, although I do think I was successful in reducing the frequency. I think I just accepted the fact that blindness would come some day, and my only hope was that it would be a long time coming and would be gradual.

One late afternoon I was lying on my bed. Momma was

doing her usual library job, and my older sister was caring for me. How could I notice her stepping into the shadows through the door as I was concentrating real hard to get the feelings just right and not cause sores?

How long she watched, I don't know, but just as the feelings were coming pretty good she hollered my name, "Havel Joe Wickers, what are you doing?"

Boy, talk about lost feelings, plus I almost jerked my pecker off trying to get it back in my pants as fast as I could. She came and sat on the edge of the bed, not saying another word, but she was blinking her eyes slow-like. My mouth began to feel real dry as I watched her eyes, even though there wasn't anything watery about them.

"Show me your little thingy," she said, "and I won't tell Momma."

Talk about being between a rock and a hard place. What was I to do? I'd promised, remember? Well, after another threat or two, I scooted my pants and shorts down, and let her gaze at my pecker. She looked long and hard, then stood up and started to leave the room.

"Don't I get to see yours?" I asked, thinking that would be only more than fair considering all that had happened.

She stopped just short of the door and turned toward me. She reached down and picked up her skirt and tucked it up under her chin. I was looking at her blue-colored under panties when she reached slowly down and pulled the top band down and back up very quickly. Heck, she didn't have any pecker at all that I could see.

One night when the wind was howling something fierce, and some trucker had taken my side of the bed with Momma, I crawled in between my sisters. I lay there quietly for a few minutes soaking up the warm seeping through their nighties, listening to their easy breathing as I held mine against their waking and finding me. On most mornings I would wake before either of them and slip back to my own cold bed on the couch, no harm done.

For some reason, being the warmth or the comfort of the bed, I did not wake up as usual. I was having a violent dream about Rex, the bully who lived up the street, and how he was holding me down so hard I couldn't breath. I woke up all whimpery and sweaty and found my big sister's arms wrapped around me tight as a rope on a busted calf.

A touch of those feelings started down close to my pecker, but for some reason it just didn't seem right. Darn, it felt so good lying close to her, feeling warm and safe, and me smelling her sleepy breath, I hated to move.

First thing I knew she cracked an eye, then two and was staring at me, undecided like. I thought about making a run for it, back to my cold bed on the couch, but she wasn't lessening her grip any so I stayed. Next thing I knew, she was sliding one hand down my bare belly to the elastic on the top of my shorts where it stopped for a minute before she slipped it inside and grabbed my pecker. Whoo-ee.

"I got to pee," I said, and slithered from the bed, tripping over several of my cars and trucks on the way to the bathroom.

Looking back, I'm not sure but what my life peaked during my sixth year on this planet. In fact, it was a big year for all of us. Where my older sister got the money for it, I don't know, but sometime that summer, she and my smart sister plastered a big poster over the head of their bed. Nailed it right to the wall with finishing nails. The poster said Mariel Hemingway at the bottom, and here was this beautiful girl with bushy eyebrows staring down at the three of us.

I think I fell in love with her little up-turned nose the minute I saw the poster, but in addition, the mood of her eyes, upsetting at first, caused me to begin to cry. Both my sisters came to me and put their hands on me and told me everything was all right.

"Don't you like the picture," my pretty sister asked. Then to the poster, "Mariel, don't you think our brother is kinda cute?"

The dark eyes from the face on the wall continued to look at me, pulling me from the inside, and I turned and fled from the room.

From then on, whenever I was in my sisters' room playing cars or, if they had twisted my arms hard enough, dolls, it was always, "Mariel, to you like this dolly's dress?" or "Mariel, what do you think we should serve for lunch?" Or when my older sister was getting ready for school that fall, it might be, "Mariel, do you think this blouse goes with this skirt?" or "Mariel, do you think the boys would appreciate this skirt or these slacks?"

And sometimes, "Mariel, will you watch Havel Joe Wickers for us while we go to the store?" My sisters would leave the room giggling, with nothing left for me to do but stare up at those constantly watching dark brown eyes. Sometimes, lying there on the bed looking up at that poster, following with my eyes the curve to her hair, her nose, I would pretend that the freckles on her shoulders were tears that had fallen from those huge eyes, and in those moments I would feel sorry for her, and I think sometimes I would admit I loved her more than just a little.

One evening, my sisters were playing dress-up. They were using the bed as a stage. They had strung a wire from one side of the room to the other and had draped a light blanket over the wire using it as a curtain for the stage. I was supposed to be the audience, and the intensity of my clapping would denote which outfit the sisters were wearing was the best. You know, popular appeal or something like that.

They chose the weirdest stuff to wear: tablecloths, gauze curtains, shoes borrowed from Momma's closet. I was getting tired pulling the curtain back and forth, the acts kept changing so fast, and my hands were sure as heck tired of clapping. I know Mariel was tired of all the strange getups. I could tell that by the disapproving way she was looking at me, those heavy eyebrows falling closer to her dark eyes.

It was about this time that my older sister asked me to show my little sister how I could get a funny look to my face by rubbing my thingy. I wasn't much for doing it in front of my little sister, nor in front of Mariel for that matter, but her threat of telling Momma made me give it a try.

I was just standing there with my sisters sitting on the bed peeking out from behind the curtain, with Mariel looking over their shoulders, trying to get that feeling to come. It took a little while, considering the circumstances, and just when it was coming on real good, we all heard footsteps coming toward the bedroom door. Momma had come home from her library work early, and we had not heard her coming into the trailer.

I knew I needed to stop, but it was too late, I had to keep going the feeling was so good, and I could tell by my little sister's expression that my face must have turned all sorts of weird.

Thinking quickly, my pretty sister jumped from the bed, jerked my pants in a way somehow causing my pecker to disappear in an instant, and all my Momma saw as the door opened were the three smiling faces of her dearest children and a scowl from Mariel. I was still vibrating from head to toe feeling really strange, weird, but I smiled my best. It was then that I saw, I swear, from the corner of my eye, Mariel giving me a wink.

I must have been eight or nine, I kind of forget the actual date, when the pretty sister came home from school all excited. Mariel was in a movie named *Manhattan*, and it was playing at the local theater. She and my smart sister ran for the bedroom slamming the door in my face. I could hear them talking to the poster as if getting all the facts about the movie from Mariel herself. My knocks on the door were ignored as they babbled on and on with Mariel. Hollywood, I gathered from the screams and excitement in their voices, was strangely weird.

When Momma got home from work, the begging started,

pleas, really, for the sisters to be allowed to go to the movie. Books, not movies, not television, had been the main entertainment in our family, but they were asking for an exception: after all, this was Mariel!

First thing I knew, the three of them disappeared into the bedroom, door again closed, and the conversation continued. I don't know who was the most persuasive, Mariel or the sisters, but when they emerged, I could tell they were going to the movie.

"What about me?" I asked as they exited the room, chattering a mile a minute.

The answer came Saturday night when, after an only partially-eaten supper, we all excitedly walked down to the theater together. The sisters were arm in arm in front, Momma and me bringing up the rear.

We snuggled into the creaky old theater seats, passed one box of popcorn back and forth, and impatiently waited through the commercials and previews for the movie to start. The black and white film finally began, and it was quite a while into the film before we saw Mariel, sitting with this old guy, his glasses falling down, having dinner with some other people.

There she was, our poster come to life: cute up-turned nose, bushy eyebrows, pretty face. I about fell out of my seat when she spoke: her voice tiny, uncommanding, and kind of squeaky. She had been speaking to me for years, and I hardly recognized her new voice; it was so different I began to feel real strange.

I don't think, at that age, I understood the movie. First, Mariel was so much taller than the guy, it made no sense to me, but as the movie progressed, somewhere in the back of my young mind a seed was planted that being a shorty like me wasn't all bad.

Then there was this scene where the short guy was trying to persuade Mariel of something that she wasn't having anything to do with. First thing I knew the tears were rolling down her face toward her freckled shoulders although they were, in the movie, covered with a shirt. I looked over at Momma, and I'm not sure that there wasn't a tear in her eye too. Right then and there I felt so bad that I had to lean over and put my head against her shoulder. Although I'd finally been weaned, what I needed so badly at that moment was for her to pull up her blouse so I could take that tit in my mouth and wait for the milk to flow warm and slow.

Idaho winters in Free Fall are usually just ordinary. You know, cold, a little snow from time to time, and wind enough to blow you into Wyoming. But in 1983, we were snowed in for six days, right in Free Fall. The snowdrifts were so deep we could hardly get out of the trailer, let alone to the grocery store. We were living on beans and Kool-Aid.

My pretty sister was really upset, thinking this storm would be the end of her love life since her boyfriend couldn't, or wouldn't, as she said, struggle through the drifts to come see her. My smart sister was enjoying the heck out of the storm by curling up in any corner and reading book after book. I swear in those six days she read near a hundred of them. Sometimes, I wasn't sure she even stopped to eat the beans.

Momma, on the other hand, was just taking it in stride, puttering around the trailer rearranging things, changing this picture or that, dusting. She emptied drawers, making piles of useless stuff we'd acquired, stuff she said someone else needed more than we did. Although by the end of the week, I think she was missing the trucker some 'cuz she got real snappy with us kids.

Me, I was busy being glum. This was the kind of storm that usually put me in bed between the warmth of my two sisters, but ever since I started junior high, they wouldn't let me in their bed. I was feeling a bit morose, and more than a bit betrayed, and it was entirely my pecker's fault.

The last time they let me in, near morning I was sleepily thinking about getting up and getting back to my couch before Momma was awake. As usual, my pretty sister had slipped her hand down my shorts and was holding my pecker, and I was enjoying smelling the sleepy warmth of her skin. I could see the breasts she was growing through her gapping, mis-buttoned pajama top, when my pecker started getting big. Lately, it had been getting bigger and bigger when I rubbed it to get the feeling, but not as big as it was getting now.

In the dim morning light, I looked up at Mariel and pleaded to her to help me do something, anything to get that swelling down, to go away. But the more earnestly I pleaded the bigger and harder my pecker got. My sister's eyes opened, sleepily, then big and round, not squinty like when she was playing sexy. She gave my pecker a little squeeze, and the dern thing spit all over everything. My shorts were wet, as was her hand and even the bed.

She screamed, waking my little sister and Momma too, and shoved me from the bed to a hard landing on the floor. I heard the door to the trailer slam as the trucker left in hurry, and Momma's footsteps heading for the bedroom. There was no way even with God's help that I was going to make it back to the couch.

I grabbed the chenille bedspread, wrapped it around me, and quickly developed a stupid-where-am-I look. The bedroom door burst open, as I was explaining my sleepwalking, not knowing where I was, and other such garbage. I stumbled past Momma and fell exhausted onto the couch.

As I said, storm or no storm, I'd been feeling just a little down lately, and a whole lot betrayed, and the worst thing was, my pecker paid no mind to my feelings and kept getting big at any strange and unexpected moment.

Junior high was hard for me, but not as hard as high school. The only good thing about either was I got to play basketball. Basketball replaced my road building, and I applied the same skills to the game as I had on those marvelous roads and bridges. Anyway you looked at it I was good. It was too bad I was so short, or I might have gone on to bigger things.

I could shoot well from outside, especially from the corners, and my free throw average was near ninety-eight percent. But where I really shined was defense. I had more steals than any other kid in Idaho, and that was finally enough to make my Momma proud. And maybe my sisters too, but it was kind of hard to tell about them. My beautiful sister was going steady with some jerk that worked at the gas station, and my smart sister still couldn't get her nose out from behind her books.

The only bad thing about basketball was the after-practice shower. I'd stay on the court practicing my corner shot or my free throws, hoping the showers would be empty. Coach would come up and yell at me to get to the showers because "I want to get home to the wife and kids, darn it."

Trouble was, there was always somebody still showering, and they always had to make some comment, like "How'd a shorty like you get such a big pecker?" or "When you gonna get some hair to cover up that monster?"

Sometimes it would be simple like "Look out, here comes Pecker-Boy," or "Don't pick up the soap, Pecker-Boy's behind you." You know, dumb things like that. Sneaking a look here and there, I didn't see that mine was any bigger than most of the boys, particularly the older ones. Only the fat kid had a teeny tiny one, so little that you could hardly see it between his fatty thighs.

Then came the particularly harassing night in the shower when the big, older guys had taken me down and measured it. Embarrassing, is what it was, and I was still stinging and red-faced, and not knowing what to do about it or how to keep it from happening again. Especially the getting bigger part while they were lining up the ruler.

Coming home late, those thoughts were quickly shoved to the side. I knew something peculiar was going on the minute I set foot in the door of the trailer. Momma was already home from the library, and I could hear her rummaging around in the tall bathroom cabinet, the one where we put important but not talked about stuff. For example, it was where my beautiful sister hid her tampons, and where my smart sister hid her math books. Me? I didn't have anything to hide that would fit on a shelf.

I stood at the bathroom door and watched Momma, jaw tight, high on a step stool, paw through bottles of left over pills, tubes of ointment, and dark, half-empty bottles of liquids. Finally, she seemed to have found what she wanted and came down with a green tin in her hand. She walked quickly past me as if I wasn't even there, and disappeared into the sisters' room, banging the door behind her.

I quietly shuffled closer to the door, trying to hear what the heat of the conversation was all about, but the threatening voices were too low for me to hear. My beautiful sister about mowed me down as she fled the room, heading for the bathroom. Momma was sitting on the edge of the bed looking up at Mariel, reminding me of a movie I had once seen where this nun who was in a lot of trouble was looking up at some crucifix, asking for divine guidance. I was sure hoping Mariel was more help for Momma than that crucifix had been for that nun.

My sister stayed in the shower an awfully long time, whether to hide from Momma or for something else, I didn't know. Not long after she disappeared through the door, this awful smell started escaping from under the door, bad enough that Momma finally came out of the bedroom and stuffed an old tee shirt in the crack between the door and the floor. The smell was pretty bad, all right, and it reminded me of the state highway weed sprayers, only worse.

There were just three of us for supper that night. Momma stirred her food round and round the plate, but didn't eat much. My smart sister ate more than usual, and I just sat there watching it all, wondering, after that gosh awful smell, if my beautiful sister would ever be the same again.

Come the weekend, and still no sight of my beautiful sister from the depths of the bedroom, I did the unpardonable: I interrupted my smart sister as she sat in the corner reading a book about the life of Albert Einstein. Rather than the usual tirade about human rights and her undeniable right to privacy, she answered my question with one word: crabs.

"Crabs?" I said to myself, and out loud to my sister. She ignored my further questions, nose back in her book, but I knew what I was going to do tonight. I was going to the library. After Momma got home from work, that is.

Spring and all the ordinary beauty that floods into Idaho came early that year. As our closest neighbor Jack Longnecker had predicted, I had just finished an outstanding freshman basketball year, and before I knew it, my beautiful sister had graduated from high school and was on a bus to St. Louis to go to school. She'd picked a small liberal arts college "to get her bearings," with a promise to come back and finish at the big university in Moscow, Idaho.

After waving her good-bye, I couldn't shake this deep, empty feeling, and I didn't know what else to do but go home and crawl into her bed. Quietly settling under the covers, I slowly rubbed my pecker until the feeling welled strong and hard, and I let it spend on my pants and the sheets, and I didn't even care as tears flowed in rivers down my cheeks to join the wet spots already there. The tears were so strong, my vision so blurred, I failed to notice, under those bushy eyebrows, Mariel's sympathetic gaze.

The rest of high school was kind of a blur for me. I remember two things: I continued my outstanding play at basketball, winning the Most Valuable Player Award in our last game at the state tournament even though we lost the final, and Miss Harmon, the student teacher in Social Studies.

Miss Harmon had eyebrows that looked like Mariel's, only they were trying harder to grow together in the middle. Most days she wore slacks to class, and a bright colored blouse. She often tied a scarf in her hair to hold the curly brown mass away from her face. Surprising even to me, it was her rump that I remember the most.

Short as I was, I'd have to jockey for position to get a good look as she moved back and forth in front of the class explaining this civilization or that one, or even as she explained why this country was now called this or used to be called that. Sometimes she perched on a high stool and pointed at the charts on the wall with a long pointer. I could see a line through her slacks, and that made me wonder if it was made by her panties and if so, what they looked like, as you never saw my sisters' panties through their slacks.

One day Miss Harmon showed up in a dress, black with flowers and pretty darn short. She perched on her stool, and all the boys, including me, were transfixed by her legs. She moved them this way, and then that way. She crossed her legs, and then she uncrossed them. Down from the stool, she paced back and forth explaining the Russian example of communism or something I couldn't concentrate on considering there was no panty line to be seen, none anywhere.

My imagination was working in overdrive by this time, and what little logic I had seemed to point to the fact that she must not be wearing any. Panties, that is. I was leaning out so far into the aisle to see the view I almost tumbled, when about that time that my pecker really started to grow. I slid my notebook over my lap, but I could tell it wasn't going to be enough.

Now I'd seen my pretty sister half-dressed a few times, and if truth were told, even naked, but half-dressed she always had her panties on. I raised my hand, frantic now to get Miss Harmon's attention and to ask for an excuse for the bathroom.

I ran down the hall, through the door and into a stall. I closed the door, but the lock was broken, pulled down my pants and tried to pee. Nothing would come through that big thick thing so it seemed the best thing to do was rub it a little to get it to go down in size. The feeling was just coming good when the bathroom door opened and I heard Jerry the Janitor whistling a merry tuneless tune as he started banging the garbage cans around.

At least the noise fixed the swelling and it quickly disappeared. At last, it sure felt good to pee.

I spent the summer between my junior and senior year working at the gas station down the block, the same one where my pretty sister's old jerk boyfriend used to work. With my beautiful sister gone, the rest of the summer, especially early mornings and at night, was spent trying to catch my smart sister naked as she went between the bathroom and her bedroom.

Ever since I began high school, the couch had become my permanent bed. Not that the trucker was there most nights, but as Momma said, it was time I had a bed all to myself. This worked fine for me, as it seemed lately, I needed to get the feeling more and more often. The worst part was I had to be careful not to get the leavings on the couch.

Anyway, lots of nights I would lie there trying to keep my eyes open until my sister used the bathroom that last time before she turned out the lights and went to bed. Trouble was, she didn't know when to quit reading and go to bed, so most nights I was asleep before she went by. And the mornings were worthless since I had to get up and go to work before she was up.

The weekends weren't much better, especially the mornings since she read later and, therefore, slept later in the morning. Still I tried. She was so different from my beautiful sister, who was either careless or liked to show herself. Why, I didn't even have to try with her and I'd seen her several times on her trips to the bathroom and back. Once, in fact, a long time ago, she had invited me in to the bathroom to wash her back, saying she had hurt her arm and couldn't do it. Her breasts were pretty small, and her tits were a nice rosy color. I couldn't help but notice that they had a nice jiggle when I scrubbed her back.

It seemed hotter than usual that summer. Maybe it was because the gas station was hot with all that blacktop around it, and the awnings had rotted away years ago and had never been replaced. Anyway, one evening as I finished supper alone while the smart sister was in her room reading, and Momma was working late at the library, I got to thinking about ways to cool off. When I was little, I could wade in the creek, but I was bigger now than the creek itself.

I showered to get some of the sweat washed off, and I was standing in the living room in my shorts cooling off. I wandered over to the bedroom door, and there she was, book in front of her face, something about dynamic tension and algorithms. Looking back, I don't know what I was thinking, but I walked into the room and lay down on the bed next to her. She didn't say anything, but she rolled over putting her back to me.

I must have been there ten or maybe even fifteen minutes, comfortable in that old bed, wondering how my beautiful sister was doing in St. Louis. We hadn't had a letter in a while that I was aware of. I looked up at Mariel. She pulled her brows even tighter together in the middle, but she didn't seem to have anything to say either. Then my mind drifted over to thoughts of Miss Harmon, which brought on thoughts about her rump, and even her legs. I think my pecker started to get a little bit enlarged, but I really hadn't paid any attention I was so lost in thoughts of Miss Harmon and how she crossed her legs first this way, and then that way, sitting on that high stool.

With thoughts of Miss Harmon's rump clear in my mind, you know, the line of her brief panties and all, without even knowing what I'd done I'd reached out my hand and placed it on the rump belonging to my smart sister.

Without missing a paragraph, probably not even a word, my smart sister said in a low monotone: "Do that again, and I'll kill you."

I jerked my hand away and rolled onto my back and lay very still, catching my breath. Soon, I got quietly up and softly walked from the room where it seemed a whole lot cooler than it had been even fifteen minutes ago. And the strange thing was, my pecker was the smallest it had been for years.

My senior year in high school was pretty much ordinary. Basketball was ordinary too. I continued to lead the scoring, especially with my corner shots, and again I had more steals than any other kid in Idaho. My teammates continued to make remarks about my pecker, but I managed to avoid getting measured again.

I had one date with the girl that lived three trailers over from ours. It was one of those girl-ask-boy dances they had at the school once or twice a year. Thinking back, I was pretty nervous about never having been on a date before. I really longed for my beautiful sister, as she would have been able to tell me how to act and what to do. Whether she could have told me how to keep my pecker small, I don't rightly know. I did know that my smart sister had never had a date, so it wasn't worth asking her for advice.

Of course I could have asked Momma, but how do you ask your Momma questions like that, especially the one about the size and all. Anyway, neither of us, me nor the girl three trailers away, had a car, so when she stopped to pick me up, we just walked over to the gym, where the dance had already started.

I had on a soft flannel shirt and a new pair of Levi's I'd been saving for graduation. The girl looked real pretty in a pink cotton dress. Neither of us knew how to dance, especially me, but we managed to watch the others awhile and then we finally gave it a try. She didn't have much to say, and neither did I, so we just kind of shuffled around the floor, bumping into some of the other couples, which caused us to bump into each other.

That bumping around, and the time we stopped a minute so she could pick up a corsage that someone had dropped, started causing me some problems that I hadn't planned on. When she bent down to pick up those flowers, the top of her dress kind of fell away from her chest, and there I was, looking right at her bare breasts, all soft and tender looking. They weren't too big, but her tits were rosy, and they had a nice shape to them as she grabbed for the flowers. Whoo-eee.

My pecker began straining the reliable Levi fabric. By then, she had the flowers in her hand, and we were dancing and bumping again. I know my pecker was poking her on every turn, but she either didn't notice or she didn't care. How was I suppose to know which is was, and after thinking about it for awhile, I wasn't sure that it mattered? All I knew, I had to get to the bathroom.

I took off across the dance floor, leaving the girl from the trailer standing there. I got to the bathroom and into the stall, but there were no longer any doors to shut. They had been removed in some far-fetched administrative decision. I managed to get my pants open and had just started rubbing it a little to make it go down some in size when the bathroom door opened and someone went to the urinals. On the way he said to me, "What'cha doing in here, Pecker-Boy?" At least that solved the problem.

My beautiful sister used to make a big deal about her first kiss. Why is a first kiss any different that any other kiss? Like the last kiss for example? After dancing a few more times, the girl from the trailer and I walked home. She reached for my hand as we crossed the highway. It felt small and warm in mine, and she would periodically give a squeeze as we walked silently along.

When we reached my house, she took a few more steps, dragging me along, past our front door and kind of out of the beam from the porch light. The glass part of the cover over the light had been broken for years, but I had never noticed the weird shaped shadows the light cast on the gravel along the steps.

The girl turned me from my interest in the shadows, and the first thing I knew her lips were pressed against mine. I guess I should have closed my eyes like they did in the movies, but I was busy looking at the fact that she was quite a little taller than I was. It reminded me of Mariel's movie where she was taller than the old guy, and I guess I started to grin, because the girl pulled her lips away for a minute and looked down at me with a somewhat quizzical look before she smashed her lips against mine. This time she moved them around some, and I wasn't sure if she was trying to put her tongue in my mouth or if she was just licking her lips.

She leaned against me as she did this and I could feel her small breasts against my chest, which caused my pecker to push right back against her legs. She still didn't seem to mind, but it was about then that the front porch light began to blink on and off in a kind of code-like rhythm. It sure did distract the girl, and it wasn't long before she said good night and headed through the shadows in the direction of her trailer.

Later that night as I lay on the couch trying to get to sleep, I thought about her thin blonde eyebrows, and her straight blonde hair. I guess I hadn't looked at her eyes, 'cause I didn't think they were brown, nor very large, but I couldn't be sure. Then I wondered if she had freckles on her shoulders, and I thought about her breasts, wondering just a little if they would be extra warm if I had touched them, and how good would one of her rosy tits feel if I was able to put it in my mouth. Anyway, I decided right then and there that there was a difference between a first kiss and any others. In fact, a really big difference.

After graduation, things seem to slow down. Maybe it was the heat, as the summer seemed drier and hotter than usual. The leaves on the willows outside of our trailer seemed less green, and maybe even a little curled.

I was still working at the gas station, and was trying to decide what to do about school. Momma expected me to go to college, probably at the University of Idaho, but I wasn't sure. I liked cars a lot, and was thinking a little about being a mechanic. Jack Longnecker, our closest neighbor, said I should go and become an engineer, you know, a road engineer. Why, he said I'd be a natural at it, near as he could tell.

One evening while I was weighing the pros and cons of one over the other, my beautiful sister showed up just as the sun was sliding down behind Goat Bluff. Momma was already home from the library and was busy fixing supper. I heard a car slide to a stop in the gravel in front of the trailer, and suddenly the front door flew open and there she was. Her eye makeup was a little melted, and her lipstick seemed a little crooked, but she looked good even if she was a little pale. For all I knew, the sun didn't shine as bright in St. Louis as it did in Idaho.

She and Momma clung to each other for the longest time, which thinking back seemed kind of funny. When she was living here, they seemed to fight like cats and dogs. Never loud or anything, but they sure did have their times. I suppose being gone awhile gave everyone a little different perspective, including me.

My smart sister came out of the bedroom where she had been reading, and didn't even bring the book. When my beautiful sister was finished hugging Momma, she turned and did the same thing to my smart sister. I was kind of hanging back in the corner, watching, but when she was finished with that hug, she came for me. She smelled like cigarettes and some stifling perfume, but it still felt good to have her smashed against me like that, warm and curvy.

She wanted to know how I'd been, and was I still taking showers at school. She'd somehow forgotten that school was out now for about two weeks, and I had already graduated. She was interested in what my smart sister was reading, and how things were at the library.

We soon sat down for supper, and the talk went on and on. I noticed she didn't have much to say about school in St. Louis, other than it was still there, but the more she talked, the more I realized that she was just talking. I didn't know why, but somehow I knew she wasn't listening at all. I could see the tired lines around the corners of eyes, and I noticed her nervous habit of spinning her glass between drinks of water. She didn't eat much, and it wasn't long before she asked if she could shower and go to bed. She said she knew it was early, but she was tired from the road.

For the next few days, each afternoon when I came home from the gas station there would be a note on the door saying to please be quiet, sister was sleeping. And sleep she did. For three days straight. Could you believe it?

On the third evening, I stood at the bedroom door, which was cracked open a little, and saw her there in bed. Because of the heat, she had kicked off any sheet or blanket, and was lying there in her pajamas, head on a pillow, her hair streaming over the pillowcase. I guess they were pajamas although they seemed to be just panties and a little fluffy top. I could see her legs, covered rump, and her back as she was lying with it towards me. I understood the heat, as I'd left my shirt off since cold showering after work, and I was still warm.

After watching her for a little while, I looked up at Mariel. She was looking back at me with the saddest eyes I had ever seen. Mournful, they were, and I wasn't sure but thought I saw a tear forming in the corner of her big brown eyes. It sure made me feel bad, especially because I didn't know the cause.

Maybe it was because of Mariel and her mournful eyes, but suddenly I needed some comfort, and I just walked right on into the bedroom and lay down on the bed next to my beautiful sister's back. Even though she was turned away from me, I could smell the warmth of her skin, and I thought about the last time I had been in bed between my two sisters. You know, before I was banned.

I started to get a little nervous, remembering, and honest, I was thinking about getting up and getting as far away from that room as I could. But before I could make my move, my beautiful sister rolled over and looked at me. She didn't say anything, she just kept looking into my eyes for the longest time.

I was getting even more nervous as my pecker had started to get big, and I sure didn't want problems like the last time. Just as I turned to leave, my sister took me in her arms—you know, just kind of pulled me in toward her until I could feel her breasts against my chest through her little fluffy top. I could really smell her skin now, and darned if my pecker wasn't getting bigger by the second.

She was squeezing me like there was no tomorrow, and I found myself putting my arms around her and squeezing her back. It felt real good, all tight and close like that, and in spite of my good intentions, that feeling started to rise up out of nowhere. I began to sweat like the devil as her tits were tapping little rhythms of invitation into my bare chest.

Maybe she sensed it or something, because just about then, my beautiful sister let go of me and was holding me more at arm's length. Roller balls of tears were pouring down her cheeks forming puddles on the pillow before they slowly soaked away. I swear I was getting splashed from in front and from above, but I was too busy squashing the feeling to look up at Mariel now.

"Havel Joe Wickers." my beautiful sister said kind of under her breath, still looking at me through the rolling tears. "Havel Joe Wickers."

The feeling was slowing down faster than my heartbeat, and I stole a glance at Mariel. She didn't look any happier, but I saw no tears so I looked back at my sister. She gave me a slight smile, then kissed me full on the mouth. Not a long one, mind you, but a dead bulls-eye, and neither me nor my pecker knew what to think, other than it seemed like we should both be getting the heck out of that bedroom. Had I known then what I know now, that it would be a long, long time before I would ever smell my beautiful sister's warm skin so close, I would have stayed longer in that bed. But I didn't know.

My beautiful sister stayed in that bedroom three more days, and Momma was taking food in to her. My smart sister was curled up in the corner of my couch reading some book about quantum physics. Without even looking up, and probably not even skipping a word, she said in her monotone voice, "Damaged goods."

That night, a while after supper, I sat out back of the trailer on a little wooden stump left over from a willow that we had to take down, broken as it was from a winter storm. I looked up into the clear sky and past the million or so stars that were all bunched together up there. The new moon was just a sliver, cupped and gold, and I thought a lot about damaged goods, whatever they might be.

After all that, the rest of the summer laid back lazy and ordinary. My beautiful sister took a job at the electric company, Momma continued to work at the library, my smart sister was still reading, and I, along with working at the gas station, continued my inner search for what I was going to do come fall.

But I would be amiss if I didn't tell you about another thing that happened that summer. I started to grow. In height, I mean. I'd been stuck at five foot six and one-half inches (if I stood on tiptoe) for most of my high school years. Now I was shooting up, and although my voice had long ago made a gradual change from a kid's voice to a baritone, the taller I grew, the deeper my voice became. By September I was pushing six foot, and one octave below middle C, and by the time I finished growing a few months later, I topped out at six foot two and nearly two octaves below middle C. The only trouble was, I still thought of my self as "Shorty", and sometimes, especially late at night just before I drifted off to sleep on that old couch, "Pecker-Boy."

Even though I knew I wanted to be a mechanic and work on cars, that fall I headed to the northern part of the state, to Moscow, and the university to study engineering. Jack Longnecker, our closest neighbor, came to say good-bye as if I was leaving the country or something instead of just going to college. He told me to "go teach 'em how to build them roads." And here I thought I was going to learn.

There were two problems with university life as I saw it. First and the worst was, I missed my family. I thought about writing and maybe even calling, but something always seemed to get in the way. I was living in the dorm, and it was so noisy I wouldn't have been able to hear my family on the phone even if I had called. The second problem was that someone was always wandering in and out of my room, and keeping the door closed didn't seem to discourage traffic any either.

So getting the feeling became a real problem with so many people in and out of my room and before I knew it, my pecker just seemed to go on vacation. It just crawled into a small corner of my shorts and nailed up a "Do Not Disturb" sign. That was, until I saw Emily.

Emily usually sat a few seats in front and a row over from me in freshman calculus. Her back was good and straight and I liked the way she sat in her chair. You know, not slouched, her feet together kind of at the side. Her brown hair fell evenly over her shoulders, and she had a cute up-turned nose. I would sit, half listening to the instructor and wonder if she had freckles on her shoulders. Emily, I mean, not the instructor.

The main problem was she didn't even notice I was watching her. I dreamed of ways to introduce myself, but they all seemed so dumb. It was only by chance that she stumbled over my feet (they had grown enormous in proportion to my height) as I was trying to cram my frame onto the chair behind the desk.

"Excuse me," she said, her eyebrows knitting together in one long furrow above her eyes, and her hand braced against my shoulder as she steadied herself. Her voice was kind of squeaky, and it reminded me of Mariel's voice in that movie with the old guy. Anyway, I liked it, and it was then that my pecker changed signs: "Back From Vacation."

The class met at 9 AM, Monday, Wednesday and Friday. For weeks, I wouldn't have been able to tell you what classes I attended on the other days, or during the different hours. And in spite of what Jack Longnecker, our closest neighbor had said, I was struggling with the class. But what did you expect, me sitting there day after day watching Emily instead of paying attention.

She, of course, would have been only one hindrance; the other was the demands of my pecker in spite of all the traffic through my room. It was really frustrating was what it was, and I think you can probably relate to that.

Things finally got back on track, sort of, when one afternoon I saw Emily walking ahead of me on my way back to the dorm. Anyway, my long legs caught up with her, and then we were kind of walking along together, Emily and me. It felt great being with her like that, and although she wasn't as fast a walker as I was, we were doing pretty well together as we neared the residence hall. I opened the door for her, and she gave me a great smile, a thank you, and left me standing there holding the door.

That night, lying in my bed, I thought about how I would ask Emily out. You know, for a Coke or coffee, or maybe dessert. Well, not coffee 'cuz I couldn't stand the taste, but certainly for a Coke. But then I got to worrying about how I didn't have a car and how could I expect Emily to walk with me for a Coke, so I just put it aside, rolled over, and went to sleep.

In hind sight, I should have gone home for Christmas that first year, but I had taken a job at one of the local garages, "Bud's," and truthfully, I liked the work. Old Bud was in his eighties, and still getting grease on his hands. He sure knew a lot about cars, and as he said when I inquired about the job, "all that smarts don't give me the strength I need." He hired me to be his strength.

As much as I missed my family, I thought Bud needed me more. I did call home on Christmas Eve to wish everyone a Merry Christmas, and it was sure good to hear Momma's voice. My smart sister didn't have much to say, which was no great surprise, as I could imagine her with a book in her other hand, reading as we spoke. My beautiful sister wasn't there, but out on a date with some jerk, or at least that's what my smart sister said. I knew the minute I hung up the phone that I'd made a big mistake by not going home, but it was too late now. All I could do was go up to my room, lie on my bed, and try to remember Mariel looking at me from the poster. It was the best I could do at the time.

I did a lot better the second semester. The schoolwork came on good and strong and I learned some interesting things. I kept an eye out for Emily, but didn't see her anywhere. We certainly didn't have any classes together and any chance meeting her walking toward our residence hall didn't pan out. So I did the next best thing and buckled down and studied real hard. And working with Bud was a learning experience all its own. You see, Bud refused to work on any car newer than 10 years. He said they just don't make them like they used to, and beyond that, he refused to discuss it.

Suddenly it was April. The trees were leafing out and flowers were bursting with pride along houses and sidewalks. People were thinking seriously about gardens. It was late in the afternoon after classes and I was helping Bud pull an engine from a '67 Dodge truck. What a monster that was.

The garage door was open to the sun, and we both saw an old VW coughing its way toward our entrance. The driver was hunched over the steering wheel urging the little Bug on while the smoke pouring from behind seemed dense enough to be pushing it. It rolled just to the entrance when it wheezed one last gasp and jerked to a halt. The door opened and there was Emily, brows furrowing together above her eyes.

Bud stood wiping the oil and grease from his hands, and I just stood there hanging on to the chain from the chain lift, the engine halfway out of the Dodge. The smoke that had pushed the VW to our door passed the Bug and filled the garage with an oily, black stench. I could hardly see Emily, much as I wanted to, as she swam her way through the smoke toward us. She headed straight toward Bud and halfway there looked in my direction. A brief moment of indecision inched its way across her face as she recognized me, or thought she did, as she would admit later.

After that moment of indecision she changed course and walked up to me. I was still hanging onto the chain as if it were a lifeline.

"Do you work on Volkswagens?"

"We don't do nothing that ain't American," answered Bud who was standing behind her still wiping his hands.

She looked at me slightly bewildered. "But Volkswagens have been in America since, since, well, since before I was born."

"Don't matter, they ain't made in the good old U.S. of A.," said Bud, who had taken a few steps to her right, but was still mostly behind her.

This was news to me, so all I could manage to do was shrug, still holding onto the chain.

"Why, that kind of attitude is — is un-American," she began as she turned toward Bud. "Where are you from?"

"What do you mean where am I from? I'm from right here in Moscow and have been since coming here in 1920, by dang," Bud retorted.

"Coming from where?"

"We was comin' from New York City —."

"And before that?"

"Well, we was comin' through New York from Bulgaria."

Emily placed her hands on her hips, took two steps toward Bud and said, "And you were born where?"

"Bulgaria, by dang it."

Surprised as I was by the exchange, I suddenly let go of the chain, forgetting to put on the brake, and the engine went singing toward the floor, the chain ratcheting on the pulleys, clackety clack. I managed to get the brake on just before the thing hit the floor or the tie rods underneath the engine compartment. Anyway, that's how it came about that we fixed Emily's VW bug, although it took a little time since Bud said he didn't know a "damned thing about them German machines." That was all right by me as Emily stopped by every afternoon after her classes to check on the progress of her little VW Bug that she called "Princess."

Fortunately, I'd bought a used bicycle, as I would never have been fast enough, even with my long legs, to get to the shop after my classes and arrive before Emily walked through the door to see Princess. As it was, I was able to be helping Bud pull the valves, or lying on my back, unscrewing the pan when she came in. I still liked the way she sat, as she did most late afternoons, on a stool that Bud had brought from his office just for her to sit on. You know, not slouched, her feet together on the rung of the stool.

Her brown hair, now that it was warm, was usually pulled back from her face, and sometimes she tied it up in a ponytail. She still had that cute up-turned nose, and some afternoons it would have a streak of grease on it when she would get too close to the mechanicing we were doing. With the warm weather and sleeveless blouses and an occasional halter top, I no longer had to wonder about whether she had freckles on her shoulders because I could see them plain as day, just like little tan colored paint splatters. I swear, some days I could, if I was lying under that VW twisting some bolt or another when she came in, have my pecker lift that VW right off the jack stands. Whoo-eee!

It took us two weeks to get the Princess going after replacing the rings, bearings, regrinding the valves and replacing about half of the wiring. Of course we had to spend some time on the Dodge since it had come into the shop first. When she was finally finished, I watched old Bud take a clean shop rag or two and polish the faded blue paint of the Princess until she shined. I'd never seen him do that before, not in the time I'd worked for him.

Emily came for Princess, check in hand. I had learned from listening to her and Bud talk that she had changed majors and was now studying political science. She wanted to be in government work of some kind, maybe even the Foreign Service. She'd moved out of the residence hall, couldn't stand the noise, she said, and had a little basement apartment all to herself.

She gave Bud a hug and kissed him on the top of his greasy forehead. She gave me a wave, climbed into Princess and drove away from the garage with her hand waving out the window. Princess was really purring, if you could call the VW metallic whine a purr, and I for one was sorry to see her go. I think deep down, old Bud was going to miss her too.

My first year at the University was quickly coming to an end, and I was trying to decide on staying with Bud for the summer or going home to Free Fall, where I could probably work at the gas station. I'd about made up my mind to go home, and was heading out the door of the residence hall to bicycle down and tell Bud about my decision. I burst out the door, still wrestling with the idea, and all but ran into the side of the Princess.

"Would you like a Coke, or maybe dessert?" asked Emily through the passenger side's open window. She was leaning across from behind Princess's steering wheel, and her shoulders looked twice as brown as I had last seen them, almost covering her sprinkle of freckles. I could see the tops of her breasts above her halter-top, which were also nice and tan.

"Well, sure. That sounds all right to me," I said, my voice raising about two octaves from its normal range. I climbed into Princess, my knees jammed into the dash, and we were off down the street, off the campus and down toward Marketplace. She stopped in front of Heaven's Ice Cream Parlor and we went in, me noticing her brown legs and her white shorts as I held the door for her. We sat in a booth, and to tell the truth, all I could do was stare. I mean, I had seen Emily lots of times, but I had never been sitting directly across a table from her before.

Her skin appeared much softer than I had noticed previously, and her little up-turned nose wasn't as small as I remembered, but it was still cute.

"How is Princess running?" I managed to ask, still staring at her beautiful face.

"Beautifully, really smooth. You and Bud did a great job, and she is feeling young again."

"Do you live in Moscow, or are you staying here for the summer, or are you going home?"

She smiled sweetly, realizing, I think, that I was terribly nervous. What she didn't know, at least I hoped she didn't know, was that my pecker was all but lifting the table up in front of us. Dang, I hoped the ice cream we'd ordered would cool it off a little.

"No, I don't live in Moscow except as a student, and yes, I'm staying here for the summer."

She continued to tell me, in a very excited voice, a brief history of Moscow that she had just learned in class. How Moscow had been founded in 1877 and was known as Paradise Valley before a man named Ness or Neff renamed it Moscow because it reminded him of his hometown of Moscow, Pennsylvania.

"If you can imagine," she said.

Although I had not known, I assumed that the town was named after the one in Russia, but I was too busy watching her freckles claw their way through her tan to tell her. That and trying to control my pecker under the table since the ice cream wasn't doing the job.

"I was offered a job with the city as a liaison for the city government this summer, so I decided not to go home."

I still didn't know where home was, but what did it matter. Moscow was home for her now, at least for the summer, and I guess I would be staying the summer too. I suddenly realized that Bud, at his age, needed me more than they needed me at the station back in Free Fall.

When we got ready to leave, I made sure she was up and heading toward the door before I got up from the table. By the time I got to Princess, I was looking pretty normal. I opened the door for her and she laughed, which sounded a little like a music box, at least to me. She drove me back to the residence hall while I watched the wind blow through her brown hair, and knew tomorrow that I would call Momma and tell her that I would not be home for the summer.

By taking a few classes that summer while working for Bud, I was able to stay in the hall. It was sure a lot quieter in the summer, and I actually had a room all to myself. I'd like to tell you that Emily and I had a great romantic summer together, and I think we could have had I been a little smarter about things.

Maybe once a week, as I was biking home from the garage, Princess would pull up along side me, or sometimes she would be waiting for me as I rode up to the hall. We'd go down for an ice cream or a hamburger if we were hungry, and I would hear all about Emily's liaison work with the city. She was learning fast about the politics, and she loved it.

It was probably mid-July, after a particularly hot day at the garage, when Princess pulled along side me as I was riding toward the hall.

"How about a hamburger, stranger?" Emily asked me through the open window. I realized that it had been several weeks since I had seen her, and why I hadn't called her, I'll never know. I was suddenly embarrassed about it, and almost turned down her invitation because of it.

I'm glad I didn't, 'cuz it was one night of strange wonder for me. We ate our usual hamburger at Heaven's with Emily doing most of the talking. She made her job sound really exciting, and as I looked at the grease under my fingernails, I wondered a little if I was doing the right thing working for Bud.

First thing I knew she was apologizing to me for not having stopped by, and to think it was me that had had the same thoughts just minutes ago. Seems she had met a guy and thought she was falling for him, but she said she missed me, and besides, he turned out to be a jerk. I thought, for a minute, that tears were coming to her eyes, but then she smiled and wiggled her up-turned nose, and the sun seemed out to stay. I listened to more about her work as I realized how much I enjoyed sitting across from her.

After we'd eaten, Emily drove me home, and after parking Princess, we got out of the car and started walking down toward the water tower. She reached out her hand, and it felt wonderfully cool and small in my hand. We were silent as we walked; the stars blinking so hard you would have thought we could have heard them snap, crackle, and pop. Warm as it was, the grass we were walking on sent up coolness against our arms and faces, and the smell of the flowers along the way was intoxicating.

We reached the area under the water tower, and we stood facing each other. She placed her hand on my cheek, and I wanted to kiss her right then, but I wasn't sure how to go about it. You know, how was I to start? She must have been reading my mind, 'cuz she went up on tiptoe and her lips, like butterfly wings, brushed my lips. They finally came back to land lightly, and they tasted so sweet a shiver went down my spine.

I started to kiss back as best as I could, and the first thing I knew we were lying on the grass, pressed together like a waffle iron, and just about as hot too. We were groping each other pretty good between the kisses, and I don't know whether it was passion or me, but her tank top came sliding off her breasts, and in the starlight I was privileged to see two of the most perfectly beautiful things I had ever seen. Not to say I was an expert or anything, but even compared to my beautiful sister's they were something special.

I was enjoying the view so much I wasn't even thinking about being betrayed by my pecker who was reaching out trying to shake hands. Man alive! Even I knew that was no way to treat a lady. But before I could apologize or anything, I guess Emily decided to shake hands right back, because she was rubbing it through the fabric of my cutoffs. I wanted to tell her it didn't need any encouragement, but it was probably too late for that. So I just snuggled up close to her wonderful breasts, breathed in the musky scent of her skin, and enjoyed the feelings.

Two weeks later, Momma called. My beautiful sister was getting married, and I needed to come home since I was in the wedding. The date had been set for the last weekend in August, and could I please be there a day or two early since there was so much to do. Bud said he'd manage without me for a few days, but after I told Emily I had to go home, she seemed to suddenly turn distant.

I couldn't put my finger on it exactly, but even though she smiled and seemed excited for me that my sister was getting married, something seemed to change. The night before I was to catch the bus for Free Fall, we went out for our usual hamburger. As she often did, Emily talked about her work, smiled and acted like her usual self, but I could tell, something was definitely different.

We drove to the hall in Princess, who was running perfectly, and even though I asked Emily, she declined going for a walk. We sat, me looking at her, seeing her dressed wonderfully in white shorts, a T-shirt, and barefoot. Her skin was so tan that her freckles were hard to see. I could tell she wasn't wearing a bra, and I wanted so much to kiss her, and touch her lightly on her nipples with my lips. But even my pecker detected the change, and it was not straining at the leash, but was being totally civilized.

I was the first to say goodnight, and she leaned over and kissed me lightly on the lips. "Have a good time at the wedding, and take care of yourself." She chucked me lightly under the chin, and I found myself saying goodbye and getting out of the car. I stood and watched as Princess sped off into the night.

No matter how you go, it's a long way to Free Fall from Moscow. I climbed on the bus at nine in the evening, my small suitcase in the overhead rack. It never made much sense to me to go through Montana just to get home, but here we were, hours later in Missoula. The bathroom break and the chance to stretch my long legs certainly were welcome. Thirty minutes or so later we were about to get underway. It seems that most of the passengers from Moscow must have been heading for Missoula, as the bus was nearly empty now. Maybe there'd be room for me to sleep.

Just as the bus was pulling out, there was a loud banging on the bus door. The driver braked suddenly, sending coffee onto some laps and my knees into the back of the seat in front of me. The bus door opened and in popped a young girl left over from the hippie days, or maybe she was some crazy Mormon, I didn't know. She was dressed from head to foot in tie-dye, and beads were hanging over every inch of her body, you know, bracelets and necklaces. Her red hair was tied back with an autumn-colored kerchief, and she was dragging a very large duffel behind her down the aisle.

The driver heaved his huge body up from his seat and tried to stop her progress saying that the duffel had to go underneath in the storage compartment. She finally stopped long enough to relinquish her duffel, slung her gigantic backpack into the window seat, and plopped into the seat across the aisle from me. She was barefoot, her sandals dangling from the side of the backpack.

I immediately smelled herbs and maybe incense, a ripeness, as the waves melted from her clothes and body. She gave me a brief smile, and the light flashed on an ornament pinned in her nose. Her earrings dangled forever, and the feathers mixed with beads tickled across her neck as she turned her head.

The driver was back on the bus, the door shut, and we were again on our way. With the lights back down, the few passengers had quit gawking and were settling down for the long night ride ahead. I turned to get as comfortable as I could, placing my jacket under my head, and gathered the rhythm of the bus into my bones to prepare for sleep.

About the time I actually began to doze, some strange and exciting scent would creep its way across the aisle, and my eyes would open and I would glance at the redhead. She was reading, the reading light pouring past her kerchief onto the white pages of her book. I looked past her, and out the windows as the headlights illuminated a sign telling us we were back in Idaho.

As I closed my eyes, I felt a light, warm touch on my arm. Opening my eyes, the redhead was motioning me toward the back of the bus. She smiled as she pulled out a large, rainbow-colored Afghan from her backpack and headed down the aisle. I got up and followed her, not knowing what she wanted. I think my pecker had a premonition, as I felt it pushing against my pants.

She was waiting for me, Afghan held up, open, inviting. She

had removed her kerchief and her hair was tumbling uncontrolled around her face and across her shoulders. I sat down, and the rainbow enfolded me, already warm from her body against the air conditioner of the bus. My head whirled as the scents and touch and soft kisses enveloped me. She took my hands and placed them on her breasts, now bare beneath the rainbow, and my fingers tread gently toward her erect nipples.

She expertly opened my pants button and zipper with astounding speed, and before I could mumble a word, she had encased my pecker within the warmest, softest, most sacred place known on this planet, and it showed its gratefulness by staying huge and erect for a very long time as she quietly moved back and forth before showering its thanks. All I could do was bury my head between her breasts, and breathe deeply of the herbs and incense, as if they were a shrine, and pray my thankfulness for this unasked blessing.

The morning sun brightened the rainbow, and as I opened my eyes, I could see the Tetons to our left. The redhead was still asleep, her hair and the Afghan cushioning her head as the sun kissed the silver bead in her nose. I managed to get my pants back on without waking her, but then I didn't know what to do. I started to pull the Afghan down, but she was still naked from the waist up, her blouse somewhere lost beneath us.

I reached for her hand, and she began to stretch luxuriously, like a cat just up from her nap. Her eyes opened, clear and green, her smile was sweet and slow, and freckles played tag across her nose. She leaned forward and kissed me lightly on the lips as she slipped her blouse on. I stood, also stretching, and I walked back to my seat and gathered up my jacket.

In fifteen minutes, I was standing outside the drugstore watching the big bus pull away. The redhead was reading, or sleeping, her hair brilliant gold strands in the sunshine pushing against the window. It was then that the thought came to me—I should have asked Emily to come home with me. I stood watching, squinting into the morning sun, and from somewhere deep, a sigh slid slowly over my lips and fell into the dust around my feet.

I walked the six blocks to our trailer, my little suitcase feeling even lighter in my hand. The summer was dry, as usual, and the willows were protesting about the lack of rain, curling their leaves. I stood in our drive and looked at those leaves, waving gently in the morning breeze, rubbing easily against the end of the trailer, and marveled at how small the place appeared. The porch needed painting, and I wondered how in the world it could have become shabby-looking so soon, in less than a year.

When I reached the door, I was suddenly overwhelmed by peculiar, unsure feelings that left me wondering whether I should walk right in or knock first. Momma must have heard me thinking, because the door opened with a bang of the screen door against the trailer's side and Momma wrapped me in a huge hug, rolling me from side to side. She must have been standing on her tippy-toes, because the top of her head was right under my chin instead of down on my chest.

"Havel Joe Wickers!" she said several times, and then, "Looks like you've grown another four feet while you've been gone."

Most fellers would probably get red in the face from such a welcome, but I was too busy trying to tell my pecker it was just our Momma, as it was getting signals mixed up and had come to direct attention.

I looked over Momma's head, and there was my smart sister standing in the doorway. I could see there was no book in her hand, and that genuinely surprised me. She might have said "hi" or something similar, but there was no hug. Pushing past her was my beautiful sister, more beautiful that ever, her dark hair curled tight, her eyebrows thick and glossy. Here came another hug, and my pecker was really confused now. Confused enough to start pushing right back, and as I felt my sisters breasts softly caressing my chest, she started laughing, stepped back, looked in the direction of my crotch and said, "My, my, Havel Joe Wickers, you've grown at least a foot." Then she laughed again, her eyes sparkling with all kinds of mischief.

We all laughed, even my smart sister, and we went inside the trailer where I got kind of woozy in the head. I guess all that blood my pecker was using left me that way, or maybe it was the wonderful smells of Momma's spaghetti dinner, or maybe even just the old familiar things pounding me from all sides. Anyway, I was glad to sit down at the little table, all crowded with food, and torn-out pages from magazines showing brides and wedding cakes and strands of pearls.

Momma handed me a plate, and then I realized I hadn't eaten anything but a sandwich since getting on the bus in Moscow. All I can say is that spaghetti tasted mighty good, and the conversation of catching up wasn't half bad either.

Of course, the main topic was my beautiful sister's wedding and the "hero" she was marrying. I remembered him from the basketball showers, and the next night at rehearsal, he remembered me too. As he was shaking my hand, he said, "How's it going, Pecker-Boy?"

As soon as dinner was finished, and the talk began to slow a little, I got up and went to the bedroom door and took a look a Mariel. I swear she was as glad to see me as I was to see her. Her little nose was still up-turned and cute, and the intense expression I remembered had softened some, maybe just for me. I couldn't help but smile at her, actually I grinned, and as I watched her freckles spill over her shoulders, I thought I saw her give me just a little hint of a smile back. It sure was good to see her, and I think my pecker thought so too, because it was the first time in quite awhile that it was totally relaxed and still feeling good.

That night, lying on the couch with just a light sheet over me, I listened to the willow's friendly tickle along the end of the trailer, and wondered why a fool dog was barking his head off somewhere in the distance. Behind me, in the tiny kitchen, my sisters and Momma were still discussing the finer parts of the wedding, but at that moment, I was wondering where that redhead was going, and if she might be coming back.

As Momma said, after the wedding was all over and we were back at the trailer with our feet propped up on pillows, the electric fan in the doorway humming its best, "It sure went smoothly."

My smart sister was still in her pretty, yellow bridesmaid dress, but she already had her nose back in some book about the Human Genome Project. She looked more relaxed than at any other time I had seen her today.

I removed my bow tie after having taken off the black jacket, and was admiring the velvet strip running up the sides of my pant's legs. It felt soft, velvety under my fingers, reminding me some of the redhead's breasts. I'd never worn a tuxedo before, and to tell the truth, I felt pretty good in it, except for the shiny, pointy shoes.

As I sat there feeling the strip, my mind shifted from the redhead to wondering what kind of job it would take to wear a tuxedo for work, but decided, since I wasn't musically inclined in any way shape or form, this one time might just be it. I felt bad for a few minutes, but was interrupted by Momma saying we'd better change our clothes and get ready to go out to eat, 'cuz she sure wasn't up to fixing anything for supper.

Late that night as I was lying on the couch ready to drift off to sleep, I thought a little about the wedding, and remembered how strange it felt to hear my beautiful sister making promises to a guy that couldn't even hit a decent free throw. And then, after the reception, as the two of them were leaving for their honeymoon in Jackson, I watched my beautiful sister climb into that car, never taking her eyes from that guy, and how I felt even stranger when she never even noticed that it was me who was holding the car door open for her.

I left by bus early the next morning without even saying goodbye to Jack Longnecker, our closest neighbor. I'd given

Momma a big hug, and she felt small and slight in my grasp, kind of like sand from the beach that you hold too hard in your hand. My smart sister was still sleeping, probably because she'd been up late reading. But even if I had told her goodbye, I'm not sure that it would have stopped the empty hole that was spreading somewhere in my stomach.

The bus back to Moscow was crammed with people, noisy, and smelly, and Moscow and my little room in the hall never looked so good to me, a much welcomed sight, until I saw the note on my pillow. It was from Emily.

"I'm sorry to have to leave you this note," it began, and then went on to explain that she had no phone number or any way to get in touch with me, and that she was sorry she couldn't tell me in person, but would try to call me later, after my return.

"This fantastic job possibility came up on the spur of the moment, and I am going to Washington, D.C., with Congressman Lilly as one of his assistants."

The printed message ended, and then she had drawn a smiley face, and signed her name in script. There was a PS: "Will you take care of Princess for me? The keys are with Bud. Treat her as if she was yours, as I know you love her too."

I lay down on my bed and looked up at the ceiling, my eyes following a crack in the plaster that rambled across and started down the outside wall. The empty hole I had been feeling suddenly expanded, and the only thing I could do was grab my pecker and hang on for dear life.

The school year started without any problems. My classes and labs kept me more than busy, so I had to cut down my hours with Bud to a drop during the week. I still worked Saturdays, and I don't think the slowed schedule bothered him any at all.

"It'll give me a chance to get my breath," Bud told me as he climbed on to a stool to rest his tired legs. He was busy wiping grease from his arms and hands. I still worried that the increased workload for him might be too much, but I was afraid to say anything that might hurt his feelings.

School had been going for nearly a month before Emily called. She said she wasn't going to need Princess, and would I do her a favor and sell the car and send her the money. Seems Washington was way more expensive than she had imagined, and she needed the money. Her job was going well, and Washington was a fantastic place.

"There is so much history here. It's as if you live between two worlds, two places, the old and the new."

There was a pause before she told me to take care of myself, and she'd be waiting for the money from Princess, and thanks a lot. If I ever got to D.C. be sure and look her up, and then the conversation was over, and the line was buzzing in my ear long before I was able to say what I wanted to say. And that was that I truly missed her, and I especially missed our walks out under the stars and lying under the water tower, and sitting in Heaven's Ice Cream Parlor watching her across the table as she told me about her day.

I put ads up on bulletin boards around the campus, and before the week was out, Princess was sold. I couldn't watch as she drove away with some guy at the wheel with a backward cap on his head. I tried to shut my ears to her sound, but darned if I didn't hear a valve miss closing just as she went around the corner. Who knows, maybe she would miss me as much as I missed Emily.

The holidays were here before you could say "Santa Claus," and Bud and I were knee-deep in restoring a worn out old '52 L-head Ford pickup. It belonged to one of the town's doctors, and it was up to us to magically return some childhood dream to him. I loved the grill on that truck. I don't know what it reminded me of, but the big headlights, and the central portion with the big enlargements were really special. Although I can't be sure looking back on it, but I think they reminded me of breasts.

We had most of the engine work done by Christmas, and it wasn't unusual for the doctor to stop by on a Friday night as we were closing to look at his dream. The Friday before Christmas, here came the doc, and following close behind was his daughter carrying presents for Bud and me. I could tell by the wrappings that Bud's present was a bottle of something, and I'd have to bet it wasn't Coca-Cola.

The smaller box, the one for me, wasn't a give-a-way, but actually I was more interested in looking at the daughter. She was one of those young women that could have been fifteen or twenty-five. Slight, like a runner, quite tall for a girl. She was wearing a stocking cap, and from beneath it her long blonde hair glistened down her back almost to her waist.

While Bud and the doc discussed the finer points of the mechanical restoration, the daughter brought the smaller present directly to me, and suggested I open it right then and there. I was fumbling with the wrapper, and she slid her bright, red gloves off to help, and there, on her left hand ring finger, was the biggest, brightest diamond I had ever seen. And next to that, almost hidden from view, was a wedding band.

My pecker, which had come to attention the minute she had walked through the garage door, took one look at those rings and decided to stand at ease. All I could do was continue to fumble with the paper, and when I finally got it open, the gift was an illustrated book by Wellington of all the famous bridges in the United States. As I flipped the pages, there were schematics, and drawings along with photographs, and I was immediately lost within its contents.

"Pardon my ill manners," said the doc, drawing me away from the architectural drawings of the New River Bridge in West Virginia, "but I want to introduce you to my wife, Claire."

I tore my eyes from the pictures of the longest single span arch bridge in the world, and looked directly into the mint-green eyes of Claire. She smiled softly, forming slight dimples in each cheek, and stuck out her hand for me to shake. I took her hand,

and it was like someone had wired me to the coil of that old '52 Ford, the charge from her hand up my arm and to my heart was so great.

For a minute it was embarrassing, as neither one of us seemed to want to let the handshake go, and the doc just standing there watching. Old Bud came to our rescue with one of his coughing fits, but by now, my face was as red as her gloves, which I bent down to pick up off the greasy floor of the garage.

We stood around and talked a little more; well, they did, I just stared, but finally good Christmas cheer was given to all, and Claire and the doc left the garage. Bud unwrapped his bottle of wine, a 1929 Vintage bottle of Armagnac, and I sat on the tailgate of the pickup and thumbed though the book. Her dimples were in my mind's eye, and even with all the grease and gasoline smells radiating in that old garage, I could still smell her perfume.

We managed to get the mechanical work all done on the '52 just before classes began again in late January. The doc had continued to check on his baby, but Claire had not returned with him. I had written a special thank-you note for the book, which I was enjoying immensely. As the work ended, I finally gave the doc the note, and hoped somehow that it didn't get lost in the big pocket in his overcoat, and would find its way to Claire. At least that's who I was thinking about when I wrote it: especially her dimples.

One night as I was studying my brains out for an upcoming advanced solid geometry test, someone hollered for me to get to the hall phone. I still didn't have a phone in my room, mainly because I didn't see the need for the use nor for the cost.

"This is Claire," the warm voice said into my ear. I don't know why, but I looked around, up and down the hallway, but no one was near. "I desperately need to talk with you," she went on, and there certainly was urgency to her voice.

I was thinking of what to say, as she continued: "I'm free tomorrow until 7 PM. I will meet you in the school library, research section. You tell me the time."

I had classes until three, and I was supposed to work for Bud until six, six thirty. "Between three and three fifteen," I answered, wondering what could be so important. Bud would be all right if I was fifteen minutes late.

I went back to studying, but dimples and mint-green eyes surrounded me, so I finally gave it up, crawled into bed, and worked on the feeling. Sometimes things just happen you can't explain no matter how hard you try.

I did the best I could on my test considering there were still dimples and green eyes all over the pages of the exam. I listened to most of my other classes, and when three o'clock came, I made a beeline for the library, research section. She had her back to me, but I knew it was she by the blonde hair racing down the back of her white sweater. She was bent over a large book, an atlas, I think it was.

I sat down across from her, and my heart took two or three irregular beats when those mint-green eyes crawled up from the book and looked at me. She had on a pair of reading glasses, and they were slipping down her nose, and seeing that, I grinned. She smiled back, and yes, there were those dimples, ever so slight. She looked even younger than when I had first seen her, and I wondered why she wasn't in school just like me.

"Here is the short version of my story. I'll save the longer one just for you if you are interested."

She waited a minute, as if for a response, but when I said nothing, went on. "My husband is a workaholic, as most surgeons are, only mine is worse. We have no children, only two dogs, but they aren't much for conversation."

She smiled at her own little joke, and, of course, I smiled too. "To be frank, I get lonely."

She stopped there, and continued to look at me, or I should say, various parts of me. While she was talking, her eyes roamed up and down my arms, across my chest, and stopped again at my eyes. Not only was my heart beating faster than normal, but my pecker was rejoicing.

"So, if you are interested, this is what I would like for you to do. I would like for you to spend some time with me, say once a week. We would talk and share ideas, you know, things we each like to do—maybe even our dreams if we really get to know each other well."

She let those words settle, and just as I was getting ready to respond, wondering when I would have the time, really, when she said, "I'm prepared to pay you for your time. Think of it as another part-time job. I'm sure I can pay as well as Bud pays you, and I'm sure he would even approve."

Maybe Bud would let me off another day a week, or let me be late one of the days I was now working for him. I knew I'd be willing to ask him—that was for sure.

"The only thing I ask," she began again, interrupting my thoughts about Bud, "is that you must not tell anyone, not Bud, no one. Do you agree?"

At this last question, her mint-green eyes seemed to snap, and I could see that she was very serious about all this talking and sharing.

I told her it sounded like something that I would really like to do, if I could find the time. What I didn't tell her was that I'd do about anything to watch those dimples come and go, and that I already knew which day Bud would have to work alone.

"Fine." she said, and brought those dimples out to play again. "I am really excited that you are willing to do this for me. I'll call you Monday night, and you can tell me when our first time will be."

She put her hand forward to shake my hand, to close the deal, and I gladly took hers waiting for that coil shock to hit me again, but instead of a shock there was a warm flow like melting solder from her hand to mine. We both smiled, and she turned, picking up her jacket. I admired her long legs and stride, as she walked out of the room and disappeared down the hallway.

Monday came slowly. I'd just gotten in from working at Bud's and was busy getting out my books for study when I was called to the phone.

"When?" she said in a low breathless voice, as if she'd run a mile just to get to the phone.

"Two thirty Tuesday," I said. The phone clicked dead. I stood looking at the receiver as some delivery boy walked by carrying a pizza.

"You can't order a pizza just lookin' at it," the guy said as he handed me a business card, then continued walking on down the hallway with the pizza over his head.

Of course Tuesday afternoon came, although there was a period during my morning lab that I wasn't sure that it would. I had been wondering ever since the last phone call where we were meeting, and I expected her to call and let me know. But the call didn't come, and I waited as two thirty approached, trying to read my book about bridges, and not getting very far as I was straining to hear the hall phone ring.

Promptly at two thirty, there was a knock at my partially-closed door, and I nearly jumped out of my skin. Funny how things like that happen. The next thing I knew Claire was standing in the middle of my tiny room, the single room I had begged and pleaded for this school year, looking at my posters of bridges and highways. Then she walked to my desk and flipped the pages on the bridge book, slid her coat off and placed it on the back of my chair.

She turned and gave me that dimpled smile, and the next thing I knew she was standing on my toes, and running her hands up my arms and across my chest. I instinctively put my arms around her and that coil shock hit my heart and molded us together, and her lips were every bit as soft as corn silk, and she smelled as sweet as clover hay drying in the sunshine.

And that is the short story of how Claire and I spent almost every Tuesday afternoon for the next year and a half. And even though she had some funny rules (no touching her below the navel, no kissing of any kind while poetry was being read, and toes are not an erogenous zone) my pecker and I learned the spiritual art of love and are eternally grateful for the lessons. But it was only when we parted at the end of my junior year that I really understood the depth of our learning.

But I'm getting ahead of myself, because maybe you would like to hear the long story of Claire, or at least the medium length one. As I think I mentioned, she felt that the doc wasn't around enough to keep her interested. But his money did, and the fact that she had grown up poorer than me helped her appreciate the finer things the doc provided for her.

But even in the midst of this, and with me helping her stay interested by listening to her talk, and share ideas, you know, things we each liked to do, and even dreams as we really got to know each other well, she had this one great fear—the fear of being alone. Now I'm talking about something as simple as being alone in a room or, especially frightening, being alone in her big old house at night.

It seems that the dogs helped when the doc was working late, but when he was gone overnight, as he occasionally was, look out, she couldn't bear it.

Claire had been out of nursing school just a year, and was working for the Gritman Medical Center as a scrub nurse in the neurological OR. That's how she had met the doc, as he was bent over the microscope all those long hours, dissecting this brain tumor or that brain aneurysm. He was recently divorced, and looking for a pretty thing to show off at the hospital parties and even the country club when he had time to go there for dinner.

Claire was impressed with his dedication, and late one night, as they had finished a long case together, they coupled in the doctor's lounge, right in the La-Z-Boy rocker in front of the glowing TV while Johnny Carson cracked jokes with Ed McMahon. When she was telling me this little bit of information, I couldn't help but wonder how that happened with her stringent rule about no touching below her navel. I was about to ask her when she told me.

The no touch below her navel rule was, I found out, just for me, or maybe really just for her, she decided, as the rule made her feel chaste, and true to her marriage vows, which I might add, made no sense to me.

As I was saying though, her greatest fear was that of being alone. She, with me listening, explored the reason, or reasons, for this: neither her mother, nor her father had died when she was young. She was not adopted, and yes, she had brothers and sisters whom she loved dearly although she never saw them as they lived on the East Coast. She could find no rational reason for the fear, but it was something that she indeed was learning to cope with.

We had been getting together on Tuesdays for about six months, when the doc was scheduled to give a presentation at some medical meeting back east. He had invited Claire to go, even insisted on it, but she clung to the idea of staying home and taking care of the dogs. An even more intense fear of being left alone in a strange hotel in some strange city was what prompted her to cry long enough for the doc to leave her home.

I had been studying late, but had finally gone to bed around one in the morning, falling immediately asleep. Mixed in with my dream of math tables and geometric shapes came the sound of music. The hall phone. I stumbled from my bed and scurried down the hall to answer it.

"You've got to come right away," Claire's frightened voice demanded. "I'm in Room 212 at the Hyatt. Hurry!"

Wondering who had kidnapped her and how she had gotten to the phone, I quickly put on some clothes, and bicycled like a mad man through the dark to the Hyatt. I stashed the bike in some bushes, sailed past the unmanned reception desk, saw the stair sign and leaped up the stairs two and three at a time to the second floor. Only when I reached the correct door did I pause, wondering for an instant what my best plan would be?

I knocked lightly on the door and stepped to the side where

I thought I would have an advantage when the door opened. It opened, and there was Claire in a long sheer nightgown, looking first to her right, and then spotting me when she looked to her left. She quickly pulled me inside, and smashed her body against mine.

"I'm so glad you could come," she whispered urgently in my ear as she rocked me back and forth.

I could taste her tears as I kissed her face, and her breasts were gently playing against my chest as my pecker was looking for an opening, kneading her in return on all her softer places. Finally, she held me at arm's length, her mint-green eyes more green then ever, and she smiled. I could, in the dim light of the room, see her dimples.

"I finally told my husband how afraid I was to say alone, so he called the Hyatt and got this room for me to stay in while he is gone, thinking that more people would be around and I would feel safe. I did for about an hour."

She paused, looking at me and finally asked, "Aren't you proud of me? For lasting an hour?"

I really don't know, even to this day, what happened that night or to her rules. I will only say this: my pecker, tired as it was, was hoping the doc would spend more time out of town. And I was hoping the very same thing.

My junior year of college was challenging and I was enjoying my career choice more and more. I had decided that bridges were my main interest, and I spent what little spare time I had designing free spans and suspensions. Sometimes, during my time with Claire, she would encourage me to draw and design, and she would stand behind me, saying nothing, until something in the design would touch her, and I would feel her tears falling on my shoulders: little rain sprinkles from some cosmic world.

Just as school was reaching its climax and I was knee-deep in finals, Momma called to remind me that my smart sister was graduating from high school, and wasn't I coming home? Luckily, her graduation was the weekend after my last final on Friday. Between classes, I called the bus station for the schedule. It still left at 9 PM: no surprises there.

I made arrangements with Bud for a week away, but telling Claire was another matter. I must have had a premonition for the violent storm that would not pass, because I waited until the Tuesday before my leaving to tell her. First there were tears, then her fists pounded my chest until she was exhausted. She fell to the floor, silently adrift and did not move for a least an hour even though I pleaded with her to let me help her to her feet.

She was so limp that although I could pull her to her feet; I could not keep her there. I finally managed to get her to a chair, from which she promptly skidded back to the floor, like syrup off a hot pancake. I sat on the floor with her, not knowing what to say, rubbing her back and shoulders. At long last, a whisper asked me how I could be so cruel as to leave her alone after all the time we'd spent together?

Explanations were of no use. I even went so far as to ask her to go home to Free Fall with me, to which came a soft feathery laugh. I was beginning to get mighty nervous because now she had stayed in my room over an hour longer than usual, and I had visions of the doc pounding on the door demanding his wife.

Of course, the doc didn't know we were together every Tuesday, did he? I tried to imagine what it would be like if he did come pounding on the door: would he be carrying a gun? If he did, I was also sure that it would be a very large one.

Eventually, Claire stopped crying, transformed back into a real person, got to her feet, and icily told me goodbye. Had I known that as the door quietly closed to my room, it would also shut on my love for Claire and I would never see or touch her again, I might have said something different or even pleaded with her to change her mind. But how was I to know that when Claire said goodbye, she really meant goodbye?

I was so worn out from finals and my last day with Claire,

I slept all the way to Free Fall. I didn't even waken during the stop in Missoula. I dreamt about red hair and rainbows and incense and herbs, but when I arrived in Free Fall, no one was asleep against the bus window as it pulled away in a cloud of dust leaving me standing there with my one suitcase in my hand.

When I reached the trailer, I didn't hesitate, but walked right in. Momma was in the kitchen, and she came into the living room and hugged me long and hard. I guess my pecker was still sleeping, 'cuz nothing happened for me to be ashamed of, which was a good thing. Momma looked thin, and I asked her if she was all right. She assured me she was, she had just been working too hard at the library, but there was something about the look in her eyes that I didn't like. It seemed that the glow I had always seen had dimmed. I'd heard about cataracts, and maybe before I returned to Moscow, I'd insist that she get her eyes checked.

We sat at the table, and she showered me with eggs and ham and fried potatoes, and non-stop conversation. Jack Longnecker, our closest neighbor, was in bad shape at the nursing home. He had had a stroke, and things didn't look good for his recovery. "Best stop and see him while you are here," she said, then, "Remember Miss Harmon? Your old substitute teacher?"

I nodded my head, thinking of her rear and her legs as she sat on that stool a thousand years ago. Seems she had come back to town to teach full-time that past school year and just after Christmas had run off with Sam Cossock, the assistant principal. Sam was married and had six or seven kids far as I could remember.

"Can you believe it?" Momma asked me.

I was busy thinking how lucky Sam was, when the door opened to the bedroom and out came my bleary-eyed smart sister. She had obviously been up much too late reading. She was dressed in Levi's and an old sweatshirt, and I was surprised to see how grown up she looked. She had always seemed mature for her age, probably because of all the books she read, but I had never really seen her look like a real adult.

She surprised me by giving me a hug, a first as far as I knew, or at least that I could remember. Talk about surprises, the hug even woke my pecker up. Then she told me how glad she was that I had come home for her graduation and I could feel my face turn red.

"She's giving the valedictorian speech," Momma said, and I certainly wasn't the least bit surprised at that.

The graduation was on Monday afternoon, and I was so nervous for my smart sister as she gave her speech that I don't remember exactly what she said. But I do remember the challenge she gave her class at the end of her speech: "When in doubt, be smart."

I was so proud of her, and not the least bit surprised to learn that my smart sister had earned a full scholarship and was going east to MIT. I guess reading all those books had been good for something. But I would be further surprised in the years to come when she would find time to put her books down long enough to marry and raise a family of four fine boys. All the while, after graduation, teaching graduate students at her alma mater.

But I'm getting ahead of my story again, and I have to get back to Momma and the doctor's appointment I made for her before I left for Moscow. She promised me that she would call me and tell me what the doctor said, and I told her to be sure and get her eyes checked too, and she promised that she would. Feeling a little better, I left for Moscow soon after visiting Jack Longnecker at the nursing home, which left me feeling as hollow and worthless as a dead pirate's wooden leg, and it haunted me all the way back to Moscow. Jack didn't know me, and we couldn't seem to find a thread of conversation between us. I wished that I had had some pictures of the bridges I was designing with me. Maybe that would have helped, but I didn't, so I had left him lost in a wilderness known only to him.

It was good to be back at work with Bud, familiar ground as they say. I found no note from Claire, and on my first Tuesday back, no word. And as I said, there never would be any, but it sure took me awhile to figure it out; to stop listening for the phone or that knock on my door.

Momma called about a week later, and she told me that the doctor had found her in good health. Oh, her blood was a little run down from working so hard, but he'd given her some medicine to build it up, and would be rechecking it in a month or so. She sounded so peppy on the phone, I thought that the medicine must be a good one to have worked so well so soon. That was late June, and little did I know that I would be back in Free Fall burying my Momma before the month of August was over.

The trailer looked lifeless without Momma. Even the willows had lost their sheen, and the screen door had fallen into the dirt along side of the porch. I hesitated by the door, unlocked it, and went in. It was neat as a pin, everything in place, everything in order. Yet something felt very wrong. I had to sit on the end of the couch and think about it for a minute, and then I realized there was not a book in the place. Later, I found out that Momma had donated them all to the library, even my smart sister's favorites.

I got up and started to prepare a good meal, and while the spaghetti was boiling, I opened the door to my sister's room. Mariel was waiting for me. The poster was faded, but the brown eyes were still penetrating, the nose still up-turned. We stood looking at each other just as my smart sister arrived from MIT. I hugged her long and hard, and the tears welled in my eyes, and I'm sure in Mariel's too, and then in came my beautiful sister, and that jerk of a husband right behind her. The three of us gathered in a huge hug, him looking over the top of us as he said, "Sorry about your Momma, Pecker-Boy."

My sisters both left the day after the funeral, after a night in the trailer wondering what to do without Momma. Even though we asked, Mariel was of no help. Finally, worn from the day, we prepared for sleep. My beautiful sister and her jerk of a husband were to sleep in the sister's room, and my smart sister grabbed dibs on the couch. I couldn't think about sleeping in Momma's bed after all these years, so I rolled up a quilt on the floor next to the couch and prepared to sleep there.

Sometime during the night, I awakened to a tapping on my shoulder. It was my beautiful sister, and before I knew it, she was snuggled on top of that quilt next to me, close, holding me strong in her arms. I could smell her skin, and her sleepy breath, and could feel her breasts, and maybe it was some noise, or the movement, 'cuz the next thing I knew, my smart sister was down there with us, her back to me, and it was as if the years, like smoke rings, had slid away into the night. My beautiful sister relaxed her grip around me as she fell into sleep, and I lay there on my back wishing Mariel could have joined us.

The trip back to Moscow was longer than any reason I could think of. Maybe it was because I couldn't sleep, no sir, not a wink the whole way. I thought about a lot of things, but mostly how tiny Momma had looked in that big old casket. It was like she had reverted to infancy or something, just a tiny doll of pale flesh. The first time I stood looking over the edge of the casket, I remember wondering whose body that really was. I certainly couldn't imagine snuggling up to it as I had often remembered doing, and it sure didn't comfort me any to think that at one time I looked forward to having one of her tits in my mouth.

Back in Moscow, I felt disconnected, isolated, weary. Only the work with Bud kept me getting up in the mornings. My last year of college was about to begin, yet I had no passion, no yearning for school. I was so far behind in my summer classes, I dropped them, and increased my hours with Bud. He didn't mind, and even seemed to enjoy the chance to sit on his stool more often, wiping the grease from his hands.

In September, school started whether I felt ready or not. All I can say is, I did the best I could, which wasn't good enough. My advisor called me in for a pep talk. It didn't really help all that much, but I did manage to finish fall semester, barely passing. I was looking forward to working more with Bud, but the week before Christmas, my lifeline snapped like I had stepped on dry twig.

We had a terrible snow, a blizzard really, that week before Christmas, shutting down businesses, breaking power lines, stalling traffic. I was able to walk the drifts, the wind had pounded them so firmly, and even though late, I managed to make it to Bud's garage that Wednesday morning, the third day of the storm. I could see tracks over the drifts to the side door, and I could see where someone, probably Bud, had shoveled a small area of snow away from the large double doors at the front of the garage.

Entering the garage, I was not surprised to find the lights off, so many lines were down, but then I realized that the place was warm, so there must be electricity. I flipped the main switch, and the lights flooded the room, and there, in the center of the garage next to an old '61 Buick lay Bud. Except for the fact he was lying on top of the snow shovel, he looked as if he had crawled into bed and had gone to sleep. There was a pleasant smile on his face, and his hands, darkened from all the grease, lay gently near his face. His cap was still in place.

I knelt down beside him, and shook him gently, hoping he was asleep, but I knew from the chalk color of his face, that he was dead. Never in my life had I openly cried. Oh yeah, tears came at Momma's funeral, but now, from somewhere inside came a cry of pain, of feeling totally lost, roared from my lips, and the tears pooled on the floor next to Bud. Sitting down on the floor, I gently gathered him in my arms, and rocked him ever so softly back and forth until I could no longer see through the tears that continued to spill from my eyes.

Bud had outlived his family, that is, his wife. They had no children. To my surprise, and maybe to yours, his handwritten will left me the garage, his house and all the tools. Yes, to me. Now I was the proud new owner of Bud's Garage. The only problem was, I didn't know much about fixing cars, only what Bud had taught me over the last three years.

And then there was school and one more semester to go. I sat near the big bench on Bud's stool and tried to think what to do. I tried wiping the grease from my hands on Bud's old rag. When that didn't work, I got busy seeing if I could finish the job on the Mustang we had been working on when Bud died. Oil pressure problems are never easy, but I was determined. I tossed the rag to the bench, got on the dolly, and with wrench in hand, rolled under the car.

Maybe it was all the snow we had that winter, but I had never seen a more beautiful spring in Moscow. I swear the flowers bloomed earlier and larger than seemed remotely possible. I had reduced the hours the garage was open to fit my school schedule, and it hadn't hurt the business what so ever. I had plenty of work. Graduation would be next week.

I glanced above the workbench from where Mariel was presiding over the shop. I could tell by her sly smile that my replacement of the Ford Probe's alternator had gone according to her high standards. I grabbed a rag, and wiped the grease from my hands, grinning back at the poster, accepting her approval. I shoved the stool closer to the bench, reached for my book on bridges and a textbook. Tomorrow was my last, and of course, my hardest final. Mariel, I noticed, continued her smile as I opened the books and began to study.

On graduation day, there was a gentle breeze swishing the leaves around, and I thought of the trailer, and of course Momma. A sudden wave of sadness washed over me, but then I knew how proud she and probably Jack Longnecker, our closest neighbor, were of me. And I knew that Bud was busting his wings up there somewhere.

That's when I knew I should have invited my sisters, but I just never got around to calling or writing them. I did think about it a few times, but I was either busy at the garage, or busy with the books. In fact, I really wasn't even going to the ceremony, but for some reason, at the last moment, I rented a gown, and with all the other excited students sat in the stadium and tried to listen to the speaker tell us how bright we were.

I received my diploma, and with the ceremony over, I was walking down the street toward Bud's Garage, my gown open and flapping in the breeze. As I walked, I was feeling the velvet along the edge of the gown, running it between my fingers. It felt soft, velvety under my fingers, and suddenly, the trees began to hum and the sun seemed to ratchet up a notch or two. I felt a strange lightness to my step and well, to tell the truth, I glanced around to make sure no one was watching.

It was about that time I heard a car pull up along side me, an Audi Quattro, and someone was leaning out the open window. Embarrassed, I stopped feeling the velvet edge of the gown and tried to walk like my feet were firmly planted on the ground.

"Hey stranger, would you like a Coke, or maybe dessert?" Emily asked me through the open window.

Come Spring

It was 1949, and I was beginning to think spring would never get here. April in Wyoming can sometimes be darn right miserable. Deep, wet snows come without warning, piling snow into drifts and freezing the ears off the newborn calves. This spring was coming slower than most it seemed to me. But then it wasn't because of the latest snow; it was because my dad had promised a new puppy "come spring."

Exactly when "come spring" was, I didn't quite know. After all, we'd learned in school that spring officially came on March 21st, and now it was closing fast on the end of April. Still, Dad hadn't said another word, and I was beginning to think I'd dreamed up the whole thing.

This evening, after supper and after clearing the table and washing the dishes as my sister, Susie, dried, I went out to the barn to feed our dog V, who was getting mighty old. "Older than dirt," someone had said, which I thought was pretty funny as we were studying the origin of the Earth in school at the time, and I could just imagine old V coming out of the Big Bang. No matter his age, two summers ago he had survived getting caught up in the hay mower. One front leg had been cut clear through, the other badly damaged. The vet had thought V should be put down, but Dad took on the doctoring and by the next summer, old V was up and running. Sure he has a limp, and the toes on one foot stick up at a funny angle, but he can still chase a jackrabbit. He's just a bit slower and he can't take the corners as good as he used to.

Finishing up my evening chores, I dropped Purina Chow into V's dish, gave him a pat on the head and stroked his back. A low growl fluttered from his throat. Old V didn't like to be messed with when he was eating. I wandered back to his bed, a bunch of old horse blankets piled in the corner of the unused granary, and fluffed them up a bit. I thought it would make them friendlier to his old bones.

It was right after V's recovery and seeing him hobble around that Dad first mentioned getting another dog. Nothing much was said again about a pup until sometime in March when Dad, one night during supper, mentioned that one of Stan Broiler's bitches was due to whelp sometime in the spring. Stan was a family friend owning a ranch about six miles from ours, and his cattle dogs were some of the best in the county, taking all the blue ribbons for herding at our annual fair.

I could feel the hair stand up on the back of my neck when I thought about the possibility of getting one of Mr. Broiler's dogs. Why, I could train him to be the best cow dog, a heeler, and a good one too! Maybe with a little coaxing, Mr. Broiler would help me get him started. The fact that I didn't know a thing about training a dog was not even a serious consideration.

Friday of the last week of April it turned warm, hot in fact, and it seemed that spring had finally come. That night at supper, I picked at my apple cobbler, one of Mom's best desserts.

"Please don't kick your shoes," Mom said touching me on the arm. Nervousness did that to me. Clearing my throat I said, "Dad, about getting a pup."

Dad looked at Mom and then at me for what seemed a lifetime before a slight smile began to form. "Tell you what, Jamie, let's call Stan and see if that bitch has whelped. Now you and Susie get the dishes done while I make the call."

I was so eager that I tipped on my chair and fell over backward hitting my head on the floor with a kerplunk, ripe, melon sound. Embarrassed, I scrambled to my feet only to trip over the corner of the rug. Down I went again, but this time only to my knees.

"Now Jamie, if you're going to get all upset about it, I just won't make the call." Dad said as he headed for the old black phone hanging on the back kitchen wall.

"That bowl isn't clean," Susie said as she handed it back to me. It was darn hard to wash dishes and listen to what was being said over the phone. Susie handed me back another dish.

"What do you think we should name him?" I whispered as I handed Susie a plate after being sure it was clean.

"First of all," she responded, not bothering to whisper, "why does it have to be a boy? Girl dogs can herd cows too."

The thought of getting a girl dog had never crossed my mind. V was male. Stan's best dog Badger was a he. A girl dog?

I watched the dirty suds swirl down the drain as Dad hung up the phone. As he turned toward me I tried to read the expression on his face while I wiped my wet hands on my pants and waited.

"She's due by the end of the week."

My heart skipped a beat.

"Now remember, we can't go and pick one out until they are six weeks old, and four pups were spoken for before we got in our bid. So, you got to hope she has a bunch of pups."

Now, my heart wasn't even beating and I felt dizzy. I let out a huge breath and my heart must have started again because my head quickly cleared. I'm not the best math student in my class, but it didn't take me long to figure it would be after my birthday in June before I got to pick a pup. Anyway I thought about it, it seemed an eternity. The only good thing I could think about was that school would be finished for the year, and I could spend a lot of time training my new dog.

That night when I said my prayers, I waited for mom to tuck me in and leave the room. That's when I tacked on a PS: "God, please make that bitch have enough pups."

School is a good enough pastime when snow is blowing, but it sure is hard to concentrate when the sun is shining bright and the world seems to be busy doing other things but learning history. To double my usual difficulty in paying attention, I had to worry about getting my pup. The good news was that Mr. Broiler had called and his bitch had whelped seven pups, which got me to thinking about taking prayer more seriously.

Still, the days dragged by at a snail's pace. Or a turtle's pace, depending on which one is the slowest. I tried, honest, but it sure came hard to do my studies when watching the leaves breaking out on the willows or dreaming about my pup come more naturally. Homework was especially hard. Somehow the days inched by and the end of May was nearing with school adjourning in one week. I would finish fifth grade—if I passed.

June came and one worry was off my mind. My report card had come, and I'd managed to escape to sixth grade. My birthday was coming in two days, the tenth, and Susie was busy in her room making something for me. At least that is what I thought because she wouldn't let me into her room no matter how hard I whined.

The weather turned unusually chilly, but that was not unusual. Mom always told everyone that the summer weather really never came until after my birthday, and I swear that is the truth. It usually rained, or sometimes even snowed, so no birthday party was ever planned that needed outside activities, and it looked like this year was no exception.

Early on my birthday morning, I made tracks through the frost covering the ground as I walked toward the barn. Looking up, the dark clouds were already boiling over Laramie Peak, and I knew it would be raining by birthday cake time. I kicked at a rock and sent it rolling through the frost, its wobbly track looking like a dying snake. I pulled my cold hands from my pockets and pushed open the door. Old V was waiting for me, wagging his tail, his front toes kicking up in that weird fashion like he was trying to wave.

I patted his head and brushed some straw leavings from the perfectly formed white V that nestled in the brown fur of his forehead. He licked my cold fingers and whined a little song. I dumped some chow into his dish and while he was eating I began to explain.

"It's not that you're that old," I began. "It's just that you need a playmate, someone you can teach all your tricks to. I'm not getting a pup because I don't like you anymore. I'm getting a pup, well because—," I reached out to pet old V again, and I heard the deep rumble begin in his throat, so I just went on talking without touching him.

"You know you can't chase rabbits like you used to, and besides, you never did like chasing after cows. Yeah, I know, they can kick hard, can't they? But some dogs don't seem to mind getting kicked."

Old V was licking up the last of the chow and looking around for more. He raised his head and I could tell he hadn't heard a word I'd been saying. He walked over to me and I petted his head and he started to follow me out of the barn, but when he saw the frost, he changed his mind and went back to his pile of blankets.

"Sorry," I said to his disappearing backside, apologizing ahead of time for the pup that I hoped was soon to come.

What seemed like a year later, although it was only five days after my birthday, Dad called me out from under the tractor I was helping him fix.

"As soon as we finish this project, we should go down to Stan's and check on those pups."

I squinted into the sun as I looked up to him and saw that his eyes were bright with mischief. Dad nudged me with his elbow.

"Don't you think?"

"Yeah," I answered trying not to show how excited I was as little fingers started fluttering inside my stomach.

We finally got the last bolt tightened about 5 PM as Dad said, "Maybe we should wait until after supper, unless you ain't feeling hungry."

His eyes were sparking now like flint against steel as we walked toward the house.

"I can wait to eat," I said knowing that there was no room for food along side of the multiplying fingers still fluttering big inside. And with that, Dad got the keys, called for Susie, and we were off down the road to Mr. Broiler's place.

Susie was sitting in back and singing to herself, which I usually liked to hear, but right now it began to drive me crazy.

"Please don't sing," I said turning my head toward my sister.

She ignored me and turned up the volume sounding more like a bleating sheep. I gritted my teeth and tried to ignore her. Sisters!

Soon we rolled into Mr. Broiler's lane, and one of his dogs, Badger, came barking to greet us. He was a big, sturdy Australian Shepherd, merle in color. Both of his eyes were "white" which gave him a sort of eerie look until you got to know him. He jumped up on me when I got out of the car and almost knocked me over with his enthusiasm for visitors. Then he jumped on Susie and did knock her over which I thought was good medicine seeing as how she wouldn't quit singing in the car.

"Here, Badger! Get off them kids. You know better than that."

It was Mr. Broiler shouting as he came from the house to meet us. "Where the heck's your manners."

Badger immediately dropped his tail stub and began to slink away, but Susie, after righting herself, called him back and began vigorously petting him.

"Now Susie, make him mind his manners," Mr. Broiler demanded as he began shaking my hand.

"So you came to pick out a pup, did you, Jamie?" Then, "Howdy, Matt," as he turned and shook my father's hand.

"Hi, Sam. So you still have some pups for us to see?"

"The whole litter is still here. I generally don't recommend taking them from the mother until they are eight weeks of age. Now, Jamie, don't get attached to any that have a string around their neck because they have already been picked."

Mr. Broiler began leading us toward an old bunkhouse. As he opened the door, I could smell a mixture of old wood and straw and something I wasn't sure of. It was a sweet smell and later I found out it was the smell of milk.

The bitch was in a crib of sorts, just big enough for her to lie down comfortably. The sides of the crib were only five or six inches tall, so she could easily jump in and out but the pups could not wander away. They were bedded on straw and it was very warm in the room. I began to feel a little light-headed from the smells and the excitement, and I sort of stopped in my tracks, letting my eyes adjust to the light.

Badger had reached the crib before us, and the bitch jumped to her feet sending puppies everywhere. She began growling, and before Badger could step back she had nipped him on the nose. Badger let out a yelp and quickly retreated.

"Now, Nellie, that's no way to treat the father of your pups. Shame on you," Mr. Broiler chided the bitch. "Come on up here slowly, Jamie, and let Nellie get a smell of you so she knows you are not going to hurt her babies."

I walked slowly up next to Mr. Broiler and let Nellie sniff my hand. I'm sure she knew I was scared. Of what, I don't know, but she let it pass and began licking my hand. The pups were jumping furiously against and up on the sides of the crib begging for petting. Susie was there in an instant cooing over each one. Nellie left me to check her out and I got down on my knees and began petting the puppies too.

Even though Dad had told me four pups were spoken for, only three had white strings around their necks. The largest and most aggressive pup demanded to be petted, but he had a string around his neck so I tried to ignore him. As I started looking over the four without strings, I noticed one of them stayed back in the corner of the crib watching the goings on. In the background, Mr. Broiler was telling me things about picking a pup.

"Some say, Jamie, that the best cow dogs will have no black on the roof of their mouths. In these merle dogs, that is sometimes hard to find, and I'm not real sure it matters."

All the pups were merle colored as was Nellie, but some had more silver woven into their black coats than the others giving them more of a blue look.

"Their colors will change some as they grow older and lose their puppy hair," Mr. Broiler continued. "Another thing to look for is a pup with some aggression. If a dog is too shy, it won't make a good cow dog. The cows will intimidate them and the first thing you know, the cow is herding the dog instead of the other way around."

After petting all the pups near the edge of the crib, I reached out across and picked up the smaller one watching from the corner. The pup snuggled in my arms and I put my face down to him and he licked my nose. He smelled good like straw and milk mixed, and I cuddled the pup more closely against my chest.

Mr. Broiler came over and opened her jaws to look at the top of her mouth. It was pink and covered with black spots.

Susie continued playing with the pups, and Nellie, seeing we weren't hurting her babies, had jumped out of the crib and was busy chasing Badger from the building. I tried to set the pup down so I could look at another, but his claws were stuck in the front of my shirt and he was clinging to me.

"And another thing, a better dog has both blue eyes and not just one."

Mr. Broiler was still teaching me the things to look for in a good pup. As the pup struggled to keep me from setting it down, I noticed that he had only one blue eye, the right one. The other was brown. As soon as the pup hit the straw, it headed back to the corner and lay down. I started looking at the other three pups without strings around their necks. The first one just didn't feel right when I picked it up and kept struggling to get down. It didn't like to be held.

I grabbed for the other one, and he seemed to like being held and kept licking my face. I glanced over to the corner, and the first pup was still lying there with both eyes on me. I set the pup down and leaned over and scooped up the first one I had looked at. The puppy clung to my shirt and melted against me as my heart melted, and the funny fingers stopped fluttering in my stomach.

I glanced at Dad, then Mr. Broiler. "I like this one," I stated, looking for approval from one or both. The men looked at each other as Susie came over and started rubbing ears on the pup in my arms. I saw my dad take out his wallet, and the two were talking so low between them I couldn't hear. Dad shook his head and said "No, I can't do that, Stan." My heart sank, thinking the price was too much for my pup.

I strained to hear as Mr. Broiler said something back to Dad, and I heard the words "birthday, for crying out loud—" Dad was still shaking his head as he carefully folded his wallet and put it back in his hip pocket.

"What do you say to Mr. Broiler, Jamie?" Dad asked.

I didn't know what I was supposed to say when I didn't know if the pup was mine. It was then I saw that spark in Dad's eyes and a grin was spreading over Mr. Broiler's tanned face.

"What are you going to call that pup?" Mr. Broiler asked me as I hugged the puppy even closer to my chest.

"I'm going to call him Henry," I said as both men started laughing. Susie was back at the crib as I looked to her for approval, but she was busy petting Nellie who had returned from chasing Badger from the bunkhouse.

"Thank you very much for the puppy, Mr. Broiler," I said quietly. "I know you said you usually don't let them go this young, but could I please take Henry with me now?"

"Well, you're right about what I said, Jamie, but I know you to be a fine young man so I think that little pup will be in good hands if you take it now. And if you think you might need some help in training that dog to herd cows, you call me, you hear?"

"Yes sir," I said as I stood up and thanked him again, and Dad and Susie and Henry and I started for the car.

We all piled in and Henry made himself a cozy little nest on my lap in the front seat, resting his head on my arm. He still smelled like straw and milk, and maybe a little bit like old wood as Dad started the car and we headed home. We were about halfway there when Susie leaned forward from her seat in back and said, "Aren't you glad that girl dogs can herd cows too?"

I turned and looked at her and then at Dad, who was looking very hard at the road ahead. I turned to Henry, who had just shut his eyes, and I picked him up by the front legs and sure enough—.

And that's how we arrived at home just in time for supper: Dad and Susie and me and Henrietta, "come spring."

The Box Social

The weather had been a whole lot cooler when the day began. Now, even though the sun had set an hour ago, it was mighty hot. Sweat seeped through the back of my shirt and I felt a trickle start down my right temple as I eased forward in my chair to let some air circulate.

The room was abuzz with folks talking and laughing in that familiar way when friends get together. It is particularly true when there is a common bond between them, and these farming people certainly had that. It was like the dirt beneath their fingernails, it was always there.

Farm Bureau was our Wyoming social life. By that I mean it was our "fun" social life. We attended church every Sunday, and that was our other social life. The serious one. Farm Bureau was square dancing and fiddlers and eating and visiting. Tonight it was a box social, which brings me to the reason I was sweating so badly.

For those of you who don't know a box social from a toadstool, I'll explain. Womenfolk put together a real nice meal: something mighty special. It might contain their favorite recipe cooked to perfection along with something very feminine to eat, like sandwich squares instead of a couple of chunks of bread with baloney pressed between. Of course, the dessert is always something to remember for days at a time.

After all this preparation, the womenfolk place all these goodies into a shoe box and then they fancy up the outside with colored cloth and ribbons and sometimes flowers if the season is right. Their plan is that the man they hope to eat with will recognize their box, because here comes the tricky part: these boxes are auctioned off to the highest bidder.

The auction provides a lot of entertainment for everybody. It separates the husbands and boyfriends of the womenfolk into two kinds: those who listen and those who don't, because you see, if some husband didn't listen to his wife, or some boyfriend hasn't listened to his girl when she tells him how her box is decorated, then he's going to end up eating with someone else—after everyone has laughed and made fun of him for not listening.

Now there are a couple more things that can happen during the auction that you might need to know. First, you have to keep your bidding hand as quiet as you can, because if the older men see you bidding on a special box, they'll run the price up on you by countering your bid. This happens all in fun, but it can sure cost you upwards in price to the point that you might wonder which is worse: not eating with your wife or girlfriend or having to see the banker for a loan.

And the second is that all the money from the auction goes to some worthy cause such as a charity or the March of Dimes or even to help some poor farming family who's having trouble making it.

I'd been sweet on Mary Rose since I sat behind her in 6th grade. I used to carry her books and even helped her when she was a crossing guard, waving the kids across the intersection while she stood in the middle of the street looking all grown up in her white safety belt with the big brass badge clipped to the cross strap. She had eyes as big and blue as Lake Marie, and a smile that made my heart skip its regular thub-dub.

I only had one class with her now that we were juniors in high school, and that was probably the reason I wasn't doing so good in mathematics: I sat and watched her instead of concentrating on what the teacher was saying. But I still liked her, and when she told me how her box was decorated, I was listening really hard. I even wrote it down in the margins of my math book, page 287, right next to the fractions.

Earlier in the day, I started feeling nervous about the time Dad and I put the tractor in the shed so we could get an early start bathing before the social. I'd been thinking most of the day that if I could get Dad to bid on Mary's box, the old guys wouldn't be able to run the price up on me. They'd just think Dad had slept through Mom's description of her box, and I wouldn't be forced past the only six dollars I had to my name.

We were walking towards the house and I said, "Hey, Dad, would you do me a favor?"

"Well, that depends on what its going to cost me," he replied, never even breaking his stride.

Darn, Dad knew me well. "It's not going to cost you anything, and it could save me a lot of money."

I explained my situation of short finances and hinted at my yearning heart. "You see, Dad, I've only got six dollars and I was trying to help out Mary Rose. I don't want her box to go unsold, but I don't want to get skinned by those old guys either. I thought if you bought it for me, it could save us both a lot of grief."

We were nearing the house before he answered. "I'll be glad to help you out, son, and I sure wouldn't want to see Mary Rose's box go unsold either."

I thought I might have heard a little bit of teasing in the last part, and I felt my face flush.

"Thanks, Dad," I said, relieved for the moment as I went on to give him a detailed description of what the box would look like. I sure hoped he was listening.

Leaning forward in my chair didn't seem to help with the heat, and the sweat kept coming. I glanced at Mary Rose out of the corner of my eye. She was sitting near the door, all decked out in a pink dress with a blue ribbon tied around her tiny waist. Why she was dressed like that, I didn't have a clue since that is the same description she had given me for her box. Of course, the box was to have a red paper poppy tied to the blue bow. I couldn't see any poppy tied to her anywhere.

"Give me a ten, a ten, a ten" the auctioneer was saying. "Sold to the man in the black hat for nine dollars and seventy-five cents." Wiping his brow he continued, "Come on, fellers, this is for a good cause. You can do better than that for a chance to eat with your favorite gal."

We were getting down to the last of the boxes, and Mary Rose's was sitting among the remaining pile. Dad had already purchased Mom's, spending nearly twelve dollars for the privilege. No wonder I was sweating.

The lump in my throat grew larger as the auctioneer picked up Mary Rose's box. "Now look at this pretty poppy. Ain't that a nice touch to keep us wondering who this might belong to? All right, gents, get out your wallets and start your bidding."

He turned the box around slowly and began, "I've got two, now three. Give me four, four, four. I've got four, now five—."

My eyes were getting blurry from the sweat pouring down my face and for a minute I felt like I couldn't breathe, forcing me to take an almost audible gasp. My hand was in my pocket fingering the five and the one I had folded there.

"I've got five, give me six, six, six," the auctioneer continued. "Come on, fellas, dig into those pockets and give me six. What about five and a quarter, quarter, quarter?

I shuffled my feet.

"Thanks, now five and fifty, fifty, fifty, fifty— sold to the big man in the blue shirt for five seventy-five, and if you won't tell his wife, I won't either."

Dad sat back down and placed Mary Rose's box on his lap next to Mom's and he made a great show of looking from one box to the other as if trying to decide which one to keep. Mom was squeezing his arm and smiling big as if to say it didn't matter to her. She'd eat with the highest bidder for her box, whoever it was, that is; if Dad decided to have it resold.

As for me, I could finally get my breath, but looking at Mary Rose and her look of not understanding started me gasping for air all over again.

" Give me a nine, a nine, a nine," the auctioneer was saying over the last box in the pile, and then, "I have ten, now twelve. Oh boy, now fifteen. Do I hear sixteen, now seventeen? What about sixteen fifty, fifty, fifty? Sold to that young feller sitting by the fire extinguisher for the grand sum of sixteen and ninety."

The old men had finally found someone to pester the price up, and I took another deep breath. I was certainly glad it hadn't been me. I pulled the bills from my pocket and started walking toward Dad. Standing in front of him, he began looking from one box to the other, again as if trying to make a decision. He started to hand me Mom's box, then smiling, gave me the pink box with the red poppy tied to the blue bow.

I handed him the bills. "Thanks, Dad."

I turned looking for Mary Rose.

Dreams

We all dream of coming into unexpected wealth. You know, "When I win the lottery" or "Maybe Aunt Martha has more money than we think," and sometimes, "I hope old what's-his-name will remember it was I that shoveled his sidewalks for five years." My dream has always been to find a big suitcase full of money, all unmarked bills in large denominations—kind of like the guys did in that movie, *A Simple Plan,* only in *my* "reel" life, I'll be by myself, and no one else will know.

Deep down inside, I used to think this dream would never happen, and if you are honest, you know your mantra is specious too. Our lives are full of little dreams we know to be false, but we need dreams to relieve our daily tedium, to survive, don't we? But perhaps I am too quick to judge your dreams as foolhardy, because my dream came true, and maybe, just maybe, if mine came true, so can yours.

Four years after I built my house on the side of a mountain, an interesting young man purchased forty acres behind and up the mountain from my small acreage. My immediate concern was that he might keep me from crossing his land, as I was accustomed to doing, to get to the National Forest. One evening, shortly after his purchase, he stopped by the house to introduce himself because he had heard I built my own home and helped a neighbor build his.

I have always been careful not to make snap judgments about a new acquaintance, as I have been proven so wrong at least ninety-nine percent of the time when I do. But as my new neighbor sat on my sofa spilling leaflets of his life, I couldn't help but notice how out of place he was, both in dress and in attitude, for a dream of a home in the rugged mountains of Colorado.

He was not wearing a necktie, but I got the distinct impression he had removed it just before he knocked on my door. His suit was Armani. Expensive shoes. His nails were polished, and I'm sure his hair had been professionally groomed earlier in the day. I liked his shirt: powder blue with dark overstitching. Peeking through the short V of the open front of his shirt, thick links of a gold chain hung around his neck. A gold watch and band, probably Gucci, and the huge diamond ring completed his elegant ensemble.

He spoke with a New England accent, clipped and precise. It seems he had squandered much of his youth on drugs and rock and roll. He had, he told me, just recovered from the failure of his second marriage, and had completed an extended stay in a drug rehabilitation center just last month. But, he told me, "I'm on my way up now. I have a good job, a new girlfriend, and with the home I intend to build here, I know I can stay clean. Denise," he said, indicating his new friend, "will see to that. She said she'll kill me if I don't!"

His laugh was harsh from the one habit he still maintained, cigarettes, although he had not smoked in my presence. I could smell the fusty smoke from his clothes, permeating the air like the smell of a burned-out forest fire late in the evening.

"Can you come up to my place tomorrow and show me where I should place the house?" he inquired after complimenting me on the structure I had built.

"I think I could do that," I replied, "but I'm not the real

expert here. Old Man Murphy over in the valley has lived in the area nearly twenty-five years. He seems to know this mountain like Trapper John knew the San Juans."

"I don't know Murphy," he said in his clipped tongue, "but I do have complete confidence in your opinion. Does eight o'clock sound okay? I'll stop and pick you up on my way if that's all right."

I hesitated for a minute and then said, "I'll just meet you there. The early walk will do me good."

"See you then," he answered, shook my hand and started for the door. He was half way out when he turned and added in a very earnest tone, "I feel the best I have in ten years. I really want to stay clean—and I know I can."

And with that, I watched him walk across my wooden deck, down the rock stairs, and open the door on his Mercedes. He left in a cloud of dust, down my lane, the car purring, sucking in the thin air and producing a gentle, expensive back-flow of exhaust.

My walk up the hill, a steep mile through the woods, was pleasant in the early light. Small puffy white clouds were already billowing over the brim of the mountain. When I got to a point just below our meeting place, I could see the very top of the mountain outlined against the deep blue sky. I walked on and arrived at the point of his acreage just as I heard the muffled roar of an engine working much harder than even the unimproved road should require.

Immediately to my left, a white Jeep appeared, a Wrangler so new I could smell the tinny, new heat odor of the exhaust system. Sam apparently had the vehicle in four-wheel drive and in the lowest gear ratio possible. He had removed the side curtains allowing me a fine view of a very attractive woman bouncing along in the passenger seat. The jeep came to an exhaustive stop, and Sam jumped from the seat.

"Good morning, Bud!" he said, as he walked around to help the lady out of her seat. "This is Denise."

Her doe-like eyes transfixed me immediately. Her hair was

shaped in a very smart, short cut, the ends curling seductively around her neck. And, oh, her complexion: olive, absolutely clear, blemish-free, and her figure was well-proportioned.

"Hi," she said, immediately endearing me to her for life by hugging me like an old lost friend, then shaking my hand. "I am so happy to meet you. Sam told me all about you, and I think you are wonderful to offer to help us with our house."

The fact that Sam and I hadn't discussed me helping with the house, just the location, did not matter; her hand was as warm as her smile. I reluctantly let go of the handshake and said, for lack of anything better to say, "Welcome to the mountain."

She was exuberant and radiant. She went on and on about the beautiful drive up from Denver. She wanted to know the names of *everything*!

"How long have you lived here?" she inquired.

"Just four years," I responded, "but I've owned the land since '76."

"Oh," she said, her eyes widening. "Are there bears around?" She glanced over her shoulder with a quick feline gesture.

Whenever anyone asks me about bears, I always hesitate before I answer. Why? Most people would genuinely embrace a chance to see a real live bear. Some people already know how pesky they can be and would rather hear that none were available. A few people would pack up and leave if they knew a bear lived in the immediate fifty-mile radius from where they were standing. The problem is, it is hard to tell which one of these people you are talking to, and even if you did know, which way would you want the story to go? So, I said, "They have a lot of trouble with bears down in the lower valley, but we only get an occasional wanderer. For some reason, they never seem to stay."

"Maybe you don't feed them well enough!" she said seriously, but her eyes were brimming with mirth. "Did you hear that, Sam, we might be able to have a bear for dinner sometime."

I didn't know whether she meant that the bear would share

a meal with them or be the meal. I started to ask, but Sam interrupted my thoughts with his interpretation.

"He won't stay around long with your cooking, dear," Sam said in a kidding manner, and with that he reached out and encircled his arms around Denise, pulled her close and did something to her ear which made her squeak. I felt my face redden, and I began to look around for the best possible site for the house. It looked as if we might need to get the house built as quickly as possible.

There was a beautiful outcropping of granite just behind where we were standing, the rocks tilting nearly forty-five degrees from some loud burp the Earth had made eons ago. The outcropping ran westward for maybe eighty feet before receding into the ground. At this altitude the winds can be ferocious, especially in the winter, but I could see a house tucked behind this natural wind break, protecting all but the very top windows of a house correctly designed, allowing an almost three hundred sixty degree of wind-protected view.

I told them my thoughts and although we looked at several alternative sites, it seemed that my suggestion was the best. Sam strode to the jeep, removed a lengthy painted stake and hammer, and drove the marker through about six inches of alluvial soil before hitting solid rock. The stake leaned and fell on its side. I busied gathering rocks and soon had the stake properly anchored. Denise had climbed to the top of the outcropping and was sitting, perched, watching as we secured the stake.

"When do we start?" she called down.

"Soon, darling, soon," Sam shouted up to her, and blew her a kiss.

I had been so taken with Denise I had not looked at Sam: not, at least, in a direct way. As he stood smiling up to his soon-to-be bride, I realized he was quite casually dressed, and if I subtracted from my mind the fact that all the articles of clothing down to and including his shoes were new, he was dressed very appropriately for the mountain. He had not shaved since last we'd met, and his short, dark whiskers gave him a rugged outdoor look. He was wearing Levi jeans and a T-shirt emblazed across the front with BLACKHAWKS. His sturdy, hiking boots were leather with Vibram soles; appropriate mountain gear. The gold chain was not visible.

Denise, on the other hand, was wearing an off-white, silk blouse and sleek black slacks. Her shoes were expensive leather flats, and in addition to a mountain of a diamond on her left hand, she accented her wardrobe with a single strand of pearls. She was certainly not dressed as Ms. Mountain Lady, but she seemed much more comfortable in the terrain than he.

The altitude suddenly felled Denise, bringing on a severe headache and slight nausea. This vibrant woman was quickly reduced to tears. I suggested we hurry down the mountain to my house where she could lie down. Although I didn't mention it, I keep an oxygen tank in my storage room just for occasions such as this. We all piled into the Jeep and Sam drove as sensibly as possible, reaching my house in about ten minutes.

"The first thing we need to do," said Sam when we were still bouncing along, Denise holding her head in her hands, "is to get this road smoothed out."

It sounded like a good idea to me, and I'm sure, had she been able, Denise would have agreed. We helped Denise into the house and settled her on the old soft couch adorning my living room. I got the oxygen from the storeroom and turned on the tank. I handed her the mask, and she automatically placed it over her face as if she had done this routine a thousand times before. I adjusted the flow to four liters. Sam was pacing back and forth, his boots thumping on the hardwood floors.

"Do you want some aspirin for your head?" I asked Denise.

"I'd like some," she muttered behind the mask, "but will it hurt the baby?"

"Baby?" I thought to myself. Hadn't Sam told me the previous night that he had just gotten out of rehab? Oh, well, I was never very good at math, and anyway, what did it matter?

I looked at Sam, as I didn't know the answer to her question. He shrugged his shoulders and continued his pacing.

"I don't know," I told her.

"I'll wait and see if it goes away with the oxygen," she said, her voice still muffled by the mask.

Not knowing what else to do at the moment, I busied myself in the kitchen preparing a light lunch of shredded beef sandwiches with mayonnaise, potato chips and carrot sticks. Sam was still pacing, but with a less aggressive stride. Denise sat up on the couch, holding the mask to her face. Her color was decidedly less white than it had been on our way down the mountain, returning slowly to that rich olive color so attractively worn. She smiled weakly at Sam, who stopped his pacing and came to sit next to her. He put his arm around her as she leaned her head on his broad shoulder.

Sam began talking, dropping more pages of his life. "I started drugs when I was twelve," he said to me, "and I was in rehab the first time when I was fourteen. What a dumb, stupid kid I was." He paused. "Did you ever feel like you didn't fit in?"

He was directing the question to me.

"Yes, I guess so."

"I mean, I never had any real friends, just those punks I spent time with doing stuff."

He looked at Denise as he spoke, and he held her closer. "Man, I was married at eighteen. Some hooker I'd met. It only lasted a month."

Denise gave no response either verbally or physically, and I surmised that she had heard all of this before. Why Sam was telling me, I did not know, but soon Denise was feeling much better, and even decided to try a little bit of the lunch I had prepared. As we were eating, Sam continued his narrative, and before our lunch was over, I was to find out that his parents were cold and distant, and very, very wealthy. They had made bundles of money in the restaurant business, owning several in various parts of New York City. Most of the big money had come from the decision to franchise the restaurant theme, and his father had covered eastern America with his name.

Apparently his father was still in the franchise business, relocating to Chicago, and was now dealing in record stores and video outlets. An avid hockey player in his youth, his father, upon finding his son to be a "klutz" in sports, had taken his pleasure by buying shares in a professional football team. The Detroit Lions, I think Sam said, but had recently traded his part ownership for complete ownership of the Blackhawks. All this, Sam said in a non-judgmental way, was his father's vicarious way of participating in sports instead of spending time with his son.

This led to a dialogue about his older brother, the "perfect son," now vice president of the franchise operation. Sam had been given a job at one of their local video rental outlets with the promise of manager if things worked out.

"Things will work out, Sam," Denise told him as she squeezed his hand, giving us both a radiant smile, indicating that she had overcome the worst of her altitude sickness. We finished our lunch and by 2 PM, they were roaring down my lane, Denise waving wildly out the open side of the Jeep. In their wake, Sam had left several gift certificates for movie rentals from his store.

It was two days later that Sam knocked at my door. I heard him coming, the now-familiar whine of the Jeep objecting to the gear ratio, as he pulled up my lane and stopped in front of the garage. I was disappointed there was no Denise, but I understood: pregnancy and nausea could not be all that much fun, no matter how beautiful the drive. Rolled in his fist were house plans. We spread them out on a small table, Sam excitedly pointing out the details.

It was a huge house; forty-five hundred square feet of bedrooms, baths, walk-in closets larger than my house, a huge family room, a den and a playroom for the baby. It seemed gothic, and I was sure that this house would not "nestle" behind the rock outcropping: it would overwhelm it. It was more of a project than I was capable of handling, and I mentioned this fact to Sam.

"Not to worry," Sam said. I'm going to sublet all the work in order to speed up the project, but I want you to be the superintendent, supervise the entire project. The pay will be good and you won't even have to leave the mountain."

Over coffee, we discussed the order of things to come: road, improvement, site excavation, foundation, framing, sheathing, roofing, siding and finish work. In between, the plumber and electrician would perform their magic.

"If all goes well and the mountain cooperates, you could be in this house in a year," I told him. His eyes lit up and his smile broke the stubble on his face.

"If we really push hard, is there any chance we could be finished by the time the baby comes?" he queried.

"December?" I asked, rather incredulously.

"Yeah, December."

"I don't see how it's possible," I said, shaking my head, thinking of the relatively skimpy building season the mountain usually allowed. The snow had melted out early this year, but weather is fickle and we could be under several feet of snow in three more months, hardly enough time to even get the house enclosed for interior winter work."

"Money is no object," Sam said matter-of-factly. "Let's see what we can get done. See if you can get the right people lined up. I'll call you on Monday."

"Sounds good to me," I said, but something in his manner, the look on his face, caused me to wonder. "If it were my place, I'd have the well done first to be sure there is a good close water supply."

"You're the boss," he assured me with his smile.

I spent the afternoon on the phone and was lucky to get commitments from most of the people we would need. The well driller, an old friend of mine near Bailey, was willing to put in the well within three days of my call. The same concrete contractor that had poured the foundation to my garage would make himself available, and would begin Monday with the excavation work, starting with improving the road. The framers, referred by the concrete man, were harder to pin down, but promised to work us in as best they could. That would get us started.

"Whew!" This was to be my year, my sabbatical, to lay back, rest, do nothing but work on my writing. After years of lecturing at the university, I was looking forward to an easier, slower pace: a gentle ebb and flow with the seasons. Now, things were suddenly complicated, and it was beginning with a very busy summer.

The Monday after my conversation with Sam arrived as fresh as the month of June had two weeks earlier. By mid-afternoon, Sam had not called. I dialed the number he had given me: no answer. I dialed again several times during the waning afternoon and late into the evening with the same result. When he didn't call on Tuesday or Wednesday, I called my construction crews and put them on hold for the time being, except for Peter's Excavation Company who had, on my word, started smoothing the road. On Thursday, I halted the bulldozer in mid-work. I wrote Peter a check and promised him I would be back in touch as soon as I heard from Sam, explaining I could not imagine what in the world had happened to him. I sensed an unhappy man as I stood watching him load his dozer on a huge flatbed truck, and in addition, I felt oddly shaken, uneasy.

It was the middle of the following week before I heard anything from Sam. I had spent the day clearing some trees that had blown down during the winter winds. I had taken a leisurely shower and had quickly fallen asleep, snuggling exhausted in my bed.

Much to my surprise, I was so deep in sleep, I did not hear a car in my lane, only pounding on my door. It took me a few minutes, jerked from such deep hollows, to realize where the noise was coming from.

"I'm coming," I hollered, but the pounding continued until, only in my shorts, I turned on the porch light and saw a disheveled Sam through the window in my door. He stopped pounding only as I opened the door and Sam slunk through the passageway and sat, totally limp and defeated on my couch. His white summer suit was wrinkled from head to foot, his shoes unshined, the open shirt stained with a spill of coffee or some other drink. His face bore stubble of at least three days, and there where huge bags under his eyes. He looked wane, terrible.

"Coffee?" I asked, moving to the kitchen to put on the pot.

"God!" he said several times. "I've been in Chicago, and unbelievably, my father said no to my house plans!"

What made no sense to either of us was the fact that his father had purchased the land for Sam with the intention Sam could develop it in any manner he wanted. The only stipulation placed by his father in the beginning was that Sam had to stay clean, and apparently, clean less than two months was not a long enough measure of clean.

"How long is clean?" I asked a dejected Sam.

"Probably until the end of time," Sam spoke wearily. "The same thing happened with my second marriage. We had a kid, and I was really down. My wife was working, supporting us. I was back into drugs big time. My father said that if I went to rehab he would bail me out financially. I didn't want to go, but my wife pleaded. I looked at my son and knew, even through the euphoria of the stuff I was on, something had to change. I went to rehab for three months, and I came out clean as a whistle, but that wasn't good enough for my old man. My wife and I struggled to hold it together, but the bailout never came, and she finally packed up our kid and moved back to Iowa. I got the divorce papers in the mail."

Sam was rocking back and forth, holding his face in his hands as his story spread out across the floor, as if looking for a place to escape. He cried, he yelled, he cursed his father, and I began to wonder if he was on something other than anger and grief.

The coffee was done and after I put on some old sweat clothes, brought him a cup, thick and black. He sobbed as it cooled, the cup precariously teetering in his hand, until he finally drank some and began to quiet down. The rocking slowed and along with his sobbing, eventually stopped.

"God," he said again, wiping his nose on the sleeve of his white suit jacket.

"Where is Denise?" I asked.

The question seemed to stabilize his mood, and for the first time he looked directly at me.

"She's at her place, I guess. I called from O'Hare and gave her the bad news. I said I was coming straight here from the airport, so I haven't seen her. She wants me to come home as soon as possible, as soon as I finish talking with you."

He used the bathroom and was gone a long time. I'd had three cups of the tar I'd made before he reappeared, looking tired, but much better. His mood had calmed, and except for the stubbled face and wrinkled clothing, he appeared quite normal.

"Can we look at the positives," I said, always trying to be helpful.

"Well," he began, pacing around the living room in a slightly agitated manner, "Denise still believes in me." He paused, then continued, "The hell with my father. If I work hard, I'll soon be manager and making decent bucks. Maybe I can get the architect to scale things down a little and I can do the whole thing myself, without any help from him."

He stopped walking, then more to himself, "Yes, the hell with him, I can do it myself— me and Denise, we can do it."

He had removed his suit coat while in the bathroom and had thrown it on the couch when he began pacing. Even though it is always cool at our altitude, he had sweated through his shirt; large stains evident under his arms. He turned to me and smiled; more of his old self, picked up his coat and started for the door.

"I've got to get to Denise's and talk things over with her," he said as he reached in his jacket pocket and pulled some crumpled papers from its depth. "Thanks, Bud," he said and kind of threw the papers my way, opening the door to leave.

"It's awful late. You're welcome to crash on the couch until morning," I said as I reeled in the papers.

"Thanks," he said again, "but this is too damned important."

He was gone leaving me with five or six badly crumpled coupons for video rentals.

Remembering, it must have been mid-September when Sam again pounded on my door. Denise, standing in his shadow, was ripe with child. Her eyes retained their sparkle, and both of them looked wonderful. After my hearty welcome, Sam spread new plans across my table, scaled down plans, smaller dreams.

"What do you think?" was his expectant question.

"Quite a change— hmmm— for the better, I'd say. This house will really nestle in behind the rock ledge." Still looking at the plans, I continued. "I really like the way you've merged the library into the family room, and the nursery is situated in a much better and more convenient location."

Sam looked pleased. Denise, her doe-like eyes watching my every movement, smiled.

"Do you think we can still get started this fall," Sam asked with an almost pleading tone.

In my mind, practicality won over their longing and I said, "It would be chancy to start a house this time of year. We might get the excavation done, but then if it snowed before we got the foundation poured, the mountain will cave in with the spring thaw and we'd have to start over again next spring."

Sam shook his head, listening. I went on. "The more prudent thing would be to drill the well, work on the road, and then hit it hard as soon as it melts out next spring."

They stayed for lunch, a simple plate of peanut butter sandwiches and vegetable soup, and somewhere in the conversation I brought up the bill I'd paid for the partial job on the road.

"Oh my gosh," said an embarrassed Sam, and he rushed out to the Mercedes and returned with a check written to me for more than the figure I had mentioned.

"Hey," I said in protest, "I only want to be reimbursed. Take it and write me another one."

I shoved the check back to him, but he threw it on the table and said the matter was closed. Our conversation returned to his dream. Denise, serene as a saint, took a nap on the old couch as we talked.

"I'm assistant manager now, and the video store is performing well in rentals. In fact, we are the lead store in Denver now," Sam said with pride. "Denise has moved past her nausea and her pregnancy is going well. It will be hard to wait on the house, but I think your plan is the best. We'll do it your way."

"I'll call Peter tomorrow and see when he can come back, and I'll get the well-driller lined up again if I can," I promised.

"Let me call them. There is no sense of you doing this piddly stuff," he replied. I went to the desk and rummaged around until I found the phone numbers he would need, and before we knew it, the sun was gone behind the saddle. There was no dusk: light, then dark. Denise awoke and they were gone; her olive skin, her doe-shaped eyes lingering in my imagination.

A few days later, as I was knocking off the grass seeds around the house with a hand cutter, I saw the well drilling rig work its way up the rough road toward Sam's property. It looked like the names I had given him had paid off. His idea to make the calls would, I thought after my last experience, be best. He could call and more accurately schedule work as he could afford to do it. As the truck ground its way up the road, I was happy to see Sam and Denise were beginning their dream.

Fall was certainly in the air; crisp, blue sky and a breeze with a slightly sharp edge. The weather gods have been especially good and there were only traces of an early snow left in shady places.

I had taken a varied steeper route for my walk, and I was out of breath. I leaned for a moment on the nearest tree.

After searching the horizon, I began to concentrate on the terrain of my own mountain: Snyder's Point and the sloping saddle. I watched the swaying of the trees in the wind, hypnotic in motion. I was surprised to see a small trailer house on Sam's property, perched east of the building site we had staked out. After the surprise, my second feeling was one of being left out. They had not included me in this part of their plan, and as I turned the event over in my mind, I thought I knew why. Trailer houses were forbidden on the mountain.

It wasn't my business, I reasoned, yet, I would hate to have their actions develop into a trend. On the other hand, with their house building starting soon, I was sure the trailer would be only temporary. I could tolerate that, as probably would my neighbors.

Late in November, on an ugly gray, cold day, a loud knock on my door rescued me from an exasperating period of writing. It was Sam with Denise standing as close behind him as her huge stomach allowed. Their story went like this: Around midnight, after work the night before, Sam had driven the Jeep up to the trailer thinking that with the baby due, he would have one last chance to spend a night on the mountain before things "got crazy". He had unknowingly left the Jeep's interior light on, and, early this morning, when he went to start the Jeep for his return to the city, the battery was dead.

He had called Denise on his cellular phone, and she had driven the Mercedes up to the beginning of their road, and he, having hiked down to meet her, realized that it was all for nothing as the Mercedes could not go up the road to give the needed jump. They decided to ask for help.

"If you could just give us a lift up and jump the Jeep, we'll be on our way," Sam said in an uncharacteristically apologetic manner.

"Sure," I said. "I just took an old battery out of the truck and didn't get the new one in, but it will only take me a few minutes to replace it and get it going. Why don't you two make yourselves comfortable in the house and I'll beep when I'm ready."

Denise was huge with child. I'm not a doctor, but I questioned, to myself of course, the wisdom of her being here at all. Her face was puffy, and her previously unblemished olive skin had taken on a reddish appearance. Her gait was a shuffle due, I'm sure, to the size of her belly and the altitude.

"We'll be okay," Sam began, "and maybe I can help."

Denise stood at the top of my drive, near the steps, arms across her stomach, as Sam followed me into the garage to get the battery. He dogged my steps down the lane to the sidelined pickup. He helped me lift the broken-hinged hood, and I hefted the battery into place behind the radiator, parallel to the alternator. He watched as I attached the cables and snugged the bolts with wrenches I'd stuffed in my overall pockets.

"Should I get some jumper cables?"

"I've got cables," said Sam as he started up the drive to help Denise to the truck.

"It might be best if you just went in the house and rested," I suggested to Denise as she started toward the truck.

"Oh, I want to come," she said, flashing her old smile, the scarf on her head slipping down around her neck. Her hair was longer, almost shoulder length, beautifully combed. She wore an oversized, knee-length, course knit sweater, gray on gray, black slacks, and winter boots. She looked peaceful yet expectant, wonderful.

"Are you sure?" I said, ever the watchful parent.

Again, she smiled as Sam helped her up into the cab. I got in, turned the key and the engine roared to life. I backed out, eased down the rest of the lane onto the main road, and turned right starting up the road to their property. The torrential rains of late summer had made the road almost impassable in places: huge washed out ruts; large, exposed rocks. The old Dodge

Power Wagon lurched and lunged, the huge engine gurgling with unused power.

I glanced at Denise who was hanging tightly on to the door handle, her huge belly flopping up and down until I could hear the rolling waves of protecting fluid. Driving as carefully as possible, I continued to monitor Denise as she attempted to hold her child still as he or she sloshed wildly, undoubtedly by this time, seasick on the high amniotic seas. Sam attempted to help hold, until at long last we came to his white Jeep parked along side of the trailer. The hood was up. No one mentioned the trailer.

Denise stayed in the truck talking quietly, soothingly to the fetus as she slowly rubbed her stomach. Sam opened my hood, attached the cables that were already hooked to his battery, got in the Jeep and started the engine.

I got out and unhooked the cables, wrapped them up and handed them to Sam. Denise struggled out of the Dodge before either of us could help her. She gave me a long hug and I could feel, against my stomach, the fetus still objecting to the ride of its life I had just provided. I helped Denise into the Jeep just as Sam thrust more coupons in my direction.

"Thanks a million, Bud," he shouted over the roar of his engine. I closed his hood, thinking, "I really should tell Sam that I don't own a TV, and I have no plans on getting one." Instead I said, "Let me know about the baby!"

Winter came, cold and windy, but no snow. I was feeling plenty guilty about discouraging Sam from building, as it was February before the first big dump of snow came. Thirty-three inches fell before the storm blew out over the plains, stopping traffic and killing a mayor's chance of re-election in the Queen City of the Plains, before it swept on into Kansas. I heard my cats crying, wanting in.

That winter, once it started, kept piling up the snow. Sometime in March, I was snow-shoeing toward the mailbox and newspaper, when I rounded the corner and there was Sam's Jeep slumped in the snow-filled drainage ditch, stuck. I started by, wondering where Sam could be, when I noticed that the windshield was heavily frosted. I pushed through the snow and tapped on the side window. There was no response, but convinced the frost indicated someone was inside, I tapped again, louder. This time a crack appeared as the window was rolled down.

I could smell the heavy odor of beer, and as the crack widened, there was a disheveled, bleary-eyed Sam with at least a week's beard in evidence, rolled into a sleeping bag.

"Why didn't you come to the house? You could have frozen to death out here!" I admonished Sam.

"Didn't want to bother," he mumbled through the beard, stirring, but having great difficulty opening his eyes. The back seat of the Jeep was strewn with architectural drawings of house plans.

"What about the baby?" I asked, "You didn't call me about the baby."

He had his eyes partially open, squinting, blinking against the whiteness of the snow.

"Fine, she's doing fine," he replied as a faint smile formed on his parched lips.

"How is Denise? Is she enjoying being a mother?"

The questions were either coming too fast, or they were too complex for Sam's current state of mind. He did not answer me, but I could tell by his expression that he was thinking of one.

"For crying out loud, Sam, you're a mess!"

His smile broadened in that slow way drunks smile when they think they are being witty and cleaver.

"Just a little office celebration," he offered, yawning a wide yawn, followed by a deep belch.

"'Scuse me," he said, belching again, then hiccupping. "Just wanted to go up and see the place."

I waited a minute, possibly for another belch, then said, "I'm going down for the paper and mail, and I'll be back in about an hour. The door on my house is unlocked. Why don't you go up and make some coffee, then we can pull your Jeep out of the ditch, and maybe, this afternoon, if you are up to it, we can snowshoe to your place."

I said all this wondering if he could even get to the house.

"Sounds good," he said, stretching, and began rolling up the window.

As I was returning from the mailbox, my neighbor, Fred Stone, who, with his wife Frieda, lives about a mile above me, stopped to say hello and ask if I needed anything from town.

"I think I'm pretty well set, Fred, but thanks a lot for asking. Nice snow, huh?"

"It's finally turning into a great winter," he said with a smile, and waving, drove on down the snow-covered road.

When I reached Sam's snowed over roadway, the Jeep was gone. I could see where someone, probably Fred, had pulled him out. The Jeep tracks went on up the main road, and I assumed he would be at the house, making coffee. When I got to my lane, I noticed the Jeep tracks went by, on to where, only Sam knew. Thinking he had just missed the turn, I figured he would soon be back as the road ends at Fred's and Frieda's house. I went up the lane, shed the snowshoes, and entered the house to start the coffee myself. Sam never returned.

I knew it wasn't my place to worry about a grown man, but what are neighbors for? As my anxiety level rose, I decided to call Denise to see if he had driven back to Denver. I dialed the phone only to find the number was no longer in service. There was no forwarding number, and information had no listing for Sam. I did not know Denise's last name.

It was mid-afternoon before I convinced myself to go looking for Sam. It had started snowing again, and if I didn't get a move on, any tracks or traces of Sam would soon be snowed over. After checking back at the place where the Jeep had been stuck, I snow-shoed up to the end of the road. He was nowhere to be seen, and I could not find any tracks bailing off into the deep snow anywhere along the road. This made me believe he had not tried to hike to his trailer, a good choice given the depth of the snow.

By now, it had begun to snow hard; huge, heavy flakes, and I came to the conclusion, that for some reason, he had merely turned around at the end of the road, and had journeyed back to the city. How I had missed him on his way back down, I could not imagine, but I had found no evidence to make me think otherwise. Unfortunately though, I had no way to confirm my opinion.

"Time to let it go," I told myself, cutting through the woods and deep powder to the house.

Aside from my brief worry about Sam, the cats and I hunkered down to enjoy the snow. On the fourth day, out of nowhere, the sour roar of a snowmobile split the middle of the white stillness, snarling through my creative thought, through the middle of some of my most creative work. I jerked to attention and moved swiftly to the window. I could see, barely, the top of a stocking cap whip through the trees in the approximate vicinity of the road to Sam's place. Later, on my walk down the hill, I saw the white Jeep, snowmobile trailer attached, parked at his entrance. At least Sam wasn't dead, frozen somewhere into a snowball, his whiskered face pale in the icy cold.

The Jeep was there for two days, and on the third day, gone. Instead of a returning snowmobile track, there were giant post-hole steps through the deep snow. I could tell by the tracks that it had been a monumental struggle. Sam must have had trouble with the snowmobile and had walked out: a remarkable feat, considering the depth of the snow.

A day and two small snowstorms later, curiosity got the better of me and I strapped on the snowshoes and followed the giant steps up Sam's road until, almost three-fourths of the way to the trailer, I came upon the floundered snow machine. It had tipped on its right side and had sunk into the deeply drifted snow. Sam had, from the huge, snowy holes and burrows, struggled mightily to right the beast, but in the end, the machine had won. Sam had thrashed his way through huge drifts to the trailer, and then, eventually, back down to the Jeep. Crazy and as dangerous as it was, I was impressed. Maybe he'd morphed into a mountain man after all.

The spring I expected Sam and Denise to begin building, the snow piled up and up until, it seemed, there was no room left. As a result, the snowy path in my lane got narrower and narrower until I could barely get my old pickup between the mounds of snow. Finally, when it began to melt, the torrents of water chased each other under the snow, reminiscent of the flash floods occurring the summer before. And the mud! When not sloshing through the snow, I was squirming in the mud. Mud, mud, and more mud. All I had was MUD! In the midst of all the mess, the hummingbirds arrived on time: Mother's Day. Flashes of color and shrills of sound pulled me from my depths of depression and I retrieved the feeders from storage, and boiled the nectar.

I heard, via my neighbor, Fred, that there was occasional activity at Sam's trailer, but he didn't recognize the vehicles parked along side, and never saw the people coming and going.

"Vehicles?" I inquired.

"Vehicles," said Fred. We looked at each other, and Fred shrugged his rounded shoulders, the straps from his overalls yanking comically at his bib and pants.

As for me, I never saw nor heard anything of Sam, Denise and whatever the baby was named.

No construction occurred on the mountain that summer. What a shame, too, as after summer's late start, it was gloriously prime; puffy clouds, deep blue skies, and showers paced just right to keep the mountain green and lush and free from fire hazard. A perfect summer, really. Near the end of August, as I was returning from my morning trip to the mailbox, I heard a car approaching behind me. I turned and seeing an unfamiliar car, I stepped to the side of the road to let it pass.

The car, an old dented and pockmarked Oldsmobile, slowed and stopped. The driver's side window was down and I was slow to recognize the driver as Sam. He was so slouched in the driver's seat I could hardly see his heavily-bearded face. There were large bags under his dull eyes, and his hair was long and badly needing a shampoo.

"Hi, Sam," I said and leaned my arm on the top of the door frame, looking more closely at him through my colored glasses. His casual clothes were a rumpled mess, and he had a bottle of beer squeezed between his knees.

"Hi, Bud," said a female voice, and I realized, sitting next to Sam, was Denise. Her hair was long, ratted, a mess. Her perfect complexion was marred with acne-like sores, and the beautiful olive skin was pallid, ashen. Dullness had replaced her clear eyes, and her pupils appeared dilated, her gaze fixed on some other world.

"How's the baby," I managed to say, stunned by their appearance.

A slight shift in gaze brushed quickly by, a small light in the desert, an almost smile from Denise.

"Oh, she's fine. Staying with Grandma today."

Sam was rocking forward and backward, taking a pull now and then from the bottle. I noticed torn and wrinkled house drawings randomly clinging to the back seat, strewn among various bottles, cans, and wrappers.

"New car?"

Sam laughed with a hoarse, rattling laugh.

"Yeah. Like it?"

Another laugh, another pull from the bottle.

"Well," I said as I stepped back, surveying the car. "It does have its charm."

A high pitched giggle from Denise. Sam continued rocking.

"See you later," said Sam as he shifted the car into drive and started forward. Denise waved a weak and limp wave, and they drove up the road leaving me in a cloud of dust.

Sometime late in the month, around midnight, there was heavy knocking at my door.

"The bear's back" I said aloud.

I pulled on a pair of pants, and although the knocking had ceased, I hurried down the stairs and to the door. I switched on the outside light, looked out the window, and there was a wild-eyed Sam, waving his arms in kinetic frenzy. I opened the door.

"You've got to help me," yelled Sam as he looked over his shoulder into the darkness for some real or imagined threat, his arms and fists flailing wildly at the night. He quickly shoved past me and through the door, still looking over his shoulder. It was then that I realized, in his wildly swinging right hand, was a very large handgun. I quickly closed the door, and by the time I turned around, he was crouched behind my big old couch, peering madly over the back, the gun in his hand appearing and disappearing as his arms moved frantically up and down.

"Get down, Bud!" he shouted to me, "They'll be here any minute."

My heart began to race and I looked for a place to hide, at least momentarily.

Sam shouted again, "Shut off the lights! Hurry! Hurry, Bud, hit the switch and get the hell down!"

I quickly turned off the lights, and against my better judgment, joined him behind the couch. He promptly hit me in the chin with his wildly failing hand. Luckily, it was with the one without the gun, or I might have been out cold instead of stars chasing around my head.

"What the heck is going on, Sam?" I demanded. "Who's after you?"

"It's the Feds, or the Commies, I don't know which. Maybe it's the cops!" And with that, he began to cry and cough a wretched, harsh cough, alternating between the two.

"Where's Denise?" I said, trying to keep my voice level, unafraid.

He stopped his crying and coughing long enough to say, "I think they already nabbed her 'cause I haven't seen her."

I crawled across the floor toward the bathroom, intending to turn on the shower light so we'd have some illumination and I could see where the gun was.

"Douse the light!" he yelled as I flipped the switch. A shot rang out, and I doused the light and hugged the floor, praying the gun wasn't pointed in my direction. I could hear movement in the dark.

"Sam," I whispered, "where are you?"

"Here!" he shouted back, as if that explanation would tell me precisely where he was.

"Put the gun down, Sam, before you kill one of us. Put it down."

"Fuck you and all the others out to get me!" he ranted. "Fuck you! The hell with all of you!"

I heard him start to cry again, and it sounded like he was moving back and forth, squirming along the floor. I couldn't tell which, but I decided it was time for me to change my position. As silently as I could, I crawled through the darkness to the den. I felt for the doorway, slid through it into the room, and felt along the bookcase until my hand touched the flashlight I stored there for emergencies. I sat up and leaned my back against the wall, out of breath, listening.

Other than the muffled crying and occasional cough, I heard nothing. There were no cars sounding along the road, no lights outside of any kind. Above my wildly thumping heart, which was pounding against my ribs, I could hear no footsteps on the deck.

It must have been ten or fifteen minutes before I heard it. Snoring? Yes, snoring! I was sure of it! Sam was snoring! I inched out of the den, flat to the floor and slowly, very slowly, slid toward this new sound. Nearing his previous position behind the couch, I shielded the light as well as I could and flicked it on, just for an instant. Sam was curled in a fetal position behind the couch, and as near as I could tell in that brief glimpse, he was soundly asleep!

In the dark, I quietly and slowly inched toward his curled

body. When I was close enough to feel his foot against my arm, I covered the light with my hand and gave it another quick flick. I could see the gun was still in his right hand, which was curled up under his chin. In that brief glance, he looked like a baby fallen asleep from hard play, a toy clutched in his hand.

Still in the dark, I positioned myself to where I thought I was near his head, and thus the gun. I had decided that, in a swift, simultaneous move, I would flick on the light and grab the gun. It was, I thought, my only chance to disarm Sam before he flipped out again. I lay there listening to my thumping heart, my blood coursing through the vessels, and took a deep breath, flicked on the light and grabbed the gun. He never as much as moved, but I was shaking uncontrollably!

Sam slept a good twenty minutes after I snatched the gun before he woke up, screaming. He was rubbing his arms as he rocked and he was agitated, threatening and sweating profusely.

"Please, please!" Sam was rocking violently. Not able to stay on the couch to where he had moved when he awoke. He slid back to the floor. "I need a fix, God, I need a fix! I'll do anything you ask," he yelled at me. "Please go to the trailer and see if there is any stuff left. It's in a black bag squeezed up behind the sink. Go, please, go!"

What a nightmare! Upon wakening, he had come after me, but I had long since disposed of the gun, dropping it down the hole behind the foundation of the garage. We had tussled briefly on the floor, and I had continued to talk to him. I'm sure the release of the drug's grip he had been using helped, but it took some doing on my part to convince him that no one was after him. I threatened to call the sheriff if he didn't quiet down, and in hindsight, I should have called. It would have been a whole lot simpler.

But I didn't call, and in between the names and threats Sam threw my way, and me holding him to prevent injury to himself or me, the long night finally slid into morning; a gray morning laced with cold drizzle and flecks of snow.

Finally, around 10 AM, after an hour of shaking and seizure-like spasms, Sam fell asleep on the floor. I covered him with an old sleeping bag, and feeling totally drained and fatigued, I stretched out on the couch above him. It was after 2 PM when movement and noise awakened me. Sam was moving erratically under what little of the sleeping bag was still covering him, and he was moaning quietly.

I stepped over him and went to the kitchen and put on some coffee—extra strong. It was ready about the time Sam opened his eyes. I poured a cup, cooled it down with water, and I forced him to drink the full cup. He sat, head bent, shaking, sobbing one minute, laughing the next, making drinking from the cup another challenge. I busied myself cooking oatmeal and frying bacon and eggs, all the while keeping one wary eye on Sam in case he became violent again.

I took a plate of eggs and bacon to him and stuck it under his nose. I immediately recognized my mistake as fetid vomit painted the eggs. I quickly withdrew the plate and went to the kitchen in search of paper towels. I wiped the floor and his face and stood looking down at one of the most miserable sights I had ever seen.

A wretched being: Sam was thin, bony in fact, and his straggly hair was streaked with gray. His clothes looked like he had been sleeping in them for a month. There was no Gucci watch, no handmade shoes and no gold chain. And he smelled worse than a pigpen: a mixture of urine, alcohol, and vomit. All we lacked was the mud.

Back in the kitchen, I sat in front of my cooling oatmeal. I'd entirely lost my appetite, taking only a few sips of coffee. I needed something stronger, but unfortunately, coffee was the strongest drug I had in the house. I looked out the window. The drizzle had turned entirely to snow, and as much as I usually admired the season's first snowfall, I could only sit with my chin in my hands and stare.

The snow, so long in coming, continued heavy for four days.

At the end of the snowfall there were sixteen inches of new snow on the ground and blanketing the trees. It was beautiful. Sam had had a rough time, but on the third day he seemed rational and mostly normal. The shaking had stopped, and he had begun to eat small amounts of food I prepared; Cream of Wheat, and later in the day, a small helping of pinto beans and rice.

On the fourth day, he was very remorseful, and on the fifth day, as the sun began melting the snow, he asked if I would take him to Denver, to his brother's house. I hadn't known his brother lived in town, as he had never mentioned it. I wondered about Denise, but I was afraid to ask, and I certainly feared for the baby.

Sam called his brother, and after a hearty lunch of chicken soup and tortillas, we left for Denver, the tires of the old Dodge crunching sharply in the snow. I drove, and except for the directions to his brother's house, Sam was silent. As I pulled up in front of the well-kept brick home on Humboldt, I could see his brother standing, waiting at the door. Sam quietly thanked me, shook my hand, and walked from the car.

"Take care, Sam," I said. This time, he left no coupons in his wake, and I felt strangely sad and distracted as I pulled away from the curb. It was an even more silent drive home, up the winding paved road that had been cleared of snow. I turned left for the dirt road, stopping at the mailbox for my mail and paper. I slowly finished the drive, one switchback at a time, until I passed Sam's turn-off, and then up my lane, the old Dodge roaring through the unplowed snow.

Quirky as they were, Sam and Denise would have fit in splendidly on the mountain, and it is sad for me to say that I never saw either of them again. A year after I had taken Sam to his brother's, Fred stopped by my house.

"I thought you might want to know about Sam," he began, "He's in rehab again. Denise divorced him, and she took the baby and moved to Chicago." Fred and Frieda had been to a star-gazing party near Snyder Mountain, and someone who had worked with Sam at the video store had shared that information.

That evening, I walked up the mountain, admiring the crop of liverworts and mushrooms along the path, and skirted to the left of my usual trail and came out through the trees along the ridge where Sam had placed the trailer. I paused by the door, tempted to go inside, but the trailer looked so sad and forlorn I decided not to enter.

I was amazed how much stuff was strewn around the trailer. There was a pair of crumpled and torn pants blown against some boulders; several shirts of various colors lay loosely under the trailer stairs. Bolts, assorted nails, bottles and pieces of bottles, several partially burned logs and boards pocked the ground. Although no cans were visible, dozens, no hundreds, of flip-tops were scattered around the trailer, and all over the graded area and into the ground under the trees. Several spent lighters lay partially covered with small rocks and soil as if buried in some reverent and mysterious ceremony. The ground was peppered with cigarette butts. I stopped looking at the clutter and gazed east over the plains. I could see downtown Denver, and a small rainsquall floating above Westminster. Looking south, Highlands Ranch sprawled up the hills from W-470, and beyond. Pikes Peak glistened in the south. I felt like a bird, circling above its prey, the view spellbinding, breathtaking.

My eyes focused on the closer carpet of evergreens along the edge of the ridge, and to the road below, snaking up our mountain; the one I hike each day for the daily news. To my left, a moderate-sized spruce was split up the side: a jagged streak; a recent lightning strike, I'm sure. The white of the tree's inner layers shown brilliant in the late afternoon sun, its underbelly soft and vulnerable like that of a newborn fawn.

I turned around just as the sun ducked behind the distant range, somewhere near James Peak, and the brilliant streaks of gold shot across the blue of the sky, reaching for infinity, piercing fluffy clouds along its journey. Sam and Denise, so young and with such promise: melted, gone. I felt sad. I felt a genuine loss. Sucking in my breath, I put my head down and turned toward home, taking the shortest, steepest path I knew, the emptiness of my feelings shadowing my heels every bit of the way.

My seasons continue to come and go, cycles of the mountain. It has been two years since Sam and Denise disappeared. My neighbor to the west, Jace, sold his property and left mysteriously in the night. I have yet to meet the man who bought his place. Fred and Frieda told me that he is very rich: CEO of one of the Fortune 500 Companies. I have seen him driving on the road, eating his dust as he passes in his huge pickup, vanity plate winking prestigiously in the sun. I have waved, and even stepped toward the roaring machine in a friendly manner, thinking that he, the driver, would stop and talk. Instead, he barely nods his head as if waving or giving another friendly gesture would cause him unmentionable harm.

Shortly after buying Jace's place, "The Stranger," as I call him, purchased three more forty-acre parcels; two above his log home, and one below. One of the two parcels above his place was Sam's. Upon hearing of the purchases, I realized my unspoken dream that Sam and Denise would one day show up at my door, banging hard, talking and laughing, daughter in tow, was completely shattered.

I've just returned from a long, lifeless meeting in Denver, and I find myself restless and needing a walk, the more vigorous the better. Since I had picked up my mail and paper on my way home, I begin walking up the steep part of the mountain behind my house. Soon I am on the old road to Sam's place. "The Stranger" quit using the road about a year ago, replacing it with a new road, one with more direct access, which begins further up the mountain. I am surprised at the erosion of the old road, so soon returning to nature: ruts, exposed rocks, and in places the grass and small evergreens are already piercing the rocky, untrammeled soil.

Further along my walk, I am rather startled to see posts supporting a heavy chain strung across the old road. In the middle of the chain hangs a red-lettered sign: *NO TRESPASSING*. I stop in my tracks and look at the sign. In all my years on the mountain, there has been nary a sign posted anywhere. I have always been welcome to roam freely through all properties, any time.

I skirt around the sign, leaving the road, and head cross-country toward a rock ledge just below "The Stranger's" cabin. Edging under the ledge to my right, I reach a notch, squeeze between two sharp edges of the ledge, and pull myself up and past the steepest portion, skinning only one elbow in the process. Feeling slightly irritated from the stinging sensation of my bruised skin, I continue through the old fallen trees above the ledge toward Sam's trailer.

I recognize my irritation is magnified by the sign I have just encountered below. My feet are pounding the ground, transferring my anger to a surprised and unsuspecting Earth. Recognizing the silliness of letting a sign set my mood, I smile to myself and feel much better by the time I reach Sam's.

My second surprise of the day; the trailer is gone. Some thief in the night; the trailer has been stolen away. On casual inspection, there is no evidence that a structure has ever been to this part of the mountain: no wheel marks, no stunted grass, no human sign; only a small leveled area. I walk to the exact place where the trailer had been, and look out over the eastern plains. The late evening shadows cast long fingers, reaching, grasping toward the distant, tall buildings of Denver. A hawk shrieks above. There is a warm evening breeze, and I can smell the scent of the new growth of pine.

My eyes, shift to the ground under my feet, and among the rocks and sparse grass I see, partially covered, multitudes of can flip-tops. A further visual search finds a few old cigarette butts, split and torn, ground into the soil; and over by the rock outcropping, a small pile of shattered glass. Gone are the pants and shirts; the bolts, except for one; and I see nary a rusty nail. The burned logs and boards have disappeared as if by magic, and as I slowly walk around the area, I am able to identify only one ragged, dented, semi-complete lighter.

Something **metallic**, like a semaphore winking in the late afternoon sun, **draws** my attention to the rock face of the outcropping **that would** have protected and given beauty to Sam's house. I **walk** slowly to the granite face, reach up six inches above my head, **and** grasp the silver splinter, only to realize it is an old spoon **someone** placed for convenience during some long ago nighttime bonfire. It is wedged rather firmly in a crack, and only when I **wiggle** it and pull in an upward manner does it come free into my hand.

I study the spoon, turning it slowly. It is simple and plain with no swirls or flowered designs on the handle. I am interested to see that it must be stainless steel or it would be tarnished by now, and the vacuity of design surprises me, knowing Sam's and Denise's flare for extravagance. I feel the smooth, cold metal as it leaves my hand, sliding into the dark depth of my front pants pocket.

I study the rock face, and above the crevice that had held the spoon is a small shelf formed from a streak of quartz blazing through the granite. Standing on my tiptoes to reach for the shelf, and with some unknown urge, I run my hand along the ragged edge until my fingers feel a soft roll of something jammed behind a most prominent bulge of granite. I tug once, then twice before the mass is dislodged, and bringing it down to my waist, I stand staring at my holdings: a bulge of stained and soiled bills.

My mouth is immediately dry, and my hands, sweating, begin to shake. A quick, spontaneous breeze kisses my neck, and a sudden chill creeps along my spine. Slowly, I begin unrolling the bills, their inner surface untouched by the elements are bright and new. I do not recognize the centered picture of a mustached man on the face of the bill. His head is tilted up in an arrogant way, and he has bags under his eyes, and he looks worn and fatigued. I read his name: Grover Cleveland.

Nervously, I lick my thumb and begin counting. "One, two, three." I clear my tightening throat as sweat pours from my face, continuing, "Four, five, six—."

Petey

Doc was looking forward to the weekend because it was "The Kid's" turn to take call. Doc called his new young veterinary partner "The Kid" because, to Doc, he seemed so young. Dr. Timothy Nair, DVM, graduated from Colorado State University School of Veterinary Medicine just last spring, and one thing he didn't lack was confidence.

Dr. Nair's confidence was good in some ways as he was not afraid to try any new procedure, and he was absolutely confident that each sick or injured patient was his friend. Doc was always asking him to slow down, just a little, because at times he thought Dr. Nair's over-abundance of confidence kept him from learning.

Doc had hired Dr. Nair right after his graduation three months ago, and generally things were going well between them. Certainly the practice was already showing signs of growth. Oh, there had been a few little mishaps, but what did he expect with a new graduate? And Doc rather liked being on call every other week, and not every night and every weekend as he had been doing for years.

This was the first weekend that Doc was leaving Dr. Nair

completely on his own, and yes, he was sure he could handle it. Doc and the missus were leaving Friday evening to drive south to Pagosa Springs. He planned on climbing into the wonderful hot springs and not getting out until time to drive back to Denver on Sunday. Ah, yes, he could smell the bubbling water now.

Dr. Timothy Nair was still wired as he got ready for bed Saturday night. Nell, his wife, had already tucked herself in and was listening half-heartedly to Tim telling her how well the clinic had gone that morning.

"I saw a good number of patients, and I think I was right on all my diagnoses," he told her excitedly. "And I even got the beak and nails trimmed on Mrs. Kern's parakeet without any problems."

He was referring to his first attempt at trimming the beak and nails on a parakeet, when the little bird had died in his hand from his over-firm grip on the little-finger-biting monster.

"I only had one minor surgery to do. This dog cut his paw on some metal lawn edging, but I was able to repair the whole skin flap. It should be as good as new if he keeps the bandage on and the owners don't let him lick the incision."

He paused for a minute as he adjusted the blanket, swung his feet into the bed, and placed his head on the pillow. "You know, they ought to outlaw that stuff."

"Surgery?" asked his wife in a sleepy voice.

"No, you know, that metal lawn edging."

Dr. Nair was sleeping soundly, dreaming he was fixing another cut foot pad, and the severed artery was bleeding badly and he could not get a ligature around it properly and the foot continued to bleed more and more as he intensified his efforts. The phone was ringing in the background and he, so sound asleep and involved in his dream, wondered why the receptionist didn't answer the damn thing.

On the tenth ring, Dr. Nair suddenly awoke with a start, sat straight up in bed, and reached for the bedside phone.

"Dr. Nair speaking. Yes,—yes, tell them to meet me at the hospital in fifteen minutes. I'm on my way."

He reached over and shook Nell.

"I've got an emergency call," he told her excitedly, as he began dressing as fast as he could. "I'll be back as soon as I can."

"What happened?" Nell's sleepy question came.

"Some parrot is having a seizure," and with that he was out the door and into his car. As he drove toward the hospital, he tried to remember everything he knew about parrots, but he had to admit, there wasn't much to remember. Most of what he knew about treating birds he had learned from Doc in the last three months, and certainly nothing about parrots.

The client was waiting for him when he drove into the parking lot of the hospital. The trunk lid, looking a little like a parrot's beak, was gaping wide to accommodate a huge birdcage.

Dr. Nair stepped from his car and walked rapidly toward the cage. In the dim street light he could see, stretched across the bottom of the cage, a huge green Amazon parrot and it didn't seem to be moving. Not even thinking to introduce himself to the client, he said, "Let me help you get this cage carried into the hospital."

The middle-aged, large-bodied, woman stuck out her hand and said, "I'm Bertha Gardner, and I want to thank you for coming out to see Petey."

Dr. Nair clumsily shook her hand, noticing that she was dressed in a green outfit close to the color of the prostrate bird. As the two of them struggled across the parking lot with the cage, Dr. Nair fumbled with one hand for the keys in his pants pocket so he would be able to unlock the door when they reached it. For a moment, he lost his one-handed grip on the cage, the cage tilted precariously, and Petey slid and then slammed against the wire side, his yellow head flopping to the side. He still did not move.

The cage barely fit through the door, and Dr. Nair was

wondering silently how in the world Mrs. Gardner had loaded the cage into her car trunk.

"My neighbor helped me load Petey into the car," the panting and puffing Mrs. Gardner explained as if she had read his thoughts.

They carried the cage through the door, the exam room, past the pharmacy, and into the back treatment room. Dr. Nair flipped on the light and opened the cage door.

"Will he be all right?" whispered the distraught Mrs. Gardner.

Dr. Nair was sure Petey was dead as a mackerel, but he hated to say it. Instead he quickly guided Mrs. Gardner back past the pharmacy, through the exam room and into the reception area.

"Now have a seat, Mrs. Gardner," said Dr. Nair as he pushed her toward a chair. I'm going to get some oxygen for Petey and give him some medicines, and we'll see what happens.

He dashed back to the treatment room, glanced at Petey who still lay in a limp mass against the side of the cage. His green feathers looked dull, ruffled and faded, his bluish-gray beak more ashen, and his eyes were still closed.

Dr. Nair wheeled the oxygen tank from the corner of the room and grabbing a small facemask from the rack on the wall was ready to administer oxygen to the fallen pet. Reaching through the opened cage door, he picked up the limp bird with his right hand. Just as he was turning the body length-wise to get him through the door, the gray folded eyelid rolled back to half mast, the thick beak opened and quickly closed on the web of skin between Dr. Nair's thumb and forefinger. The pain was immediate and very sharp, his whole hand felt immediately numb.

"Ow!" screamed Dr. Nair through clinched teeth, hoping Mrs. Gardner in the next room did not hear him.

"Is everything all right in there?" inquired Mrs. Gardner in a thin high voice.

"Fine. Fine. Everything is fine," Dr. Nair replied, the pitch of his voice almost matching Mrs. Gardner's, his jaw was so firmly clinched in response to the pain which was now stabbing its way up his arm.

Petey looked firmly into Dr. Nair's eyes, and then the bird's lids closed for the final time. Petey expired on one last breath, but his jaw remained clinched on the web of tissue. Blood was starting to ooze from the skin of Dr. Nair's hand.

Sizing up the situation, Dr. Nair used his left hand to try and pry open the thick beak, to no avail. Petey was still mostly in the cage, but as Dr. Nair shook his hand in an attempt to loosen it from Petey's death grip, the limp body flopped back and forth and out from the cage and began to fall toward the floor.

Dr. Nair jerked his right hand up in an attempt to keep Petey from falling, only to cause the firmly clinched beak to tear more deeply into his skin, and blood began flowing in a greater stream. He managed to get the bird back onto the tabletop, reached in a drawer, pulled out a screwdriver and attempted to wedge it between the upper and lower beak.

More awkward with his left hand, his attempt failed, the screwdriver slipping and imbedding itself into his skin next to Petey's closed beak.

"Holy sh--!" he began, but at that moment he realized that Mrs. Gardner was peering over his shoulder.

"What in the world are you doing to Petey with that screwdriver," she demanded.

The oxygen mask and tubing fell to the floor and hissed like a startled snake. Dr. Nair's blood dripped down the front of the cabinet to the floor and splashed on the toes of Mrs. Gardner's sandaled feet. Petey lay upside down; his feet straight in the air, toes curled. His eyes were closed, and except for the grip of his beak, he looked blissfully peaceful.

"My goodness gracious," whispered Mrs. Gardner stepping backwards, and then began to fall toward the floor as her eyelids fluttered violently.

Dr. Nair instinctively grabbed for Mrs. Gardner to help break her fall. Following Dr. Nair's grasping hand, Petey flew through the air like the good bird he was and smacked Mrs. Gardner full across her face. She slid to the floor with Petey following, pillowing in on her ample bosom. Dr. Nair's hand followed, still attached to Petey's beak.

Dr. Nair grabbed for a towel on a nearby rack, wet it in the sink and applied it to Mrs. Gardner's forehead. Petey followed his every move. Mrs. Gardner's eyes fluttered again, and her eyes began to focus. Dr. Nair got Petey back on the table in the most comfortable position he could as he examined his hand for further damage.

"Oh, my," said Mrs. Gardner. "How's Petey doing?"

She lay on the oxygen tubing, with hissing coming from somewhere near her pelvis. She reached up to move the damp towel across her forehead, and her eyes began to look more normal.

"Well, Petey's doing, ah, Petey's not doing very well. I'm afraid what I mean is Petey's not going to make it, Mrs. Gardner."

"He was such a fine pet. What do you think caused his seizure, Doctor?"

Mrs. Gardner was now in a sitting position, and the oxygen whistled from somewhere under her, desperate to escape.

"I think Petey had a stroke. Yes, a stroke would make him act in such a bizarre fashion. The more I think about it, I'm sure he had a stroke." He waited a minute, observing Mrs. Gardner sitting on the floor, the oxygen still whistling from somewhere beneath her.

"Now please don't get up until you are sure you are no longer dizzy. Then, Mrs. Gardner, whenever you are feeling better, I'm afraid I'm going to have to ask you for some help."

His whole right arm ached, clear to his shoulder. At least the blood flow had slowed considerably.

Very soon, Mrs. Gardner was standing, tears sliding down her cheeks in measured droplets. She kicked the oxygen tubes out of her way as if it were common practice, came to the exam table and began stroking the yellow feathers on Petey's head.

"Poor baby," she said. Then, as if seeing the situation for the very first time, "Oh, you poor boy! Look at your hand. What has my Petey done to you?"

She pulled on Petey's beak and head.

"Ow," cried Dr. Nair, trying not to shriek, although now his whole hand was feeling more numb than painful. "I think if we work together we can get Petey to let go."

With heads together, Dr. Nair grasped Petey's top beak with a pair of pliers in his left hand as Ms Gardner worked the screwdriver slowly between Petey's beak and began to pry. It took several tries, and the sweat was beginning to replace the tears on Mrs. Gardner's face, but finally Petey's death grip was broken. The bird lay quietly on the table cupped in Mrs. Gardner's hands as Dr. Nair placed his hand in the sink and began to let cold water pour over the wound and swollen area of his hand.

"Oh," he said in relief.

"My, my," said Mrs. Gardner.

They looked at each other and smiled, just the two of them, not Petey. When Dr. Nair looked at Petey, the twist and angle to his beak could have been a smile, or a sneer. Dr. Nair dried his hand, and Mrs. Gardner helped him apply antibiotic ointment and a bandage. His hand felt better. He reached and turned off the oxygen, which was still hissing in the corner where Mrs. Gardner had banned the tubing with her foot.

Dr. Nair found a small bright blue towel in the towel drawer, and gently took Petey from Mrs. Gardner, wrapped the bird in the towel and lay the package in the center of the bottom of the cage. Mrs. Gardner let out a sigh, and then before he knew it, she smashed him against her bosom in a powerful embrace.

"You did the best you could, Doctor," she said to him as she pressed him even closer, "You took wonderful care of Petey during his last moments here on Earth."

She finally released him, and just in time as Dr. Nair was

having trouble breathing and was beginning to regret shutting off the oxygen.

He helped her get the cage through the door and into the still gaping cavern of her trunk. He tied the trunk lid to the cage with an old shoestring she has given him for the task. The night was brighter, turning to dawn. Dr. Nair opened the car door for her and shut it after she had squeezed into the driver's position.

"It doesn't matter what your charges are. Just send me the bill," she said as she backed the car and turned into the street, all the while waving her hand and arm out the open window in good-bye. "Thank you so much," were her parting words as she spun gravel getting into the street, the car rapidly disappearing into the growing light of day.

Dr. Nair re-entered the hospital and walked to the record cabinet behind the receptionist's desk. Sorting through the G's, there was no Gardner in the files. There was one Gardener, but a different client, one he knew. There was no Gartner either. His right hand began to throb with growing pain. He quietly shut the file cabinet drawer, turned out the hospital lights, locked the door and got into his car. The sun was just coming up as he turned the car from the parking lot toward home.

The author lives and works in Denver, Colorado, where he shares gardening duties with his wife, Shirley. When he is not writing, he busies himself searching for perfection in his veterinary orthopedic specialty practice. Additional information is found on his Web site, www.flyingthree.com.